D1190402

BLUE RIDGE SUMMIT FREE LIBRARY
P.O. Box 34
Blue Ridge Summit, PA 17214-0034

SAND AGAINST THE WIND

SAND AGAINST THE WIND

CATRIONA MCCUAIG

THORNDIKE
CHIVERS

This Large Print edition is published by Thorndike Press, Waterville, Maine, USA and by BBC Audiobooks Ltd, Bath, England.

Thorndike Press, a part of Gale, Cengage Learning.

Copyright © Catriona McCuaig 2008.

The right of author Catriona McCuaig to be identified as the author of this work has been asserted by her in accordance with the Copyrights, Designs and Patents Act 1988.

ALL RIGHTS RESERVED

The text of this Large Print edition is unabridged.

Other aspects of the book may vary from the original edition.

Set in 16 pt. Plantin.

Printed on permanent paper.

LIBRARY OF CONGRESS CATALOGING-IN-PUBLICATION DATA

McCuaig, Catriona.
   Sand against the wind / by Catriona McCuaig.
     p. cm. — (Thorndike Press large print clean reads)
   ISBN-13: 978-1-4104-0850-1 (alk. paper)
   ISBN-10: 1-4104-0850-7 (alk. paper)
   1. World War, 1939–1945 — Wales — Fiction. 2. War widows
— Fiction. 3. Parent and child — Fiction. 4. Family — Fiction. 5.
Coal mines and mining — Fiction. 6. Wales — Fiction. 7. Large
type books. 8. Domestic fiction. I. Title.
PR9199.4.M4253S36 2008
813'.6—dc22
                                                2008012090

BRITISH LIBRARY CATALOGUING-IN-PUBLICATION DATA AVAILABLE

Published in 2008 in the U.S. by arrangement with Robert Hale, Limited.

Published in 2008 in the U.K. by arrangement with Robert Hale, Limited.

U.K. Hardcover: 978 1 408 41207 7 (Chivers Large Print)
U.K. Softcover: 978 1 408 41208 4 (Camden Large Print)

Printed in the United States of America
1 2 3 4 5 6 7 12 11 10 09 08

You throw the sand against the wind,
And the wind blows it back again
William Blake

CHAPTER ONE

'Good grief, Nellie! I thought I'd never get here. Talk about a slow boat to China!' Mari Lucas smoothed down her rumpled skirts and smiled wearily at her friend. 'I hope you put the kettle on before you left the house. I'm gasping for a cuppa!'

'Good thing I didn't, then,' Ellen Richards retorted, 'else it would have boiled dry by now and set the whole place on fire. I was beginning to think you weren't coming after all! What are you waiting for, then? Give us a hug!'

The two women held each other for a long moment. 'Wish I could have let you know the train was late, then you needn't have come down to the station so early. We started off from Cardiff on time but then there was some sort of flap on. These two plain-clothes coppers came into every carriage, asking to see our identity papers, and

7

as it wasn't a corridor train that all took time.'

'What were they looking for, did they say?'

'Not a dicky bird. We'll never know, I suppose; that's the maddening part. I did wonder if it had something to do with spies. You know how we're always hearing stories about the Nazis coming down by parachute, disguised as nuns?'

'They'd stick out like a sore thumb if they did that here,' Ellen told her, grinning. 'There's precious few nuns in Cwmbran. They're mostly Methodists in these parts. Never mind all that; let's get you home and make you that cup of tea!' She picked up her friend's cardboard suitcase and led the way out of the station yard, still talking nineteen to the dozen. 'Sorry we couldn't fetch you in the car, but I should think you'll enjoy the walk after sitting in one place for hours. If you collapse along the way I'll just leave you where you drop, and Mariah will come for you with the wheelbarrow when she gets a minute.'

'Oh, you! How is your Mariah, anyway? Missing her husband, is she?'

'Of course she is, and worried sick at times, with him being a pilot in the RAF. She keeps busy, though, out gardening for hours every day, and she gives me a hand with our evacuees, which is a big help.'

'That's about all we can do, nowadays,' Mari replied. 'Keep busy, I mean, so we don't spend too much time thinking.' She broke off as they came within sight of the lovely old house. 'I say, you fell on your feet when you came here, didn't you, Nell? Living in the lap of luxury like this. It's a far cry from the houses in our terrace, I can tell you; two up and two down, and an outside lav.'

'I'm not exactly the lady of the manor, you know!' Ellen retorted. 'I'm a glorified servant, that's all. As far as the outside world knows I'm just the housekeeper at Cwmbran House, and that's the way I hope it will stay.'

Contrition showed on Mari's homely face. 'I'm sorry if I spoke out of turn, Nell, but you know what I mean!'

'Yes, I know what you mean. Come on, let's get you inside and settled. I can do with a good strong cuppa myself.' She quickened her pace as they neared the front steps and, biting her lip, Mari was obliged to follow.

The two women had grown up in Cardiff, where they had gone to school together. Later on they had taken jobs in Lloyd's, the big department store. They'd had dreams of marrying in due course and setting up home near to each other. Remaining as close friends, they meant to share the upbringing of any children they might have. However, fate had something different in store, in the shape of the Great War. The conflict had taken Ellen's brother, Bertie Richards, leaving her without a soul in the world to call her own. Grieving and desperately lonely she had given in her notice at work and fled down to Barry, where she had happy memories of a seaside outing with Bertie and their parents.

That was when she had met Harry Morgan, the wealthy owner of the Cwmbran colliery and the mansion in which she now lived as his housekeeper. In an unguarded moment the two had come together, and their daughter, Mariah, was the result.

Ellen suspected that if Mari had got wind of the situation at the time she would have been deeply shocked. Back in 1917 nice girls weren't supposed to get themselves in situations like that. In fact, Ellen counted herself fortunate that she hadn't ended up in the workhouse, which was where many girls in trouble had to go.

Nowadays it was a different world. Both of them were mature women, mothers of grown daughters, and they were aware that life wasn't all black and white. Furthermore, Mari was agog to get to the bottom of what she thought of as a romantic story.

That evening, when the two of them were alone in Ellen's comfortable sitting-room, sipping a celebratory sherry, Mari raised the subject again. 'I can't believe it's been all of a year since I was here last, Nell. Remember how I turned up in the middle of Mariah's wedding? Not that I meant to gatecrash. It's just that when my little brother told me he'd seen you, I couldn't wait to get in touch. Without stopping to think I just hopped on a train and came looking for you.'

'And I'm glad you did. You don't know how many times over the years I've thought about contacting you, but I didn't dare, in case my secret came out. And now, of course, it has.'

'Poor Mal. He didn't mean to upset the apple cart, you know. He felt terrible about having blurted out that your Bertie hadn't been married, when everyone here thought he was your husband, and you a war widow. I hope it didn't cause trouble for you, Nell.'

Ellen shrugged. 'It could have been worse. Harry's daughter hit the roof, of course, and I can't say that I blame her. It was an awful shock to find out that her beloved

11

father had gone astray, and still worse to learn that Mariah is actually her half sister. The worst of it is, she's convinced that Antonia — that was her mother — must have known about Harry and me and been devastated by it.'

'Which wasn't true.'

'Of course it wasn't true! As I've explained, there was no question of us having an affair, and if Antonia hadn't died giving birth to Meredith I shouldn't have come anywhere near this house. It was only when they feared for the child's life, when she wouldn't take to the bottle, that Harry asked me to come. As far as anybody knew I was a young widow with a new baby of my own and so the perfect choice to act as wet nurse for his daughter.'

'But you stayed on after that.'

'Not without some misgivings, I can tell you. But when Harry offered to have Mariah brought up alongside Meredith I looked on it as a godsend. What would you have done, Mari, faced with a choice between that and taking her away to a life of poverty? And Mariah is his daughter, you know. She was entitled to his support.'

'Mm. I must say I'm surprised that he didn't ask you to marry him, after a decent interval. He was a widower, after all.'

Ellen didn't answer for a long moment. She had dreamed of that, but all hope had died when he'd suggested leaving Mariah with him while she went back into the world on her own. Then, when she'd refused to give up her child, he'd offered her the post of nanny to both girls, on a salaried basis, and she'd jumped at that. Years later, when they no longer needed a nanny, she'd graduated to becoming housekeeper, when the former chatelaine had retired and been pensioned off.

'We get along quite well as we are,' she said at last. 'I have thought once or twice that I should move on, but somehow I've never quite summoned up the energy. Then this war came and I seemed to be needed here. Half the servants have left to join up, and then we were landed with half a dozen evacuees, so there you are!'

'And poor Meredith lost her husband in the war, of course. I'm sure she's been glad to have you to lean on.'

Ellen made a face. 'To take it out on, you mean! I try to be patient with the girl, but it's not that easy. And now we're worried about Mariah's husband as well. I can only hope and pray that he comes through this rotten war in one piece. We're all in the same boat, though, aren't we? If we're not anxious about our loved ones in the services we're fretting about what's going to happen if the invasion comes. That Hitler wants stringing up, that's all I can say!' Mari stifled a yawn, the sight of which brought Ellen to her feet. 'Just look at the time! If we don't get to bed soon we'll never be up in the morning, or at least, I won't. You're welcome to have a lie-in, of course. That's if you can! The boys are up with the lark and they don't care who knows it. And then there's Henry, Meredith's little boy. He's got a pair of lungs on him like you wouldn't believe. He's up in the nursery, of course, but he still manages to make his presence felt all over the house!'

Mari struggled to her feet. 'Aye, I am feeling a bit cross-eyed. I'm glad we've had this little chat, but there's something else I want to discuss with you, when we get a moment to ourselves, and it has to do with getting that man Hitler right where we want him!'

'Goodnight, then,' Ellen told her, smiling, when she had shown her friend into the best guest room. 'God bless! See you in the morning.'

CHAPTER TWO

It was the middle of the following afternoon before the two women found time to talk again. In the meantime Mariah took their visitor off to inspect the gardens while her mother did some indoor chores.

'Oh, the lovely rose garden!' Mari cried, shocked at its disappearance. 'I did so admire that glorious display when I was here before, and now it's all been ploughed under. It's enough to make a person weep!'

'You can't eat roses,' Mariah told her, although truth to tell she had shed a few hot tears herself when the deed had been done. 'We'll replant it all after the war, Harry says.'

'If you can find the nursery stock, that is!' Mari's face was grim. 'Anyway, there are more important things to talk about than flowers. I wanted to have a word about your mother.'

'Mam? What do you mean?'

'Well, about her secret having come out last year. Does she mind very much? I feel responsible, seeing as it was my brother who set the cat among the pigeons.'

Mariah blushed. She still hadn't quite got used to the fact that Harry Morgan was her father, and not poor Bertie Richards. 'You know Mam! She never says too much about it, but yes, I know it weighs on her mind pretty heavily.'

'I suppose everyone round about knows the truth now?'

Mariah considered this. 'No, not really. I'm sure Meredith wouldn't mention it to a soul. As far as she's concerned the whole thing is a disgrace, and the fewer people that know about it, the better.'

'But the servants. Surely they know all about it?'

'If they do, they're keeping their thoughts to themselves. Harry holds all the cards, you see. Outside of this house, and the colliery, there's not much chance of finding other employment locally. That's enough to stop tongues wagging. Anyway, the staff here still refer to Mam as Mrs Richards, and they treat her with respect. That wouldn't happen if they'd changed their opinion of her, would it? You can always spot dumb insolence.'

'All the same,' Mari persisted, 'it can't be easy for her. She must feel as if she's treading on egg shells all the time, waiting for something to happen. That's why I've come to see her.'

'I don't know what you mean. I assumed it was because you wanted to resume your old friendship, now that you've finally found out where she's living.'

'That, too, of course, but I want to take her back to Cardiff with me, and I'm hoping you'll back me up.'

'That would be nice. It's years since Mam had a bit of a holiday.'

Mari hesitated. 'That's not quite what I had in mind. I want her to come to me permanently, or at least for the duration of the war. Do you think she'll come?'

'Oh!' Mariah was taken aback. 'I don't know, Auntie Mari. I've been on at her for years to leave Cwmbran and strike out on her own, but something has always happened to prevent it. I get the impression that she means to hang on here at all costs. Go ahead and see what you can do, by all means, but don't say I didn't warn you!'

'I think we can squeeze another cup out of this pot,' Ellen murmured, lifting the lid and peering inside. 'Perhaps it'll stretch if we water it down a bit.'

'No more for me, *diolch*,' Mari told her. 'I wouldn't mind another of those biscuits, though, if it's going begging. Now, Nell, I've something to say, and I'll thank you to hold your peace until I've got it out. All right?'

'That sounds ominous!'

'Well, it's like this. Our Sandra is going in for nursing, and our Vera's all set to join the Wrens. With my Will away at sea that leaves me sitting in an empty house, see? And I don't fancy taking in any ordinary lodgers to be at their beck and call all day. In any case, I can't see my hubby agreeing to let me have strange men living under our roof when he's not around to keep an eye on them!'

Ellen thought she knew what was coming. 'And you want to offer a room to Mariah, is that it? A place where she and Aubrey can spend time when he comes home on leave? That's very good of you, but there's plenty of room for Aubrey here, and Mariah has her war work, as you know. If she goes to Cardiff she'll get called up in no time, and then you'll be back to square one in any case.'

'Who said anything about Mariah? Of course she doesn't want to leave here! Na, na, it's you I'm talking about!'

'Me!' Ellen looked bewildered. 'What on earth are you talking about, Mari Lucas?'

'Now I'm on my own, I mean to do a bit of war work myself. Remember how we worked in munitions together in the last war? At least, we did until you did a moonlight flit! I thought we could do it again, eh? Help to show Hitler what's what. And this time we'll have my nice comfy house to go home to, instead of that pokey little hostel like before. What do you say? It would be a bit of a laugh, *bach!*'

'Oh, Mari, I couldn't possibly! Surely you can see that?'

'I can see that you're still looking over your shoulder in case your story gets out and makes you the talk of the Cwmbran chapel!'

'We don't go to the chapel. We belong to All Saints' church.'

Mari gave an exasperated sigh. 'Church, chapel, what's the difference? If it ever got out that Mr Harry Morgan had fallen from grace it would be the talk of the Amman Valley! And no prizes for guessing who they'd label the scarlet woman!'

'Thank you very much, Mari Lucas! And I thought we were supposed to be friends!'

'Oh, Nell. Don't get hold of the wrong end of the stick, there's a love. You know I don't think badly of you. I'm on your side, see? And isn't it time you got away from here? You're still a young woman. Wouldn't you like to meet somebody nice and get married? There's not much chance of that in Cwmbran, is there?'

'You've been talking to Mariah!'

'Na, na. Well, I did mention this to her, as a matter of fact, but it wasn't her idea. Do say you'll think about it, *bach*. We could have you packed in no time and you could come back with me on the train tomorrow.'

Ellen rubbed her eyes. 'I'm afraid you'll have to excuse me, Mari. I can feel a headache coming on. I'll have to go and lie down for a bit.'

Mari threw her hands wide. 'Now I've offended you.'

'No, you haven't. I know you mean well, and I'm grateful, but I can't do as you say, and that's all there is to it.' She stumbled out of the room, brushing away a tear as she went.

'Any luck?' Mariah whispered, when Mari returned to the garden.

'Unfortunately not. I'm afraid I didn't put it very well, and it's put her back up. I'm going to have another go later but I don't have much hope of getting her to change her mind. What's the matter with her, girl? Is she still eating her heart out over Harry Morgan? If he cared about her at all he'd have proposed marriage years ago, but he didn't, so it's about time she moved on!'

Mariah tried to hide a smile. 'Of course she's not still carrying a torch for him. What an idea! Why, she's well past forty, Auntie Mari!'

'So am I, Mariah Mortimer, so am I!'

Seeing the grim expression on their friend's face, Mariah was dimly aware that she'd put her foot in it somehow, but she couldn't for the life of her fathom why. She hastened to put matters right. 'I expect that Mam is stuck in a bit of a rut. After all, she's lived here for more than half her life. She'd be lost without this place.'

Alerted by a puff of smoke in the distance, Ellen picked up her friend's suitcase and made her way to the end of the platform. That was where the third-class carriages would be when the train stopped. She could think of nothing more to say. She'd enjoyed Mari's visit but last-minute farewells were always awkward.

'Now you will come to see me in Cardiff?' Mari insisted. 'Just for a bit of a break, like.'

'Yes, one of these days,' Ellen told her,

not meaning it.

Ten minutes later, watching the train steaming away, she heaved an enormous sigh. The visit had unsettled her. Why should she leave Cwmbran when she was needed here? If they all thought she was weak, that was too bad. It was her life and nobody was going to push her into doing what she didn't want to do. If Harry ever gave her notice — perhaps if he married again — that was a different matter. Then she'd have to put a brave face on it and get out, with as much dignity as she could muster.

On the other hand, perhaps she was missing out on life, washed up in this backwater, comfortable and secure though it was. Shouldn't she do something about that before it was too late? Making up her mind was just too difficult.

'Perhaps I'll do something about it after the war,' she decided. 'If it ever ends.'

CHAPTER THREE

Mariah Mortimer stood up and stretched, in an unsuccessful attempt to straighten out her painful back muscles. Digging for Victory was all very patriotic in theory but in practice it was sheer hard work.

'Want a drink, miss? I'll get one for you, if you like!' The small boy grinned up at her shyly, eager to be of service.

'No, thanks, Evan.' She ruffled his spiky red hair. 'I'll have a nice cup of tea when we get finished here. I'm looking forward to that. Only ten more rows to hoe, isn't it? We might be able to find a glass of pop for you boys, since you've worked so hard.'

She glanced at her six young helpers, wondering how they'd ever managed before taking on these evacuees from Swansea, where the bombing had been severe. Until their arrival she'd been struggling on alone in this gigantic vegetable garden, all the outside servants having been called up. One ancient groom had been brought back out of retirement but he had his hands full looking after the horses and had no time for gardening as well.

Taking their cue from her, the boys retreated to the shade of the privet hedge and she let them go. Slacking off for five minutes wouldn't do any harm; they'd work all the better after a break.

She gazed up at the old house, which seemed to glow in the late spring sunshine. Could there be anywhere in Wales more beautiful than Carmarthenshire at this time of year? Cwmbran was a coal mining community, producing anthracite, known locally as the black diamond, but sheep-farming was also carried on here and the surrounding countryside was peaceful and delightful.

The large dwelling was the property of Harry Morgan who, it seemed, owned half of Cwmbran, as well as being involved in other business interests. The outlying farms also formed part of his estate so he was a force to be reckoned with in the district.

Mariah had come here when she was just a few weeks old and had never known any other home. It was unthinkable that some day, if the threatened invasion came, it could be taken over by some smug Nazi and its current inmates turned out, or worse.

She gave herself a mental shake. Those were defeatist thoughts, and she should know better. A shout interrupted her reverie.

'Look, miss! It's Dewi Williams! Coming up on his bike, see?'

Sure enough, a Boy Scout was weaving his way up the drive, trying to control an old boneshaker of a bicycle that was much too big for him. Mariah was suddenly aware of a cold feeling in the pit of her stomach.

'Wonder what he wants, then? Hey, Dewi! Whatcha doin' here, boyo? Come to help with the potatoes, have you?'

Ignoring the shouts of the younger boys, the scout let his machine fall to the ground and strode over to where Mariah stood waiting, like a statue carved in stone.

Having given her a smart salute he fumbled in the pocket of his uniform shirt and pulled out a small orange envelope.

I'm going to be sick, Mariah thought, swallowing hard. Please don't let it be Aubrey! Please don't let me break down in front of the boys!

'Aren't you going to open it, miss? Go on, it might be something important!' The boys were clustered around her now and she had to stop herself giving a sharp retort. Of course it was important. Telegrams in wartime always were!

With trembling fingers she tore the envelope apart and scanned the contents on the small form inside.

'What is it, miss? It's not Mr Aubrey, is it?'

'No, no. It's Mrs Fletcher's grandfather, in Herefordshire. I'm afraid he's dead.' Poor Meredith, she thought. She is so fond of him. She's sure to go to pieces when she hears about this.

'Did a bomb get him, miss?'

'No, you little ghoul. Apparently he had a stroke.' She fumbled in the pocket of her britches, hoping to find a coin for the messenger, but there was nothing there but a hankie and a half-chewed toffee. 'If you'll come up to the house with me I'll find sixpence for you, Dewi,' she told him, but he shook his head virtuously.

'We don't take tips, miss. This is our war work, see?'

Mariah nodded. All over Britain the scouts were doing sterling work as part of the war effort. '*Diolch yn fawr,* Dewi,' she told him, turning to her helpers, who were standing about with their mouths open. 'I have to go in, boys. Can I trust you to carry on without me? You'll be in charge, Dai.' The child assured her that he could manage.

Mariah's mother met her at the door.

'What is it, *cariad*? I saw the boy from my upstairs window. Tell me nothing's happened to our Aubrey!'

Mariah placed the slip of paper in Ellen's outstretched hand. Ellen gave a sigh of relief. 'Paul Meredith. That's all right, then! Oh, you know what I mean, girl! I'm sorry he's dead, of course, but he was getting on a bit. Even without a stroke he couldn't have gone on much longer. What I really meant was —'

'Yes, Mam, I know.' Mariah didn't want to dwell on the fact that the telegram might have been bringing bad news about her husband. That could still happen.

'Who is going to tell Meredith about her grandfather, then?' she asked. 'Obviously she has to know right away. "Come at once," it says. "Funeral Thursday."' The two women frowned at each other. They knew from experience that the girl was likely to have hysterics, and who better to take out her distress on than the messenger?

'Harry,' Ellen said. 'Harry will tell her. After all, he'll have to go to the funeral. Paul was his father-in-law. You take this up to his study, *cariad*. I know he's in there. I saw him come in about half an hour ago. For goodness sake wash your hands first, though, and tidy your hair. You look like you've been working down the pit!'

'Surely it's not that bad, Mam!' Mariah laughed, but she did as she was told. Ellen was not only her mother, but she had also been their nanny, and when she spoke in that tone of voice you jumped to it!

'This isn't unexpected,' Harry Morgan remarked, when Mariah had shown him the telegram. 'The old boy wasn't young any more, and there had been one or two false alarms before this. It had to come some day, of course.'

Mariah said nothing. She knew that Paul Meredith was barely twenty years senior to Harry, who had been quite a bit older than his wife, Antonia. It followed that if Paul was dead, then Harry might wonder about his own mortality.

'I'll telephone my mother-in-law at once,' he decided. 'Naturally she'll expect us to be there for the funeral, but she'll want re-assurance. She fusses so much in the normal run of things that she's sure to be all of a dither now.'

'Hadn't you better say something to Meredith first? Mam thinks it would be better coming from you.'

Moments later, Mariah heard loud sobs coming from the morning-room, where

Meredith was writing letters. She tiptoed down the hall and stood outside the door, listening.

'Poor, poor Grandpa! I can't bear it, Dad! You mustn't ask me to go to the funeral. I won't do it, I won't!'

Harry made soothing noises. 'You can't not go, *cariad.* Think of poor Henrietta! You're all she has left now. She'd be heartbroken if you weren't there to see her through this.'

'You'll be there, Dad.'

'And so will her only granddaughter, my girl! Think how you would have felt when Chad was killed, if none of us had been here to support you.'

This brought forth another flood of tears, but at last Meredith pulled herself together and, typically after a storm, began to throw her weight around.

'Nanny! Where are you? Come here at once. I want you!'

Ellen appeared, grumbling. 'What is it now?'

'I suppose you've heard about Grandpa? You'll have to look after Henry for me while I'm gone. Of course, this would happen right after I had to get rid of that wretched nursemaid!'

'Of course I'll look after Henry for you,

Meredith. A funeral is no place for a two-year-old. And I'll take him now, shall I? You'll want to go and pack, and I daresay you'll want me to press your black frock?'

'Yes, and you can see to the veil on my black hat. I can't think how it got torn.' She flounced off, sniffing into her handkerchief. Ellen raised her eyes to the ceiling.

CHAPTER FOUR

The church was full. Paul Meredith had been, if not exactly popular, a man who'd had a finger in many pies. A church warden, a some time member of the local council, and, latterly, a magistrate. Former colleagues had come to pay their last respects.

Harry Morgan was seated in the front pew, sandwiched between his daughter and his mother-in-law. There was a strong smell of moth balls which caused a tickle in his nose. Most of the congregation wore pre-war clothes, brought out only for funerals and weddings. New garments cost 'points' and in any case there wasn't much to buy in the shops.

The vicar was droning on, reminding them of Paul's work in the community. Harry's mind wandered. Here in this same church he had stood at the altar, waiting for his bride to take her place at his side. Antonia's funeral had been held here, too.

Here his motherless daughter had come to be christened, at the express wish of her sorrowing grandparents. Now the cycle of life had moved on. The local newspaper had printed a lengthy obituary, describing Paul's achievements and saying that he had "gone to join the silent majority".

Meaningless words, Harry thought. What would be said about him when his turn came? He'd led a fairly blameless life, really, except for that one slip, and he'd done his best to put that right, hadn't he? He'd given Ellen Richards a home, and he'd brought up their daughter alongside his legitimate child. Mariah had wanted for nothing. Of course, if Antonia had lived, that would never have happened.

'Dad!' A dig in the ribs and a loud whisper brought him back to the present. Had he spoken aloud? But no. He was meant to be giving a reading, and had apparently missed his cue. He hauled himself to his feet and approached the lectern.

Back at the house refreshments were being served, the meagre spread being presided over by Mrs Crossley, the Meredith's cook general. The 'funeral bake meats' consisted of weak tea and some dubious-looking sandwiches.

'And we wouldn't even have had those if some of the Mothers' Union hadn't come up trumps,' Henrietta Meredith mourned. 'This rationing business is the absolute end!'

Only half listening, Harry looked across the room to where his daughter was chatting to a young woman from the village. Having a good old moan by the look of it! He hoped the other girl wasn't getting an earful about the servant problem. That wouldn't go down well if she had no help in the house, and few people did, nowadays. He recalled the scene he'd witnessed two days ago.

Gladys, little Henry's nursemaid, was getting told off by Meredith. It was hard to say who was making more noise; the two-year-old or his furious mother. Fortunately Ellen had swooped down on the shrieking child and borne him off to her sitting-room, with promises of a sweetie for a good boy.

'I have told you before, Gladys, I will not have Master Henry subjected to corporal punishment!'

'He had it coming, madam, him deliberately trying to flush my gloves down the lav! And all I did was give him a slap on the hand to let him know it was wrong.'

'He's just a little boy. He doesn't know any better.'

'Then how's he supposed to learn?'

'You reason with him, Gladys. Explain gently that he's made a mistake, and mustn't do it again.'

'Begging your pardon, madam, but that's all wrong. Spare the rod and spoil the child. That's what the minister said in chapel only last Sunday. A good smack on the bottom never did me no harm, see? That boy's got a temper on him, madam. He needs to be curbed.'

Meredith drew herself up to her full five foot four inches. 'How dare you speak to me like that, Gladys Jenkins! You'll kindly allow me to know what's best for my poor, fatherless boy. And you can apologize at once, or you can pack your bags and go!'

'That suits me, madam! I've been thinking about joining the ATS anyway. If it hadn't been for Mrs Richards asking me so nice, I never would have come here in the first place. It's ridiculous having three people to look after one little boy. Why, my mam brought up seven on a miner's pay, and nobody to help, and look at you, with a houseful of servants and nothing to do all day! It ain't right!'

Spluttering with rage, Meredith took hold of the nursemaid's shoulder and propelled her towards the door. Incensed, Gladys let fly a volley of abuse as she stumbled across the carpet. Smiling to herself, Ellen thought it just as well that this last salvo was in Welsh, which Meredith couldn't understand. Some of the words weren't fit for her delicate ears!

The upshot was that Meredith was left without anyone to look after the boy.

'Can't you take charge of him, Nanny?' she pleaded.

'No, I can't! My nannying days are long past, and being housekeeper in a place this size keeps me on my toes, especially with a reduced staff. You'll have to look after him yourself, my girl. Other young mothers do it.'

'That's because they have no choice. People like us don't have to.'

Ellen said no more, but of course she couldn't argue when Paul Meredith died and she was asked — no, told — to look after the child while his mother attended her grandfather's funeral. She made up her mind that a replacement for Gladys would have to be found, sooner rather than later. She had too much to do in the house, and she wasn't as young as she used to be.

The gathering was over at last and the mourners had departed, shaking the widow by the hand and making meaningless comments.

'Anything I can do, you have only to ask.'

'We shall never see his like again.'

'He was a wonderful man. Always there when you needed him.'

This last comment set Henrietta off. As soon as the door had closed behind the last visitor she broke down. 'Always there, was he? Well, he's not here now, and I certainly do need him. Oh, what am I going to do?'

'It's all right, Grandmamma! We're here,' consoled Meredith.

'Oh, you're here now, but you'll be going back to that Cwmbran place tomorrow, and then I'll be all on my own in this house.'

'You'll have Mrs Crossley,' Harry was unwise enough to remark.

'Mrs Crossley? My cook?'

'I only meant she'll be company for you. And being a widow herself, she'll be understanding.'

'Huh!'

Harry felt the need for a stiff drink. Nothing like that had been served to the company and he wanted one now. 'I think we all need a little pick-me-up,' he ventured. 'How about you, Mother-in-law? For medicinal purposes, of course, after your stressful day.'

'Well, perhaps a small sherry, then. Will

you do the honours, Harry?'

The drinks cabinet, such as it was, was kept in the drawing-room. The door was closed now, but after the funeral it had been filled with mourners, as had the dining-room and the morning-room. When the family retired to Henrietta's small sitting-room on the first floor, Mrs Crossley had shut all the doors 'to hide the mess', saying she'd clear up later. She'd been on her feet all day and needed to sit down with a nice cup of tea and a bit of peace and quiet.

Harry sniffed. Was that smoke he smelled? Many of the guests had been smoking, but surely this odour was more than tobacco? He opened the door and jumped back, choking, as a gust of smoke billowed out from the drawing-room. Banging the door shut again he raced for the telephone in the hall, bellowing up the stairs as he went. 'Fire! Get everybody out!'

Meredith appeared at the top of the stairs, frowning. 'What did you say, Dad?'

'The house is on fire. Do as I say, can't you? Get the women out, and hurry. Yes, operator, a fire at the Larches. Send the fire brigade at once!'

'I must go back for my jewel case. Let me go, Meredith!' Henrietta, struggling in her granddaughter's grasp, was hustled down the stairs as Mrs Crossley appeared on the landing, clad only in a sturdy petticoat and lisle stockings.

'Grab a blanket or something,' Harry ordered. 'Don't waste time getting dressed. If the fire spreads to the stairs you may be trapped up there.'

Within minutes the fire brigade arrived, and Harry and the three women were standing outside at a safe distance as the men did their work.

'They mustn't go tramping through the house with all those hosepipes,' Henrietta wailed. 'Tell them, Harry! Oh, my poor house! Why did this have to happen, today, of all days!' She buried her head in Meredith's shoulder, leaving a wet patch on the black silk. Meredith patted her on the back, speechless in the face of this new tragedy.

Out on the road a little group of neighbours had gathered, brought out by the clanging of the bell on the fire engine. Harry gazed at them, grimly. For once he agreed with Henrietta. Why did this have to happen now?

CHAPTER FIVE

Little Henry Fletcher was toddling about, giving high-pitched squeals as he went.

'Oh, my head!' Ellen massaged her forehead, pulling a wry face. 'He's been doing that all morning!'

'Have you tried distracting him?' Mariah asked. She had come indoors to fetch a clean hankie, and found her mother in some distress.

'Of course I have! Nothing works. He doesn't want a story, and he hurls his toys at the wall, laughing like a maniac. He's got himself thoroughly worked up. I've tried to put him down for a nap, but he only pops up again, like one of those tumbling kelly dolls. He's worked out how to climb out of his cot now, and I'm afraid he'll hurt himself.'

'Never mind; his mother should be back soon, and you can hand him over to her.'

Ellen grimaced again. 'That's just the

problem! I've had Harry on the phone. He's on his way home today but Meredith has to stay on. Something about a problem at her grandmother's house. I couldn't make out what he was saying because of all the noise on the line. Anyway, the upshot is that we're stuck with Master Henry until goodness knows when!'

There was a loud crash. Mariah swung round to see that the subject of their conversation had clambered on to a chair and was busily engaged in sweeping ornaments off the sideboard.

'Henry, no!'

The child looked at her slyly and put out a chubby hand to grasp a china shepherdess that was the pride of Ellen's heart. Mariah leaped forward and smacked him on his well-padded bottom. Howls of rage filled the air.

'Now you've done it!' Ellen sighed. 'I can't put up with this much longer, and that's a fact. We'll have to get a replacement for Gladys right away. I want you to pop down to see Megan and see if she knows of some likely girl. I want this fixed up before the sun sets tonight!'

'Meredith won't like it,' Mariah observed, removing an electric flex from the child's fingers with some difficulty. 'She'll want to interview the girl herself.'

'And if I know her, she'll find something wrong with anyone who applies. No, we'll have to handle this ourselves.'

So Mariah found herself cycling down to the village, in search of her mother's best friend. It was pleasant to be pedalling along with the wind in her hair, having a rest from the back-breaking routine of hoeing potatoes.

Luck was with her. When she let herself in to the miner's cottage where Megan lived with her husband and children, she found that the older woman wasn't alone.

'Oh, I'm sorry! I should have knocked, but I didn't realize you had company.' She looked uncertainly at the pretty girl whose face was stained with tears.

'There's nice it is to see you,' Megan smiled. 'Nothing wrong up by there, is it?'

'It's Henry,' Mariah told her.

'Oh, aye?'

'Well, you know what he's like, and he's driving Mam to drink. Meredith had to go to her grandfather's funeral, and she's dumped the baby on Mam.'

'I heard that Gladys Jenkins has been given the boot.'

'I think you'll find it was six of one and half a dozen of the other. She and Meredith had a right old set-to, from what I could gather. I was outside at the time, so I missed all the excitement. Now Mam wants me to ask if you know of anyone who might be free to come and take charge of the little imp.'

'I might do, at that. This is just what you've been looking for, isn't it, *cariad?*' She smiled at her young visitor, who brightened up at once. 'This is Myfanwy, see? Myfanwy Prosser. She's having a hard time of it at home, and she wants to get away. You have experience looking after children, haven't you, *cariad?* Come on, now, tell Mrs Mortimer all about it.'

'Oh, yes, Mrs Mortimer. I'm the eldest of seven, see. From the time I was five I helped look after the young ones, especially when Mam was feeling bad. One little boy would be nothing for me!'

'You haven't met him yet!' Mariah laughed. 'But would you be free to come? Doesn't your mother need you at home?'

The girl mopped her eyes with a bit of damp rag. 'Mam's dead,' she muttered. 'Tuberculosis, they said. She was in the san for a long time, but it didn't do no good.'

'Have another cup of tea,' Megan prompted. 'I'll tell Mrs Mortimer all about it. Drink up, now, there's a good girl.'

'But I still don't see,' Mariah began.

'It's like this. With her mam in the hospital, and not there to keep house, everything fell to Myfanwy, here. Her dada took her out of school, never mind she wanted to go in for teaching, and she had to look after the rest. Well, she wouldn't be the first to have to do it, nor will she be the last. But now the others are old enough to lend a hand, Job Prosser won't let them lift a finger to help in the house.'

'What! You mean you're expected to do all the work looking after eight people?' Mariah was incensed. Who was this man who treated his daughter like some sort of Cinderella?

Myfanwy raised a woebegone face. 'The others are all boys,' she whispered, as if that explained everything.

'According to Job, they shouldn't have to do what he calls women's work.' Megan nodded. 'Two of the boys are down the pit now, and I can see why they shouldn't be expected to do housework on top of that, but the other four are still at school, and they should be able to do something, if only to peg out the washing, but no! It's a crying shame, that it is, and I don't care who hears me say it.'

'Is this true, Myfanwy?' Of course, Megan

wouldn't lie, but Mariah wanted to hear the story from the girl's own lips.

'Yes, miss.'

'I'm Mrs Mortimer.'

'Yes, Mrs Mortimer. The worst of it is, Dada expects the house to be spotless, and his meal on the table when he gets back from work, and it doesn't matter how hard I try, the boys make a big old mess as soon as they come home from school. Then Dada sees how terrible the place looks and I'm in trouble. Took his belt to me the other day, he did, when there wasn't enough bread and dripping left to put in his dinner can. The boys had stolen it when I wasn't looking.'

Mariah made up her mind at once. 'Would you like to try the job up at the house, then? It'll be hard work, mind, running after young Henry, and Mrs Fletcher — his mother, that is — can be quite demanding. Shall we say a month's trial? You'll be paid, of course, and get your board and lodging thrown in.'

Myfanwy clasped her hands together. 'I'd love to give it a try. The only thing is, I don't know what Dada is going to say. He won't want to let me go.'

'You leave your father to me!' Megan told her. 'Go home now and pack your things. When my husband gets home from work

44

we'll go and see Job Prosser. Merfin will soon put him in his place if he tries to make trouble.'

The girl left at once, smiling through her tears.

'Are you sure we're doing the right thing, Megan? I'm all for giving the girl a chance, but the man might be within his rights to keep his daughter at home. He needs a housekeeper by the sound of it.' Mariah frowned.

'Let him marry again, then! For years she's been doing the lot without a word of thanks. Scrubbing dirty pit clothes, cooking, cleaning, making sixpence do the work of a shilling! It's modern-day slavery, that's what it is!'

'Still, he won't like it. What if he absolutely refuses to let her go?'

'She's over twenty-one. Besides, Harry Morgan is a magistrate, and on top of that he owns the colliery, where Job and two of his sons work. The man won't dare to make trouble for fear of losing his job.'

So after tea that evening Myfanwy Prosser arrived at the house, wet and shivering after walking up from the village in the rain. She was met at the door by one of the 'Swansea Six' as the evacuees were known, and she blinked at him in surprise.

'Who are you, then? I thought I was coming to look after a two-year-old, but you look far too big!'

' 'Course I am, I'm Dai, aren't I!' He grinned, leaving her none the wiser. 'Mrs Richards is waiting for you, see. I'm to take you upstairs to her sitting-room, soon as you've come.'

'Who's Mrs Richards, then? I thought it was Mrs Fletcher I'm working for.'

'Na, na. Mrs Fletcher is the baban's mam, but she ain't here. Mrs Richards is the housekeeper. She's in charge while Mr Morgan's away.'

Myfanwy was thoroughly bewildered by now. Who were all these people? How would she ever get their names straight? She was relieved when Ellen received her with a pleasant smile. 'I'll show you to your room so you can get out of those wet clothes, and then we'll have a nice cup of tea and you can tell me all about yourself.'

Perhaps this job wouldn't be too bad, after all, she thought.

Chapter Six

Harry went forward to meet the fire chief, who was coming out of the house, looking pleased.

'Good news! The fire is out, and fortunately it was confined to that one room. If you hadn't discovered it when you did it might have been a different story.'

'Have you any idea what started it?'

'It looks as if it began in an armchair, near the window. Was someone smoking in there earlier today?'

Harry shrugged. 'We've just buried Mr Meredith, and a number of people came back to the house for refreshments. I know that a few of them did light up, but whether anybody accidentally dropped ashes or a stub down the side of that chair is anybody's guess. I suppose we'll never know.'

'Yes, well, it was unfortunate that it happened in that particular chair, so close to the window. The curtains caught quite quickly, I should imagine.'

Henrietta stood with her hand over her mouth as the firemen emerged from the house, dragging a dripping hose with them. She seemed incapable of speech, and it was Harry who thanked the men for their prompt appearance and good work. When they had driven away he turned towards the house, intending to assess the damage before the women saw it.

'Wait for me!' Henrietta quavered. 'I want to see!' Supported by Meredith on one side and Mrs Crossley on the other, she crossed the lawn, trembling as she came.

'Oh, look at the mess they've made!' she cried as they entered the hall.

'Just wait there!' Harry instructed, as he squelched his way towards the room where the fire had been. Needless to say, it was an absolute disaster.

'Oh, I say!' Mrs Crossley's eyes were bright. 'Bit of a mess, isn't it?'

Harry resisted the urge to snap at the woman. His mother-in-law had come up behind him and was wringing her hands, moaning softly.

'What am I going to do, Harry? Oh, why did this have to happen to me? How on earth am I going to manage without Paul to see to this?'

'It could have been much worse,' Harry reminded her, his tone brisk. 'It's just this one room. Your insurance will pay for this, and the rest of the house isn't affected at all.'

'Except for the smell! The whole place will reek of burning!'

'I'm sure you have friends who will gladly put you up for a few days until the place is aired out, Mother-in-law.'

'Dad, no! Of course she doesn't want to impose on friends when she can come to us! You'll come back to Cwmbran with us, won't you, Grandmamma?'

'Well, if you're quite sure . . .'

'Of course we are. Aren't we, Dad?' Meredith shot a meaningful look in her father's direction.

'Er, yes, of course. Glad to have you.' This was going to cause complications, but what else could he say?

Even though her immediate future was settled, Henrietta couldn't stop fretting about her house. 'This whole room will have to be torn apart and redecorated. And look at the furniture! All smelly and waterlogged! How am I to replace all that, then?'

'Building supplies is in short supply,' Mrs Crossley remarked. 'And how are you going to find the workmen? They're all away in

BLUE RIDGE SUMMIT FREE LIBRARY
P.O. Box 34
Blue Ridge Summit, PA 17214-0034

the services now. And the shops is full of rubbish these days. Utility, they calls it, plain stuff, just thrown together, like as not. You'll not find nothing good like you've been used to, Mrs Meredith, and that's a fact.'

'Now don't worry about all that,' Harry put in, seeing that Henrietta was just about at the end of her tether. 'Mrs Crossley can see to things here while you're away, I'm sure.'

But the woman obviously enjoyed spreading doom and gloom. 'Oh, I don't know about that, sir! It'll take more than one pair of hands to sort this lot. And all for what? The next thing we know is Hitler will be coming to drop a bomb on the whole place and that will be the end of that! No, shut the place up, I say, and if it lasts out this war it can be put to rights afterwards.'

'Nonsense! There hasn't been any bombing in these parts, Mrs Crossley, and that's defeatist talk. As for closing the house for the duration, that's quite out of the question. Do that, and the next thing we know squatters will have moved in, people who really have been bombed out of their homes. Give it a few days and then start to work cleaning up the debris from the fire. That room may well have to be shut off for the duration, but the rest of the house will be fine.' Seeing that the woman was about to argue, he put up a hand to stop her. 'Hire someone to help you, Mrs Crossley. If you can't find an able-bodied man, bring in a couple of Boy Scouts. Where there's a will, there's a way.'

'I need to sit down,' Henrietta gasped.

'You'll go straight up to bed,' Harry ordered. 'Meredith, help her with her things, and open all the windows. Give her a couple of Aspro, if you have any.'

'I have some in my bag, Dad.' Meredith rummaged inside her pre-war leather hand-bag and produced a strip of Aspro, which still held several tablets. Protesting, her grandmother was led away.

Harry turned his back on the housekeeper, if that's what she called herself. She wouldn't last five minutes in his own house-hold. He wouldn't tolerate such insubordination from his own staff.

He closed the door firmly on the wreck-age. It was solid oak but was charred on the inside. That, too, would need to be replaced. He cursed the careless person who had brought this about. Nobody needed some-thing like this to happen, on top of a be-reavement.

'I've got her settled, Dad. I think she'll

sleep now. What a rotten thing to happen. I feel quite shaken up myself. Where do we go from here?'

'I'll have to head home, *cariad.* As you know, that was always my plan. I have things to see to. I suppose you'll want to stay on for a bit, to give your grandmother a hand? You'll have to make that Crossley woman toe the line, for one thing.'

'It's not just that, Dad. Grandmamma will want to pack, and it won't be just a question of throwing a few garments in a suitcase. If she's coming to us for an indefinite period she'll want all kinds of things that she can't leave behind. Family photos, favourite books, that sort of thing.'

'Yes, yes!' Harry grumbled. 'You can see to all that, surely, without bothering me with minor details?'

Meredith's mouth trembled. 'What have I done? No need to jump down my throat, is there?'

Her father was contrite at once. 'I know, *cariad,* I know. I didn't mean to snap, but you've got to admit, today has been hard on all of us. First the funeral, and now this!'

She looked at him, realizing for the first time that her handsome father was beginning to look old. It wasn't just the grey in his thatch of hair, or the laughter lines on each side of his mouth. No, it was a look of worry; more than that, a sadness in his expression. Yet he was only sixty-six. That wasn't old nowadays. Perhaps this was what war did to people. It made them old before their time. She went to him and gave him a hug. 'It'll be all right, Dad, you'll see.' She wasn't sure what she meant by that, but it seemed like the right thing to say. He patted her shoulder in return.

When he reached home he was greeted by Ellen, who assured him that everything had gone well in his absence. Nothing untoward had happened at the colliery, the crops were coming along well in their extended kitchen garden and, best of all, she had taken on a new nursery maid, by the name of Myfanwy Prosser.

'That's good,' he murmured absently.

'Is anything wrong, Harry? Was Mrs Meredith very upset after the funeral?'

'I've left her in a very distressed state. Something most unfortunate happened after we all came back to the house.'

Ellen gasped when she heard about the fire. 'There's dreadful! Oh, that poor woman! What will she do now?'

Harry hesitated. 'That's what I have to explain, Ellen. Meredith has invited her to come and stay here, and under the circumstances I could hardly refuse to go along with that now, could I?'

'Of course you couldn't. Well, this is a big enough house. I'm sure I can manage to stay out of her way for a few days.'

'Except that it won't be just a few days, *cariad.* It may well be for the duration. Perhaps it will become a permanent arrangement, I don't know.'

Ellen's chair scraped the floor as she sat down suddenly. 'Oh, Harry!' She put her face in her hands as she rocked herself back and forth.

He watched her, guessing what was going through her mind. He searched desperately for something helpful to say. 'We'll manage, somehow.' Even to himself, the words didn't sound convincing.

Ellen looked up at him then, her face troubled. 'And how is she going to react when she finds out that Mariah is your daughter?'

CHAPTER SEVEN

Myfanwy Prosser was delighted with her new situation. So far, the little boy was no trouble at all. Every time he started to meddle with something that was not his concern she simply picked him up and swung him around while he shrieked with laughter. Then she diverted his attention elsewhere. When your sole task was watching one small child there could hardly be a problem. Not like the old days, when she'd had her little brothers to look after while doing all the housework at the same time.

Well, they were old enough to look after themselves now. She had done her bit and she was free to make her own life. No more cooking and scrubbing from dawn until dusk, keeping house for eight people! Predictably, Dada had been furious when she'd told him what she meant to do.

'What!' he'd shouted. 'You want to go working for them up at the house, leaving us to fend for yourselves? You're wanted here, my girl, and here you shall stay!'

'I've done my bit, Dada. You can't say I haven't. Now it's time for me to make a life for myself, away from here. This job is the beginning.'

He shook his head angrily. 'You're my daughter. It's your duty to stay at home to look after us all. That is what your mam would have wanted you to do.'

'And I have been here, up to now, but the boys are all growing up and they don't need me as much. Samuel will be joining you down the pit before long, and the three young ones are old enough to fetch and carry. Baby Micah is eight years old, Dada.'

'Women's work!' he grunted. 'I'll not have them doing that. What would folks think? And what about the pit clothes? Have you thought of that? What man is going to wash his own filthy garments? Bad enough we have to spend all the hours of daylight down in the bowels of the earth, without getting busy at the wash tub, an' all!'

Myfanwy sighed. What man, indeed! 'There's three good wages coming into this house, Dada. Four when our Samuel gets taken on. Surely you can hire a woman to tackle the washing? Mrs Harries, for instance. With her brood she'd be glad of a

56

bit extra, I think.'

'No son of mine is going to tip up his wages to some washerwoman!' Job roared. 'What's left over after paying for their keep is used for a bit of baccy and that, and why not? They work hard for their money, and I'll not see it taken from them!'

'All right, Dada. I'll send some of my wages home and you can pay Mrs Harries with that. All right?' If she hoped that her father would be impressed with this generous offer, she was to be disappointed.

'There's stupid, girl! You working for them up there, to pay for a woman to come in and do your job here! Just stay home and get on with it and we'll all know where we are!'

'I didn't say I'd tip up the whole lot,' Myfanwy said, edging closer to the door in case he fetched her a wallop. 'That's why I'm going, Dada. I want a bit of money in my pocket. I've never had sixpence to call my own, never mind I've been slaving away here ever since Mam died.'

'That's what all this is about, is it?' he growled. 'I never heard such talk. A daughter, being paid for looking after her father, as is her bounden duty? You've got a roof over your head, haven't you, and food on the table, all paid for by me and your brothers, while you stay home all day? We work for a living. You don't.'

Having been brought up in the chapel, Myfanwy knew the biblical injunction, that a soft answer turneth away wrath. A meek agreement was certainly in order here, but something came over her and she faced him down defiantly. 'You've no idea what I do all day, Dada, with never a word of thanks from you, or the boys. It's "where's my clean shirt?" and "Have you darned my socks? and "Hurry up with the tea, I'm going out". Even the young ones get threepence a week pocket money.'

The worm had turned with a vengeance. Job Prosser looked at his daughter in amazement. 'Pocket money! And what would you do with pocket money, hey? Buy lipstick, I suppose, and go about looking like a harlot!'

'At least harlots get paid for their efforts!' she retorted, skipping nimbly round the table as he came at her with his fist raised. Suddenly all the fight seemed to seep out of him. 'There's no reasoning with you, girl, I can see that. Go then, if you must. How sharper than a serpent's tooth it is to have a thankless child!'

When her father quoted Shakespeare at her like that it was usually the prelude to a long lecture outlining her shortcomings. She had already heard enough on that score. Silently she picked up her carpet bag and left. By the time she reached the sanctuary of Megan Jones' house she was in floods of tears.

'I see you've made the break, then,' Megan greeted her.

'I suppose so, but I feel so guilty, Mrs Jones.'

'No need for that, *bach!* You had to leave home some time. Plenty of girls your age are married already with babies to show for it.'

'But I promised Mam, when she was dying, that I'd look after them all.'

'And so you have. You've brought up the little ones, and they've turned out a credit to you. It's not every girl could take on the job you've done from the age of twelve and do it as well.' Megan took a swig of tea, and pulled a face. 'There's glad I'll be when this war's over, and that's a fact. There was a time when the only use for old tea leaves was for sweeping the dust off the floors. Now we have to save them for the next brew because of this old rationing!'

'That's another thing,' Myfanwy remarked. 'I'll have to take my ration card with me and give it to the housekeeper up there, won't I?'

'Of course you will. How are they going to feed you otherwise? I suppose you've been giving bits and pieces to the children and going short yourself.' She saw by the expression on the girl's face that she had hit the nail on the head. So what? She did the same for her own youngsters, as any mother would. 'One thing, you won't go short of food up there.' She smiled. 'Mariah — that's Mrs Mortimer, you've already met her — she grows enough vegetables to feed a regiment. She's got help of course; the Swansea Six are keen as mustard.'

'The Swansea Six?'

'That's what they call them. Evacuees. Six little boys from Swansea, sent here after the bombing. Living in an orphanage, they were.'

Myfanwy was horrified. 'Hitler sent planes to bomb an orphanage?'

'I don't think so; not that I'd put it past him. No, I think that once the bombing started they sent the children away as a precaution. Mind you, one of those little tinkers told me they'd been praying for a bomb or two to hit the orphanage and their school! You know what children are.'

'But aren't I just going up there to mind Master Henry, Mrs Jones? I don't think I want to take on six little boys as well.'

'Na, na. Mariah does all that. Besides, they don't seem to need much looking after. No, you'll only have to worry about one two-year-old, temper tantrums and all!'

Myfanway picked up the bag which held her few possessions, including the Welsh Bible which had belonged to her mother. 'I'd better be going, before they give the job to someone else! *Diolch yn fawr,* Mrs Jones.'

'I'll see you out,' Megan murmured. She hoped everything would turn out well.

All that was three days ago. Mr Morgan had been away in England, attending his father-in-law's funeral, but he was back now. So far Myfanwy hadn't set eyes on him, and she wasn't sure she wanted to. She had gathered from her older brothers that Harry Morgan was a power to be reckoned with, almost next to God, which in a community ruled by the chapel was saying something. His daughter, Mrs Fletcher, still hadn't returned home. She had stayed on to help her grandmother, apparently.

Myfanwy looked down at her neat uniform with satisfaction. She was wearing a starched white apron over a lavender-coloured frock. These garments had been worn by the previous nursemaid, Gladys, but as they went with the job she had left them behind when she flounced off.

'They're too big, of course,' Mrs Richards had said, 'Gladys being taller and stouter than you, but we'll soon alter them to fit you. At least the cap will do.'

It would, indeed. Myfanwy gazed at herself in the looking glass. Didn't she look a picture, with the froth of lace perched on her glossy dark hair, the ribbon streamers dangling down behind. It was pre-war, of course; all the garments were. You couldn't get quality like that now, and nobody wanted to spend their precious clothing coupons on servants' uniforms. She giggled.

'What's the matter?' Ellen smiled.

'Oh, I was just thinking about what it said on the radio, Mrs Richards. You know, all this "make do and mend". A woman was telling people if they wanted a new frock and didn't have the coupons they should cut up some old curtains to make one!'

'Stranger things have happened, *bach.* As a matter of fact, I've got my eye on those velvet curtains in the drawing-room. Make me a lovely ball gown, those would!'

Myfanwy's eyes opened wide. Then she saw the twinkle in Ellen's own and knew it was a joke. She smiled back happily.

CHAPTER EIGHT

Mariah was aware that her mother was very unhappy. In a way, she felt responsible, although she knew that was foolish. Nothing had really gone right for Ellen since the truth had come out about her relationship to Harry Morgan, and now, with Antonia's mother coming to stay for a prolonged period, life was likely to become very difficult.

By now, Mariah was coming to terms with the fact that her father was not Bertie Richards. Happily married to Aubrey Mortimer, she was learning not to worry about who her father was. Aubrey accepted her for herself, and that was all that mattered. Besides, she had never known poor Bertie so she could hardly view his loss with any degree of pain.

No, it was Ellen who was suffering yet again.

'Perhaps it won't come out,' Mariah said

hopefully. 'There aren't many people who know about it, after all. I expect you're worrying over nothing.'

'Meredith will tell her.'

'You don't know that, Mam. I'm sure Harry will have a quiet word with her.'

'Fine words butter no parsnips with that young woman, Mariah.'

'Then we'll just have to wait and see, won't we?' But it was the waiting that was hard. Over the years Mariah had tried to persuade her mother to leave Cwmbran, to strike out on her own somewhere, but Ellen had her own reasons for staying put and time had passed with no changes being made. 'Perhaps you should think about leaving now, Mam.'

'Oh, yes? And where do you propose I should go, when there's a war on? I'm a bit too old to join up.'

'I'm sure there are plenty of things you could do. With so many people in the services now there must be lots of jobs available.'

'Perhaps.' Ellen primmed her lips and Mariah knew that the subject was closed. She wished she knew more about the events leading up to her mother coming to Cwmbran, but she had been told only the bare minimum. Painfully embarrassed, and not meeting Mariah's eyes, Ellen had muttered something about she and Harry having 'come together only the once, and never again'.

That one time was enough to give her Harry's child and, left alone in the world with nobody to turn to, she had been forced to approach him for help. He had brought her to Cwmbran to run the little sweet shop at the end of the terrace where Megan Jones and her husband lived, prepared to say that he was doing a favour for an old friend whose godchild was a casualty of the war. That was the Great War, as they called it, of course.

As things turned out, his story hadn't been necessary. Young Mrs Jones, coming into the house and seeing Bertie Richards' photograph on the mantelpiece, had assumed that this was Ellen's late husband, killed in action. On being addressed as Mrs Richards, rather than Miss, Ellen had let the mistake ride. Nobody here knew that Bertie was her brother, and it was only a little white lie. Where was the harm, if it saved his sister and her coming baby from shame? Bertie would not have minded; she was sure of that.

'You know what happened next,' Ellen had reminded Mariah on that dreadful day, when it all came out. 'Mrs Morgan died giving birth to Meredith, and they were at their wits' end here in the house when the child didn't thrive. They tried everything; tins of stuff you can buy in the shops, goats milk, everything. They thought she'd die. As a last resort they decided to bring in a wet nurse and Harry saw his opportunity.'

And that had grown into an opportunity for Ellen. She had stayed on as nanny to the Morgan baby, after the hired one had failed to give satisfaction, and the little half sisters had shared a nursery. Harry Morgan had brought in a governess to teach his daughter, and had offered Ellen the chance to have Mariah educated in the same way.

'That's when I should have left, as he meant me to do,' Ellen had explained. 'And many a sleepless night I've had since, asking myself why I didn't go when I had the chance. I couldn't bear to leave you behind, though, so I refused. That was when he offered me the job of housekeeper, so I gave in, and stayed.'

Be sure your sins will find you out. That was a favourite saying among the chapelgoers of Cwmbran, and, sure enough, Ellen's deception had been uncovered, during this present war. Some months earlier a young footman, now in the army, had come to visit, bringing a comrade with him. As luck would have it the other young man was from Cardiff, and a former neighbour of the Richards family. On seeing Bertie's picture in Ellen's sitting-room he'd blurted out, in all innocence, that Bertie Richards had never been married.

An appalling scene had followed, during which Meredith had shrieked like a fish-wife, disgusted with her father and blaming everything on Ellen, the 'other woman'.

'Do you really think she'll keep quiet, Mariah?'

Mariah came out of her reverie with a start. 'Meredith? I would hope that she had enough sensitivity not to mention it to her grandmother. Not only has the poor soul just lost her husband, after more than fifty years of marriage, but she's had the shock of nearly losing her home as well. On top of it all there's this beastly war. Nobody can stop worrying over that. Anyway, Mam, why should the subject even come up? As you said before, this is a big house. Just stay out of her way and it will all work out. You'll see.'

'I hope you're right, that's all.'

As things turned out it was Mariah who came under scrutiny. She was working outside as usual when Harry's car drew up bringing his daughter and mother-in-law from the station. She knew she wasn't needed just then, and she wanted to get to the end of the job she was doing before she went inside for a well-deserved rest.

'We're finished for today,' she told the Swansea Six at last. 'Run along and play, but don't make too much noise when you come in for lunch. Mrs Fletcher's visitor has arrived and she's an old lady who's just lost her husband. Let's give her a bit of peace and quiet, all right?'

They ran off, laughing, to the tiny club house they'd made for themselves out of old boards and fallen branches. They looked like characters from a *Just William* book, with their cheerful, grubby faces and their socks falling down around their ankles.

'Oh, for a nice hot bath, with lots of soap suds!' Mariah sighed, stretching to rid herself of the cramp in her back. There wasn't much chance of that, though. In compliance with government guidelines Harry had carefully painted a line around both bathtubs to show how much water they were permitted to use. Anyone using more than three inches was being unpatriotic, as he never stopped reminding them.

On her way upstairs she thought she heard something fall and smash inside the morning-room. Turning back she peered through the doorway, surprised to see Henrietta Meredith gazing down at an ornament, which lay on the floor in pieces.

'You, there, girl! Fetch a dustpan and brush and see to this mess!' Taken aback, Mariah didn't answer and Henrietta frowned.

'Shouldn't you be in uniform, girl? And what on earth are you wearing? No maid of mine would be allowed through the doors with muddy breeks like those!'

'I've been in the garden all morning. I was just nipping up to change.'

'Never mind that now. Kindly do as I say, and fetch a dustpan. After that you can make me a cup of tea, but make sure you give your hands a good scrub first.'

Resisting the urge to say 'who do you think you are?' because she knew all too well who the woman was, Mariah took a deep breath. She gave the embroidered bell pull a tug that was too violent for the ancient fabric. Luckily it stayed in one piece.

'I have rung for a maid,' she pointed out coldly. 'I'm sure that whoever comes will be more than happy to assist you.' She stalked out of the room, head held high, leaving Henrietta standing with her mouth open.

'What on earth is the matter with you?'

Ellen wanted to know when her daughter banged into the room, snatching a towel from a pile of clean washing as she came. 'You look like you've had a real barney with someone.'

'And if I haven't, it's only because I was well brought up by you!' Mariah fumed, pulling her jersey over her head as she spoke. 'That woman!'

'Mrs Meredith, I suppose. Don't tell me you've run afoul of her already? I did warn you to be careful.'

'It wasn't my fault, Mam. She managed to smash an ornament in the morning-room; heaven knows what she was doing with it, checking for dust, I expect, and when I popped in to see what had happened, she went for me. She called me 'girl' and started giving orders left and right, like Mr Churchill's secret weapon. Bring me a dustpan she said, and after that you can make me a cup of tea, but be sure to wash your hands first. And as for my britches, I shouldn't be allowed over the doorstep wearing those. I suppose I'm meant to be hoeing the garden wearing my ball gown!'

'Surely it can't be that bad!' Ellen was half laughing, but the incident did not bode well for the future.

CHAPTER NINE

Meredith Fletcher had come home after the funeral to find that a nursemaid had been installed for little Henry in her absence. She was in two minds about this. On one hand it took the pressure off her, but on the other it irritated her that Mariah seemed to have been responsible.

'I should think you'd be grateful,' Ellen sniffed. 'Mariah had to drop everything to go down to the village to see if Megan knew about a suitable girl who'd be willing to come at short notice. It's a piece of luck that it's worked out like this.'

'But who is this girl? We don't know anything about her.'

'According to Megan, Myfanwy is a perfectly respectable young woman. Her father and brothers are employed by your own father.'

'I should have been able to interview her before she was given the job,' Meredith insisted. 'Henry is my child, after all. I'm responsible if anything goes wrong.'

'Then go and interview her now. She's here on trial. You can always send her away if things don't work out.'

Meredith flounced off to the nursery. She found her son lying in his bed, looking like one of those cherubs in Victorian paintings. Myfanwy stood up respectfully.

'I've just got him down, madam,' she whispered. 'Doesn't he look a picture?'

Meredith's heart softened towards her. She saw a fresh-faced young woman, not many years younger than herself. Perhaps she might do. But first impressions weren't always the right ones. She beckoned to the girl, who followed her out to the passage.

'I'm Mrs Fletcher,' she began. 'I'd just like to ask you a few questions.'

'Certainly, madam.'

'Have you any experience of this sort of work, Myfanwy? That is your name, isn't it?'

'Yes, madam. That's what my name is, I mean.'

'But your experience?'

'Not professional, like, but I have brought up six younger brothers.'

Meredith was taken aback. 'You've brought up six children! Are you orphans, then? I understood that you have a father in the employ of Mr Morgan.'

'That's right, madam. But our mam died when I was twelve, see, and my brothers were all younger than me and I had to take her place in the house. I did all the house-work and the cooking, and I looked after the boys as well.'

'Good grief!' Meredith said faintly, re-membering herself as a petted twelve-year-old girl, without a care in the world, waited on hand and foot and given every advantage. 'I'm prepared to take you on trial, Myfanwy,' she said at last. 'But if I find we're not suited, I'll have to think again. Do you understand me?'

'Oh, yes, madam. Mrs Mortimer explained that to me before I came. I'll do my best to give satisfaction.'

Meredith returned to her sitting-room, feeling that she'd been outsmarted in some way she couldn't really fathom. Her grand-mother was waiting for her, wearing a frown which promised trouble.

'I've just met the most extraordinary young woman downstairs,' she remarked.

'Oh?'

'Wearing filthy trousers and carrying shoes quite caked with mud. Her manner was very offhand, I thought. She spoke to me quite rudely.'

'Oh!'

'Is that all you can say? I'm sorry to have to say this, Meredith, but the standard of service in this house is not at all what it should be. You must keep your servants up to the mark, dear, or they'll walk all over you. I had a little accident, and this person, whoever she was, flatly refused to fetch me a dustpan! Then I rang and rang and when someone finally put in an appearance it was a maid almost as old as I am. Ruth, she said her name is.'

Meredith hid a smile. Ruth was in her fifties; she had started in service there during the Great War and had been with them ever since. Henrietta made a point of never disclosing her age, but she had to be approaching eighty.

'I trust that she provided you with the dustpan you wanted, Grandmamma?'

'Yes, although she took her time about it. I don't know why you put up with this lax behaviour, Meredith.'

'It's this beastly war. Most of the servants have gone off to join the forces. We don't have enough to look after a place this size. We've had to shut off some of the rooms for the duration.'

'I asked who that girl was, and why she was in such a grubby condition, and she said, "Oh, that's Mrs Mortimer, madam. She's been doing the garden", and then I understood. She's a member of the Women's Land Army, I suppose, and you've got her billeted on you while she does her war work. Very commendable, I'm sure, but how annoying for you having to put up with strangers in the house. And I hear that you have six small boys as well, evacuees from Swansea.'

Meredith waited until her grandmother had run out of breath and then she strove to explain. 'Mariah isn't a land girl, Grandmamma. Don't you remember her? She was my bridesmaid when I was married.'

'Of course I remember your bridesmaid, Meredith! Do you take me for a fool? But that was the housekeeper's daughter, wasn't it? Surely her name was Richards?'

'That's right, but she's married now.'

'Then why is she still living with you?'

'Because her husband is a pilot in the air force. He doesn't want her to join up because they'd never both get leave at the same time. He can always come here if he gets the chance, although that doesn't happen very often. It's too far to come when he just has a forty-eight hour pass.'

Henrietta pursed her lips. 'So in the meantime she's taking advantage of you, staying on here? I hope she pays well for the privilege.'

Closing her eyes slowly, Meredith searched for the right words. 'This is her home, Grandmamma. She's welcome to stay here as long as she wants to. Anyway, she's needed here. She grows acres of vegetables and she looks after our evacuees.'

It appeared that Henrietta had ignored the last part of this statement, because she stubbornly pursued her original train of thought. 'I've always believed that your father made a bad mistake, letting that girl be brought up with you. Oh, don't bother to tell me that her mother saved your life when you were an infant! Perhaps she did, perhaps she didn't. After you were weaned Harry should have given the woman some sort of parting gift and let her go back to where she came from. Then you would have been brought up by a fully qualified nanny, instead of — what was she — a shop assistant!'

'I believe I did have a proper nanny in the beginning,' Meredith remarked. 'I'm told that she was a rigid sort of person who couldn't get on with the other staff. Dad had to dismiss her.'

'So what? Nannies grow on trees. We certainly didn't have any trouble finding one when your own mother was a baby.'

Henrietta had to be diverted from this subject. Meredith saw her chance and mentioned that she had just hired a new nursemaid for Henry.

'Oh, yes? What happened to the other one, Gladys somebody?'

'She wasn't at all suitable. She actually smacked poor little Henry, and when I took her to task over it she dared to answer me back. I had to dismiss her.'

'Very right and proper, dear. Now, do I get to meet this new girl and see for myself if she will do?'

Meredith rang the bell, and when Ruth finally appeared, breathless after labouring up two flights of stairs, she was asked to send Myfanwy in. The nursemaid appeared, smiling shyly.

'This is my grandmother, Mrs Meredith, from Herefordshire. She'll be staying with us for a while, and of course she looks forward to spending time with my son. I know you will be pleased to help her whenever she asks to see Henry.'

'Oh, yes, madam.'

Henrietta, sitting very upright in her chair

looked down her nose. 'What is your name, girl?'

'Myfanwy, madam. Myfanwy Prosser.'

'I didn't quite catch . . .'

'Muh van wee.' The girl drew the syllables out in case the old lady was hard of hearing. 'It's Welsh, madam.'

'So I supposed. Well, it's much too difficult. I shall call you Mary.'

Myfanwy lowered her eyes modestly to hide the fury in her expression. Old buzzard! Who did she think she was? The baby's great-grandma was worse than old Mrs Lewis down the chapel. She hoped their paths wouldn't cross too often.

CHAPTER TEN

Mariah settled down to write to her husband. This always represented a struggle but she had to get on with it, knowing that he looked forward to her letters as much as she longed for a blue envelope, addressed in his sprawling handwriting. It was easy enough to say how much she missed him, yet she instinctively understood that if she laid it on with a trowel, as the saying went, this wouldn't do him any good. He needed cheerful news from home to offset the stress of his work. Nor could she mention how worried she was about his safety because that was no good for morale. Added to that, what was the use of telling him to be careful? If your number was up, as the men put it, that was that!

She tried desperately to find something interesting to say. The Swansea Six were always good for a laugh. When they weren't working with her on the land they were off looking for spies. Nobody was safe from their inspection. Even the postman, panting up the drive with his sack of mail, had almost come off with his bike as a gang of small boys rushed him, yelling: 'Stop! Who goes there?'

Luckily he was a cheerful soul who went along with their game, shouting: 'Sioni Evans, On His Majesty's Service,' and giving them a smart salute when they told him he could pass.

'Is it really necessary for you to stop him again on the way back?' Mariah had enquired. 'You've done it once already.'

'We're supposed to. That's what they do in the army, miss,' young Dai Jones told her, but she had no way of knowing if this was really true. 'I'm joining the army as soon as I'm old enough,' he went on. 'I can't wait to have a go at them Nazis.'

Mariah smiled at the child. She devoutly hoped that the war would be over, and won by the Allies, of course, long before he reached the age to do any such thing.

Early one morning Henrietta Meredith happened to take herself for a gentle stroll down the rhododendron walk. Leaning on her silver-topped walking stick, a memento of her late husband, she stopped to listen to an unusual bird, attracted by its warbling note. She peered among the branches, seeing nothing.

Suddenly a figure sprang at her from the other side of the walk. 'Stand and deliver, your life or your liver!'

Her heart was beating so fast that it was a moment before she could gather her wits. 'What on earth do you think you're playing at, young man? You could have given me a heart attack, jumping out at me like that! Well, what do you say?'

'Sorry, missus.' The boy bent over and seemed to be writhing in pain.

'What's the matter now? Are you hurt?'

He straightened up then, and handed her a toy of some sort. 'I was laughing, see, 'cause you thought you heard a bird.'

Henrietta turned it over in her hand. It seemed to be a bubble pipe, but instead of a bowl it ended in a small image of a bird. 'What is it? What does it do?'

'It's a warbler, missus. You fill it it up with water, see, and you blow into it, and it warbles like a bird.' He seemed so pleased with himself that she had to smile.

'You're very young to be away from home,' she remarked. 'Does your mother come to visit you when she can?'

'Na. She went to heaven, to be with my dad. There's nobody left but me. That's why

I had to go to the orphanage. They were thinking about sending me to Canada to work on a farm, but then this war happened, so I come here instead.'

'I see.' Henrietta blinked back a tear. 'Hadn't you better run along and find your little friends? And I advise you not to jump out on people any more. You might do them an injury.'

'Except spies. It's all right to jump on them, I s'pose?'

'Yes, yes, I expect so.'

The child ran off, pretending to be an aeroplane. Henrietta chuckled to herself. The brief encounter had done her good. She recounted the tale to the family at dinner that evening and for various reasons they all found it amusing. At least it was a cheerful story to tell Aubrey, Mariah thought.

It had provided Henrietta with food for thought. 'What will happen to those boys after the war?' she asked Harry. 'The Swansea Six, as they call themselves.'

'How do I know? They'll return to the orphanage, I suppose, and they won't be the only ones. There'll be more homeless children before this war is over.'

'It doesn't seem right. That little chap told me he was on the point of being sent to

Canada, to work on a farm. On the other hand, your grandchild is going to inherit all this.' She waved her arm to indicate the great house, and the lands beyond.

'Henry is an orphan, too, if you want to look at it like that, Mother-in-law. His father is dead, in case it's escaped your notice.'

'There's no need to be sarcastic with me, Harry Morgan! His mother is still very much alive, and the child still has the rest of us. There's a vast gulf between the two boys.'

He shrugged. 'That's the way of the world. As it says in the Bible, the poor will always be with us. I shouldn't feel too sorry for our evacuees, if I were you. They're safe here with us and they're getting plenty of fresh air and good food. Save your pity for the kiddies in those countries that the Nazis have overrun. I doubt they'll fare as well.'

He knew what he was talking about, of course, but she was still determined to do what she could to make life better for the Swansea Six.

Perhaps it was unfortunate that the first step in her plan was to convert her sweet ration to their use. She was very fond of a nice toffee, but her teeth had reached the stage where she had to be careful. She was proud of still having most of her own teeth and she hoped they'd see her out. She didn't want to try getting used to dentures at her age. The boys could be bribed to help her to wind her wool. She'd been unable to persuade her granddaughter to do it.

'Must I, Grandmamma? You know how much I hate it.'

'Really, Meredith! It's not much to ask, is it?'

But sitting on an upright chair, with both her arms held out stiffly in front of her, holding a skein of wool while her grandmother wound it into a ball, was not her idea of fun.

'How on earth did you manage to get hold of all that wool, anyway? It's scarce as hen's teeth in the shops nowadays. You haven't been hoarding, I hope?'

'Certainly not! I'm as patriotic as the next person, and well you know it! I've had this by me for years, leftovers from other knitting projects. There isn't enough of any one colour to make a complete garment, but it will do for Fair Isle, or stripes, perhaps.'

But Meredith remained reluctant, so the Swansea Six were invited to help out. They were reticent at first, seeing the job as 'girl's work', but their eyes lit up when Henrietta produced a quarter of toffees.

'I'll do it, missus!' It was the small boy

with the warbler.

'Let me see your hands, then.' Henrietta shuddered. 'My goodness! Have you been down the mine, child? Go and give them a good scrubbing, and then we'll see how you get on.'

The boy, whose name was Ceri Davies, stood up well under the strain, but even he began to waver at last, and she was forced to give up.

'That will do for now, thank you. We'll have another go tomorrow, shall we?'

Much to his delight she handed over three toffees. He immediately unwrapped one and popped it in his mouth. The other two went into his pocket. It was an unspoken law in the orphanage that on the rare occasions when you were given a treat you shared it with your mates. But he had five friends and only two more sweets. That justified keeping them all for himself.

It was Myfanwy's afternoon off and she had gone into the village to see a friend. Meredith had taken Henry outside in his pushchair and the pair were sitting in the shade, watching Mariah and her helpers at work. She beckoned to Ceri, who seemed to be on the fringe of things.

'Come and keep an eye on my little boy, will you? I have to go indoors for a minute.

Don't unstrap him, mind; we don't want him wandering off.'

Ceri unwrapped his second toffee, closely observed by Henry. The child stretched out his hand. 'Want sweetie!'

'Na, na. No sweetie.'

'Want sweetie!' Drumming his feet on the footrest of his chair, Henry began to roar. Alarmed, Ceri thrust the toffee into the cavernous mouth. Anything to stop the racket before the toddler's mam came back and blamed him for causing an upset.

Looking pleased with himself, Henry sucked on the sweet, just as Meredith returned. He looked up at her, beaming. A brown stream dribbled down his chin.

'What on earth have you got in your mouth, Baby? Let Mummie see.' She tried to prise his lips open, but his jaws were clamped shut and he wriggled and twisted out of her clutch as she tried to maintain her grip on him. 'Open your mouth, Henry, please!'

He began to sob and splutter, unable to do as she asked.

She let out a piercing scream. 'Help! Somebody help! Henry can't breathe!'

CHAPTER ELEVEN

Blissfully unaware of the drama being played out up at the house, Myfanwy Prosser made up her mind to make the most of her first afternoon off. Not that the job was all that hard; money for jam, really, she mused. There wasn't much to looking after one tiny boy, not when you had other people to do the cooking and the cleaning and the laundry. She liked to hand wash his tiny woollies but that was pleasant work, and his mother liked to do any mending herself.

She went first to call on her friend Bronwen, who was a typist at the colliery office, but her mother was the only one at home. 'She'll be sorry to have missed you, *cariad,* but they've changed her day off, see. Something to do with this old war, I expect. Come on in, though, and have a *cwpan* with me.'

'That's very kind, but I haven't brought any tea with me.' By now, rationing was so tight that whenever you went visiting you took a spoonful of tea with you, in a screw of greaseproof paper. Short of an emergency, other people couldn't be expected to share their ration with you, or it wouldn't last out the week.

'Oh, we can squeeze another cup out of this morning's tea,' Mrs Evans told her. 'Now, sit down and tell me all your news. How's it going with you up above there? See much of Mr Morgan, do you?'

'Not really. He doesn't come up to the nursery floor.'

'And that Mrs Fletcher? Difficult to work for, is she?'

'Not bad. A bit starchy at times, but I try to keep on the right side of her. It's that *mamgu* of hers I have to watch out for.'

'Pokes her nose in where it's not wanted, does she?'

'She insists on calling me Mary, if you please. She says that Myfanwy is too outlandish a name for her.'

'Cheek! Well, that's the English for you. What are you going to do with yourself for the rest of the day, then, as our Bron's not home? I don't suppose you'll want to call in on your dada?'

Obviously the word had spread about their disagreement. Myfanwy pulled a face.

'He won't be home yet, Mrs Evans. I suppose I'd better look in and have a look around, maybe set the tea and that.'

'Aye, the house will be a tip, I daresay, with men in charge. Wonder what we women do at home all day, they do, but they soon feel a draught if the work doesn't get done. At least your dada's found someone to tackle the wash for him. That's something.'

Creeping down the alley behind their terrace, Myfanwy kept looking over her shoulder, expecting someone to pounce on her, calling her a bad daughter. Of course, there was nobody about. All the men were at work, and the children at school. At this time of day the women were either out at the shops or putting their feet up for five minutes. She found the spare key under the brick where it had been kept all her life, and let herself into the silent house.

Two hours' hard work put the place to rights, although she doubted whether Dada would notice the difference. The boys would be home from school before the men came off shift and they'd soon change the look of the place. An empty jam jar stood on the draining board in the scullery. It had been wiped clean but it still needed a rinse. She washed it carefully. The boys loved to go to the Odeon on Saturdays and a jam jar was a great prize because you could use that to get into the cinema, instead of money. Even a humble glass pot contributed to the war effort.

After a last look round she walked up the street to call on Megan.

'You're a sight for sore eyes!' Megan greeted her. 'How are you getting on up beyond? Come inside and you can tell me all about it.'

'No tea for me, *diolch*,' Myfanwy told her. 'I had two cups with Bronwen's mam earlier.' More like hot water with a vague taste of tea, she thought, but she didn't say it. It wasn't Mrs Evans' fault that each person's ration only amounted to two ounces a week.

'How about a Welsh cake, then, fresh baked? You'll have to hunt for the currants, mind. I only had a teaspoonful to put in them.'

In between bites, Myfanwy repeated the story she'd already shared with Mrs Evans.

'I'm sure they're glad to have you there,' Megan remarked. 'Not many girls going into service nowadays, see. All joining up, or working in the factories. It's a wonder to me they don't put us down the pit now, like they did in the old days.'

'I thought that was just an old wives tale.'

'Na, na, *cariad.* Long ago they sent children down as well, so I've heard, although whether that happened in Cwmbran I have no idea. But never mind that. How's your dada getting along without you?'

'I'm afraid to go and ask,' Myfanwy admitted. 'I did call in at the house and tidy up a bit, though. It's not bad, all things considered. I'm sure they'll manage once they make up their minds to it. Even a child can handle a broom. If only Dada can get it out of his head that I've deserted them.'

'Don't you worry about that. You've done your bit, all these years. Everybody knows that. You'd have had to leave home if you met some chap and got married; nobody would think twice about that. And now you're earning a wage you'll be able to get something put by for your bottom drawer.'

Myfanwy blushed. 'I may never get married, Mrs Jones. Not with so many of our boys going to the war and getting themselves killed.'

'Plenty of good ones down the pit.'

'I don't want to marry a miner, Mrs Jones. There's three of our family working down there now, and that makes four when our Samuel starts. Every day when I waved them off to work I used to think, What if something happens and they never come home? Cave-ins happen, and well you know it.'

Megan grinned. 'When you meet the right chap and fall in love you'll jump at the chance to marry him, no matter what he does for a living. Trust me, I know!'

Myfanwy stood up. 'I must be going. I've one or two things I want to do before I get back.'

'All right, *cariad.* Call again, next time you're down this way.'

Walking away from the village, humming happily to herself, Myfanwy felt virtuous, knowing that she'd dropped in at her old home and done what she could to help. Some day Dada would accept the fact that she was gone, and then she could visit them all on Sundays as an honoured guest.

It was a happy thought, but she had no way of knowing that far from giving Dada a warm feeling, her surprise visit had fanned the flames of his discontent. When he and his elder sons trudged home from work they were greeted by the schoolboy members of the family who were full of excitement.

'Someone's been here, Dada,' the younger boy shouted.

'Her with the clean washing, most likely. Don't yell, Pedr. I'm not deaf.'

'But look in the pot, Dada! There's *tatws,*

all peeled and ready to put on the boil.'

'And a plate of tart, still warm!' Micah enthused. 'Who did it, Dada?'

'Well, it wasn't the *tylwyth teg*, boyo! I expect it was your sister. Who else would be coming here doing the cooking?'

Far from feeling appreciative of his daughter's efforts, Job Prosser became even more resentful of what he viewed as her treachery. Wasn't it bad enough that Morgan up at the house kept them working night and day for a pittance, without stealing his daughter, too? Of course, a man like that, with a house full of servants, could have no idea what it was like to be left without a woman about the place, nor would he care if he did.

It didn't help that the Reverend Rees had stopped him in the street on the way home, asking about Myfanwy. 'I haven't seen her in chapel recently, Job. Nothing wrong, is there?'

Wrong! The question could hide a multitude of sins, Job thought sourly. 'She's gone into service, Mr Rees. Nursemaid, up at the house.'

'Ah, yes. I heard about Gladys getting the sack. So your Myfanwy has taken her place, is it?' Job grunted. Reverend Rees pressed on. 'Tell her to arrange her time off so she can come to chapel. We all need the consolation of our religion in these godless days.'

Job muttered something which might have been taken for agreement, and the clergyman nodded and passed on up the street. Wasn't it enough that his daughter had abandoned her family, without him being told off by the preacher for not seeing that the girl attended chapel?

When he reached home and found that she had been there in his absence, like a thief in the night, he felt the fury rising in his gorge. For two pins he'd take that tart and throw it in the pig bucket, but that would never do. Food was too hard to come by, and why take it out on the children, who were looking forward to their treat? Suddenly he made up his mind. He would go up to the house and have it out with Morgan. Tell him that Myfanwy couldn't stay; she was needed at home.

CHAPTER TWELVE

'Do something!' Meredith wailed. 'My poor baby! He's choking! Help me!'

Mariah leaped forward. Henry was certainly wide-eyed and red in the face, but he seemed to be in no imminent danger of choking. She rubbed her grubby hands on her britches and leaned closer to the child. A dribble of brown spittle ran down his cheek and landed on his pale-blue linen romper suit. Meredith dabbed at it ineffectually with her lace hankie.

'Out of the way, Meredith! Let me see what I'm doing!' Mariah gently prised the toddler's lips apart, trying to reach inside his mouth. She managed to get one finger around the sticky mass and gently pulled it. The toffee was well and truly stuck to his tiny teeth and it was quite a tussle to work it loose. Henry drummed his feet and made unintelligible noises.

While everyone's attention was focused

on the little drama, Ceri Davies silently unwrapped his one remaining sweet and popped it in his mouth. He was expecting trouble when that Mrs Fletcher found out what he'd done. If he got a good hiding well, there was nothing he could do about that, but he wasn't about to let them take his toffee away as part of the punishment. He began to suck blissfully, intent on making it last as long as possible.

Henry spat out the mass of brown goo. It landed on his lap, doing further damage to his clothing.

'Let's see if we've got it all,' Mariah murmured, inserting her sticky finger between his teeth again. She jumped back with a startled cry. 'The little devil! He bit me! You need a good smacked bottom, my boy!'

'He'll get nothing of the sort!' his mother snapped. 'The poor little angel! He could have died!'

'Rubbish! How could he choke on it when it was stuck to his teeth?'

'You didn't want the nasty old toffee, did you, darling?' Meredith cooed.

'Want sweetie!'

'Not now, Henry.'

'Want sweetie!' he roared, about to go into a full-blown tantrum. His mother wheeled the pushchair around and prepared to take him indoors. She stopped for a moment, turning to face Mariah.

'How did he get hold of such a thing in the first place? You didn't give it to him, did you, Mariah?'

'Of course I didn't. Do you take me for a fool? I may not be a mother but I do have enough sense not to give a toddler something he could choke on.'

Unseen by either of them, Ceri Davies slunk away. How was he supposed to know what could happen? He'd never had anything to do with babies before. At the orphanage they were kept in a separate wing.

'Well!' Mariah said to nobody in particular, as she sucked her injured finger, which tasted of caramel and mud. 'Thank you for saving my child's life, Mariah! I don't know how I'll ever repay you. Whatever should I have done if you hadn't been here to do what you did?'

Returning from her excursion, meaning to stretch out on her bed with her new library book until it was time to resume her duties, Myfanwy was surprised to be greeted by her tearful employer.

'Oh, Myfanwy, thank goodness! Here!' She thrust the furious, smelly child into the nursemaid's arms. 'There's been an accident. Henry somehow got hold of a toffee, and it almost choked him. He didn't get it from you, I trust.'

'Of course not, madam! I know better. Did you want me to have him now? I mean, I'm not back yet, officially.'

'Oh. No, I suppose you're not. But he needs a bath, and that little suit needs rinsing through. I hope it's not ruined. Look, you take him, and I'll make it up to you some other time. Next week you can have an extra hour. Will that do?'

Myfanwy hesitated. Trying to please your employer was all very well, but it didn't do to take that too far. 'Give them an inch and they'll take a mile,' Megan had warned. 'You mustn't let them take advantage.'

When no response was forthcoming, Meredith knew she'd met her match. 'Oh, very well, then,' she countered crossly. 'You can have the whole day, just as long as it's convenient for me. I've got the Red Cross ladies coming on Thursday and the WVS on Wednesday, and it's bridge on Tuesday evening.'

'Yes, madam. I'll take him now, then. Come on, Master Henry, it's bath time for you.'

'And make sure the water isn't too hot,' Meredith called after her as a parting shot.

'Test it with your elbow before you put him in.'

Meredith went to find her grandmother, to regale her with the story. Henrietta was conscious of the toffees 'burning a hole' in the pocket of her sagging cardigan. Could it have been her fault? She had managed to drop them on the nursery floor when she'd looked in to pay a visit to her great-grandson, but she could have sworn she'd picked them all up again. Had Henry, crawling around on the carpet, come across one she'd missed?

But no; Meredith was explaining how she'd taken the boy out for an airing, in the absence of the nursemaid, and it was while she'd flown into the house to fetch something that he'd got into trouble. He couldn't possibly have kept it in his hand all that time, could he? But how else could it have come into his possession? She'd forgotten that she'd given some to Ceri Davis as a reward for helping with her wool-winding.

'Oh well, no harm done,' she murmured, more to herself than anything.

'That is hardly the point, is it? I dread to think what might have happened if I hadn't come back in time.'

'Then you shouldn't have left him alone, my dear.'

'That's not fair! He was hardly alone. Mariah was out there, and those evacuees. He was strapped into his chair, and I was only away for two minutes, if that!'

'Whatever you say, dear.'

What was the matter with everybody? Didn't they understand how awful it was for a mother to have to go through an experience like that? Meredith vowed that her baby would never be left by himself again. Either she herself, or Myfanwy, would have to be at his side every moment of the day or night.

Had she but known it this decision was to be challenged in a very short while. Job Prosser, his heart full of determination, was on his way up from the village. He meant to make Harry Morgan see that his girl's place was at home. It wasn't as if the boy was motherless; if that Mrs Fletcher couldn't look after her own child it was a pretty poor lookout. Handing your baby over for someone else to look after was foolishness indeed. It wasn't as if the woman was doing war work or anything.

It was a long way round to the back door, and even Job Prosser in all his pride knew better than to present himself at the front door of his employer's mansion. Hesitating, he noticed Mariah on her hands and knees in a field of carrots, apparently thinning them out. Several youngsters were busy at the same sort of work.

'Pardon me, miss!'

Mariah got to her feet, moving stiffly. 'Yes? Can I help you?'

'Where would Mr Morgan be at this time of day?'

'Oh, sorry, you've just missed him. He had to go to one of the farms. Something about a leaky roof. Is there something I can do?'

'My name is Prosser.'

'Oh, you must be Myfanwy's father?'

'I am, and I've come to fetch her home.'

Mariah scented trouble. 'Then it's Mrs Fletcher you want to see. Your daughter is employed by her. She'll be up in her sitting-room, I imagine. Dafydd!' The boy sprang to his feet and came to stand beside her. 'Now listen carefully. I want you to take Mr Prosser up to the house and show him into the morning-room. Is that clear?'

'The morning-room. Yes, miss.'

'And then you're to go upstairs and find Mrs Fletcher. Tell her there's someone to see her, and ask if she's free. If she is, I expect she'll come down to the morning-room. If not, she may give you a message for Mr Prosser, all right?'

'And you can tell her I won't take no for

101

an answer,' Job put in.

Mariah watched them go. Then she beck-oned to one of the other boys. 'Huw, I want you to go in the back way and go quietly up the back stairs and look for my mother. Tell her that Mr Prosser is here to see Mrs Fletcher, and there may be trouble. Got that?'

The child beamed. 'Can I stay and watch the fight, missus?'

'Just you come straight back here to me. There will not be any fight. That's not the way we do things in this house.' At least, I hope not, she mused. To her way of think-ing the man was asking for trouble. Disap-pointed, the boy sped off.

Chapter Thirteen

'I'm Mrs Fletcher. And you must be Myfanwy's father. I understand you asked to see me.' It was a silly thing to say, of course, she was well aware of that, for why would he be here, otherwise? But she had to say something to set the ball rolling.

'I've come to take the girl home. She's needed there.'

'She's needed here, Mr Prosser, and I'm afraid I can't let her leave. I took her on in good faith, you know. I cannot have servants coming and going at a moment's notice. Myfanwy is here on a month's trial, and that works both ways. If when the month is up she decides she wishes to leave, of course I'll have to agree, but I hope she'll want to stay. My son has had too much upheaval already, and he seems to have taken to Myfanwy.'

His mouth dropped open. Evidently he hadn't expected this young mother to put up a fight. In the normal way of things Meredith would have panicked and started agreeing with him and apologizing, but she had had enough stress for one day. The thought of having to see to a two-year-old while she tried desperately to find a replacement for Myfanwy was more than she could bear. She might get landed with another Gladys.

'I'd better have a word with Mr Morgan, then. Do you know which farm he's gone to? Perhaps I can track him down on my way home.'

'This has nothing to do with my father.' Meredith's tone was icy. There was more of her grandmother in her than she had realized until now. 'The nursery is my responsibility, not his.' She caught sight of Ellen, hovering just outside the door. 'Ask our housekeeper. She'll back me up. And I'll tell you this for nothing, my father does not like to see me upset. I understand that you and several of your sons are employed in our colliery?' She left the threat unspoken, but it was enough to turn his face white.

She stalked off, leaving Ellen to deal with the poor man.

'That's blackmail, missus.'

'Try not to worry, Mr Prosser. I'm sure nothing will come of it. And you started it, you know, telling her you meant to go to Mr Morgan. Mrs Fletcher is right, of course. This is her business. I don't know if you're aware of it, but she lost her husband at Dunkirk. Her little boy is all she has left of Chad and naturally she wants the best for him.'

'Then she should understand how I feel about our Myfanwy! She's needed at home, Mrs er . . .'

'Richards. I'm sure you miss her, but our children do have to fly the nest sometime, you know.' Ellen could see his point of view but according to what Megan had told her, she knew that his daughter hadn't much of a life, running a household of seven men and boys of assorted ages. No wonder the girl was having the time of her life working for the Morgans.

'Do you have daughters, Mrs Richards?'

'Just the one. Mariah. You met her outside just now, I believe.'

'Ah! Then you still have her at home with you!'

'Not for long, perhaps. She's a married woman now. Her husband is in the air force. She stays here because he likes to think of her being in a safe place, but she certainly does her bit, what with all her gardening, and looking after our evacuees. Six small boys we have, from the orphanage in Swansea.' Oh, blow it! She had said too much. She caught him looking at her with his head on one side, like a robin perching on a spade handle, waiting for a worm.

'At least she knows where her duty lies, then.'

'Oh, Mr Prosser. Do try to see this from Myfanwy's point of view. Why not agree to let her spread her wings? There's so much uncertainty nowadays, with this wretched war. Who knows where we could all be tomorrow? We all have to snatch a bit of happiness wherever we can, and that includes your Myfanwy.'

'And just where does this leave me and the boys?'

'What about your older sons? Are any of them courting? You never know, one of them might get wed and bring his bride into the house. Then you'd be all set.'

'Huh!'

This had gone on long enough, and Ellen was eager to get back upstairs and turn on the wireless. ITMA was coming on any minute now, and she didn't want to miss the start. That Tommy Handley was an absolute scream! 'I suppose you could always get remarried yourself?' she ventured, greatly daring.

106

His eyes opened wide. 'You're a widow woman yourself, aren't you?'

'Yes, but I have no thoughts of matrimony. I have plenty to do here as it is.'

'Pity!'

'I'm sorry, Mr Prosser, but I'm afraid you'll have to go now. My time isn't my own; I've a job to do. Is there anything you'd like me to tell Myfanwy? I'd be happy to give her a message.'

'She knows how I feel, and she knows where to find me.' He tipped his cap. '*Nos da*, Mrs Richards.'

'*Nos da*,' she said faintly.

The door closed behind him. Moments later it opened again, and she braced herself for the encounter, but this time it was Mariah. 'What's the matter with you, Mam? You look like you've seen a ghost.'

'I'm not entirely sure, but I think I've just had a proposal!'

'What do you mean? What sort of proposal?'

'Of marriage, of course. What did you think I meant?'

Mariah gave her mother a quizzical look. 'You surely don't mean old Prosser proposed to you! You must have got hold of the wrong end of the stick.'

'Is that so! The man may be desperate,

but he's not that desperate, is that what you mean?'

'I didn't say that, Mam, but you've got to admit, it does seem odd. You don't even know the chap, so why would he march up here all the way from the village just for the pleasure of asking for your hand?'

'Oh, there's no point in saying anything to you, Mariah Mortimer! You're always so sceptical of everything. Now, do you mind standing aside and letting me pass? I'm missing ITMA.'

Mariah did as she was told, trying to hide a smile. Poor Mam! She couldn't imagine what had taken place. Perhaps she'd been given a small compliment, and had read too much into it? On the other hand it was hard to imagine the taciturn miner telling Ellen that her eyes were like deep pools, an expression she'd read in a romance novel.

Ellen, meanwhile, had fiddled with the wireless until she managed to get rid of the static, and her programme was well under way. For once, though, the antics of Tommy Handley and Arthur Askey at the Ministry of Aggravation and Mysteries at the Office of Twerps failed to amuse. She was unable to get that encounter with Job Prosser out of her mind.

Let Mariah laugh all she wanted, Ellen

had been left with the distinct impression that, given an ounce of encouragement, Job Prosser really could be brought to the point of proposing. She'd seen the way his eyes lit up when it dawned on him that she was widowed, and available.

'Don't be such a fool!' she admonished herself. 'You were the one who mentioned marriage in the first place.' She blushed, remembering. What if he'd thought she was flirting with him? She'd never be able to face him again. She despised kittenish middle-aged women who fluttered their eyelashes at men and made daring suggestions. Why on earth had she told the man he should think about remarriage? She just hoped he wouldn't start making a nuisance of himself now.

She got to her feet and turned off the wireless. Mariah came in, looking contrite.

'Listen, Mam, I'm sorry if I spoke out of turn downstairs. I didn't mean to be unkind. You're still a young woman. There's no reason on earth why a man shouldn't fancy you, even if he is wildly unsuitable.'

'I didn't say he fancied me!' Ellen hissed. 'Do keep your voice down! What if Myfanwy walked past the door and heard us making fun of her father? She might say something to the man, and then we'd be in a pickle, or at least, I would!'

'I know, Mam, but if he did . . .'

Ellen felt deflated suddenly. 'Do you know, Mariah, I've never had a proposal of marriage in all my life? Not even one. That's a sobering thought, my girl.'

'I don't know about that. Plenty of women don't get married, and I bet some of them don't care a bit. Marriage isn't everybody's cup of tea.'

'All very well for you to say. You've got Aubrey.'

'Yes, but for how long, Mam?'

'We'll have none of that talk here!' Ellen's tone was brisk. 'Go and put the kettle on, will you? I think we could both do with a pick-me-up.'

Left alone, she tried to shake off her bleak mood. She was better off than most people, wasn't she, living in this great house with every convenience. When it came to Job Prosser she was just being silly. She pitied the woman he did pick on, if he remarried. He wasn't looking for someone to love so much as a free housekeeper, and that would not be Ellen Richards. She was better off as she was, lonely or not.

CHAPTER FOURTEEN

Mariah had plenty to write to Aubrey about now. Silly little incidents as they were, reading about them would give him a sense that somewhere, far away from the events of the war, life was going along pleasantly. Decency and happiness were waiting just around the corner, in another world, as portrayed by the singer Vera Lynn, the forces' sweetheart.

Later on, Mariah was to look back on these moments as being the last happy times in that year, because it was from that day on that things took a turn for the worse.

It began with Henrietta Meredith. She had received a letter from her cook-general, Mrs Crossley. 'Listen to this,' she told her granddaughter. ' "We can't get no repairs done to your room. There isn't no materials to be had and no men neither". Really, aren't these people taught plain English in school?'

'Sounds plain enough to me,' Meredith muttered, frowning over the sock she was trying to darn. 'This is only fit for the rag bag, but I suppose I'll have to keep at it. Those boys can't go without socks.'

'Knit a square of wool and sew it in,' Henrietta suggested.

'Won't that leave a ridge in the sock? It'll rub against the shoe and bring up a blister.'

'I've more to worry about than socks! What am I going to do about my poor house?'

Meredith shrugged. 'There's not much you can do, I suppose. Anyway, you're all right here. It's not as if you're homeless, Grandmamma.'

Henrietta knew she had to make the best of it, but that didn't stop her being bored. She missed her home and her own circle of friends, and most of all she missed her husband. She went along to the Red Cross meetings but she was a newcomer, low in the pecking order, and therefore had to go along with other people's decisions. She had tried asserting herself, casually mentioning 'my son-in-law, Harry Morgan' but the other ladies were not about to give up their hard-won places on the various committees. She obediently cut up gauze and folded it into dressings but it was hardly rewarding work. Frightening, rather, because it reminded her that these squares would be used on some poor chaps suffering from unmentionable wounds.

She had tried to befriend one of the less forbidding ladies, and had invited her to tea at the house, but that had got her nowhere. 'I'm sorry, I can't accept,' the woman had said stiffly. 'I'm afraid I should not be able to reciprocate.' Such nonsense! Henrietta had gathered that the woman lived in more modest circumstances than the Morgan family and was therefore overawed by Harry's home. Snubbed, she did not issue such an invitation again.

Nor could she assume a role in the running of the house. The housekeeper Ellen Richards was in charge of that, and would of course brook no interference. Servants never did. So what was left? Henrietta could see herself doomed to spending the rest of the war knitting up endless oddments of wool and strolling in the grounds, leaning on her walking stick.

For this reason she found herself taking a greater interest in the affairs of the family, by which she meant not only her relations — Harry, Meredith and little Henry — but the servants as well. She was intensely irritated by the privileged position which Mariah seemed to occupy in the house.

'Why does she have to come down to dinner with the rest of us?' she grumbled.

'What do you mean, Grandmamma?'

'Can't she eat upstairs with her mother, if she's too high and mighty to join them in the servants' hall?'

'Mariah and I have always eaten in the dining-room, ever since we left the school room.'

'Yes, and your father should have seen to it that other arrangements were made at the time. This would not have happened if your poor mother had been alive.'

Meredith reflected bitterly that if her mother had survived her birth, Ellen and her daughter would never have come within a mile of the house, but that was water under the bridge.

'Mariah isn't a servant, Grandmamma.'

'More's the pity! I can understand why Mrs Richards was allowed to bring her child with her, being a widow, but where your father made his mistake was to let the girl share your governess. Giving her ideas above her station! There's a perfectly good school down in the village where she could have gone. And if her mother was determined not to part with her, she could have been given a maid's job here when she left school.'

Meredith sighed. Her grandmother was living in the past. Nobody lived by those old rules now, did they? But to Henrietta, born in Queen Victoria's day, they probably made sense.

'I don't see that it matters, Grandmamma. This war has changed everything for women, you know.'

'Of course it matters!' Henrietta retorted. 'I've seen the way your father looks at that girl! Smiling at her, patting her on the shoulder, all agog to listen to what she has to say. If that isn't nipped in the bud there'll be trouble there one of these days. You mark my words!'

Meredith laughed. 'I can assure you there's nothing going on there, Grand-mamma! Mariah is . . .' She bit her lip. She'd almost blurted out the truth then. 'Dad's very fond of Mariah, that's all,' she finished lamely.

Henrietta bridled. 'I wasn't suggesting that there's anything wrong, you silly girl! I simply meant that men of that age tend to get funny ideas. It wouldn't surprise me at all if she tried to wheedle money out of him. I know her type. All wide-eyed and simpering, and butter wouldn't melt in her mouth.'

'Mariah doesn't simper.'

'Why are you defending her, Meredith? I've watched the two of you together, and I've seen the way you look at her sometimes. You dislike her being here, don't you? I'm right, aren't I?'

Meredith twisted her wedding ring around her finger before replying. Years of resentment bubbled up inside her. Mariah always being treated equally by Harry when she, Meredith, should have received extra privileges as the daughter of the house. Mariah getting a new dress, a book, a pony, identical to those bestowed on Meredith. And finally, the worst betrayal of all, finding out just months ago that they were actually half sisters.

'There are times when I wish she'd go,' she admitted. 'She used to talk about going away to train as a children's nurse, and then when the war broke out she wanted to go and join up. For one reason or another, none of that happened.'

Henrietta patted her awkwardly on the back. She thought she understood. Like herself, Meredith was a widow now. Naturally she was unhappy, but there was one small irritant that could be removed.

'You don't have to put up with this in your own home, my dear,' she nodded. 'I shall speak to Harry at once, and the girl can be asked to leave. No doubt her mother will kick up a fuss but if she threatens to leave, that may be all for the best, too. You and I can run the house between us.'

'No, Grandmamma. Just leave it alone, will you? Please don't say anything to Dad. He won't like it.'

'Nonsense. If it's the vegetable gardens he's worried about, I'm sure we can get a land girl.'

'It isn't that, Grandmamma, honestly. Please, please do as I ask.'

Henrietta smiled pleasantly and sailed out of the room. Meredith put her face in her hands and felt herself shaking. This felt like a bad dream. She could not imagine what had happened to get her grandmother worked up into such a state. Perhaps it had to do with her losing her husband. When Chad had been killed, she herself had been almost out of her wits for a time, and they hadn't been married long. How much worse must it be for someone who'd been married for more than half a century?

Should she go and warn Dad that Henrietta was on her high horse? But before she could make up her mind there was a knock on the door, and it swung open to reveal Myfanwy, with Henry beaming in her arms, all fresh and rosy from his bath.

'Have you come to say night night to Mummie, darling?' She took him on to her lap, and nuzzled her chin in his bright curls.

'Mummie sing song,' he chuckled.

'All right, darling, just one,' and she began to croon to him while his nursemaid looked on, smiling.

'More, Mummie, more!'

So Meredith spent a contented half hour with her little boy, and by the time Myfanwy took him away, drowsy with sleep, the urge to speak to Harry was gone. She was rather tired herself. Perhaps an early night was on the cards. She would have a word with her father in the morning. But by then it was too late.

CHAPTER FIFTEEN

'What is all this about, Henrietta?' Harry frowned. He'd had an exhausting morning down at the colliery office, demanding to know why production was down, and the memory of it was still dominating his thoughts. The manager, Llew Roberts, had been trying to explain that a consignment of pit props had failed to arrive and Harry had felt his blood pressure rising as he ordered him to "get on the blower, man, and sort it out". Over in the corner little Bronwen Evans had bent over her typewriter, waiting for the storm to pass. It was not Roberts's fault, of course, and once he had calmed down Harry had apologized for shouting, but he was still on edge now.

'Are you aware that your daughter is deeply unhappy?' Henrietta demanded, quailing under his frown but determined to press on.

'Unhappy? We're all unhappy, Mother-in-law. It's this rotten war! But is there something in particular that's upsetting Meredith?'

There! He had given her an opening. Taking a deep breath she began on the piece she had rehearsed in front of her bedroom mirror. 'It's that Mrs Mortimer. Mariah.'

'Oh, what now? They haven't fallen out, have they?'

'Not exactly. No, but you must have noticed how they irritate each other. I think you should ask the girl to leave.' There, it was out in the open!

Harry studied his fingernails.

Henrietta waited. Into the silence she said, 'You've been kindness itself to her, all these years. She can hardly complain of being hard done by if you explain that it's time for her to move on. Meredith is still grieving over the death of her husband, and I, of all people, should know how that feels. We must do all we can to smooth her path, Harry, and if that means catering to her whims for a while, so be it. I can understand that you might be embarrassed to say anything to Mariah, so I'm quite prepared to speak to her, if you wish.'

Harry's glare was so ferocious that for a moment she felt afraid. 'Have you gone mad, woman? I won't have you meddling in matters you know nothing about. Quite apart from the fact that this is none of your business, Mariah has done nothing to merit this. It hasn't escaped my notice that ever since you arrived you've been treating her as if she doesn't belong here. Well, Mother-in-law, this is her home, and she's going nowhere, and that is my last word!'

'How dare you speak to me like that! I have my granddaughter's best interests at heart. How do you think she feels when she sees you putting a servant's daughter first? Devastated, naturally.'

'Is that what she's told you?'

'Not exactly, but I can sees she's upset.'

'Let's drop this, shall we, Henrietta?'

She didn't know him well enough to re-alize that when he lowered his voice and spoke very quietly and firmly, he was doing his best to hold on to the temper which was about to flare. She ignored the warning and continued on her chosen path. 'Can't you see that the girl is playing you for a fool, Harry? She knows she can't remain here for ever so she means to line her pockets before she goes. She's jealous of poor Meredith, of course, for being an heiress.'

Ellen had been passing Harry's study when she became aware of his mother-in-law's shrill voice. The door wasn't firmly latched and without straining her ears she could hear quite clearly what the woman was saying. Otherwise all she could make out was the dull boom of Harry's muted voice — always an ominous sign. It wasn't right to eavesdrop, of course; she made up her mind to listen long enough to make sure they weren't speaking about her, and then she'd tiptoe past. She managed to catch Mariah's name. Well, then, she'd better listen, hadn't she?

'Perhaps it is you who should leave,' Harry said now. 'I was sorry for you when you had the fire, on top of everything else, so I didn't object when Meredith invited you to stay here. However, if you're going to upset the peace of my household I'm afraid I'll have to ask you to return home.'

'You can't do this to me!'

'I can, and I will, unless you promise to behave in future.' His voice was cold. Ellen observed that he was now speaking in his best magisterial tone. He might have been facing a miscreant from the bench.

'But I'm your mother-in-law!'

'Henrietta, my wife has been dead for a long time. Officially speaking you haven't been my mother-in-law for a quarter of a century. We've kept in touch in deference to Antonia's memory, and because you're

Meredith's grandmother, but that doesn't mean that I will tolerate this sort of behaviour from you.'

Goaded beyond bearing, Henrietta seemed determined to go down fighting. 'I don't care what you do to me, but for my granddaughter's sake I demand that you send Mariah away as soon as possible.'

Ellen thrust her clenched fists into her cardigan pockets. The evil so and so! Who did she think she was? She longed to rush into the room to given her a good slap, but something made her hesitate. She gasped when she heard Harry's next words.

'I didn't want to tell you this, Henrietta, but it seems that I have no choice. Mariah Mortimer is my daughter. There is no question of her leaving Cwmbran.'

Henrietta turned white and staggered slightly. For a long moment she seemed to be fighting for breath. Then she gulped and took a step towards him. 'You wicked, wicked man! I know you're only saying that to upset me, but of course it isn't true! I shan't take any notice of you, I shan't.'

In for a penny, in for a pound, Harry thought. 'Do as you wish, but nevertheless it's true. Mariah is my daughter; Meredith's half sister.'

Out in the corridor Ellen groaned. Now

the fat was in the fire! Completely forgetting where she was going, or what she had meant to do, she fled back to her own sitting-room and began to rock back and forth in her chair, with her starched apron thrown over her head.

Back in Harry's study Henrietta's eyes flashed. She was too well bred to raise her voice in times of stress, but she certainly felt like screaming now! 'So that housekeeper person is your mistress! I might have known it!'

'No, Henrietta. Ellen is not, nor ever has been, my mistress.'

'I see. Mariah is the product of an immaculate conception, then, is that it?'

'I made one mistake. Just one mistake, which I've regretted ever since, and if you believe nothing else you can believe that.'

'What I find unforgivable, Harry Morgan, yes, totally unforgivable, is the fact that you brought your . . .' she was about to say floozie, but corrected herself in time, 'you brought your mistress into my daughter's house!'

'My house, I think, Henrietta, and Antonia knew nothing about it. Ellen did not come here until after I was widowed. I repeat, after I was widowed!'

'My poor Antonia!'

'Yes, poor Antonia. If she had survived the birth then of course I should not have brought Ellen and Mariah here. I would have made provision for them elsewhere. But that is not how things worked out. Yes, madam, I might regret having done something that resulted in the birth of a child to another woman, but I can never regret having given life to Mariah.'

'I can't help wondering how you managed to keep this quiet for all these years. What will your employees and all your fine friends think about you when this comes out? For make no mistake about it, I shall make sure that it will!'

'I doubt that, my dear; I doubt that very much. You forget that I'm a magistrate. I don't much care what people think of me, but I will not have my daughter's name dragged through the mud. If you dare to try anything I shall summon my doctor to declare you mentally incompetent, deranged by grief, if you will. And if you persist in spreading these wicked calumnies, it won't be difficult to find a second medical man to agree with him. We could have you put away, you know, and if necessary I won't hesitate to act.'

Henrietta gulped. 'I should leave at once. I shall go to a hotel.'

'I'll drive you back to Hereford.'

'No, thank you! I shall take the train.'

'Then at least let me drive you to the station.'

'That will not be necessary, thank you. Meredith can take me.'

Harry grinned. 'Then she'll have to take you in Henry's pram! Meredith has never learned to drive.'

'Surely there's someone else who can take me?'

'I'm afraid that comes down to either Mariah or me.'

Henrietta glowered at him. 'Then it seems that I must accept your offer, much as it galls me to take any favours from you! I shall go and pack now, and perhaps you'll be good enough to consult the timetable and notify me of the time of departure.'

She sailed out of the room, her head held high. Harry thumped his fist down hard on the table, bruising his knuckles. He needed a stiff drink!

CHAPTER SIXTEEN

'I can't bear it!' Ellen sobbed. 'I'll have to leave Cwmbran. I can't possibly stay here with everyone knowing what we've done.'

'Come on, *cariad.* It's not as bad as all that, surely.'

'It's all very well for you,' she gulped. 'You're a man. Other men may well admire you for fathering a child out of wedlock. It's different for women, and you know it. We have to take the blame as well as the shame.'

'It was all so long ago,' he soothed. 'We've managed to keep our secret all these years and I don't see why it should be any different now. Our daughters are aware of it, of course, but I see no reason for them to blab now.'

'Perhaps they won't, but your mother-in-law is sure to tell the world, out of spite if nothing else.'

'I very much doubt it. She's been warned that she faces being put away somewhere if she opens her mouth.'

Ellen stared at him in horror. 'No! Tell me you wouldn't do such a wicked thing!'

'*Pshaw!* You know me better than that! I wouldn't harm a hair of her head. I admit I said something to threaten her into good behaviour, but that's as far as I'd go.'

Privately he thought that Henrietta was slightly off her head or she wouldn't have got this bee in her bonnet about poor Mariah. And the present situation was partly his fault for having told her that Mariah was his daughter, and after warning Meredith to keep quiet, too!

'In any case,' he went on, 'Henrietta is determined to leave on the first train out of here. She won't stay here to be corrupted.'

'But where will she go?'

'Back to her home, I suppose. The only real fire damage was to the drawing-room, and if Mrs Crossley has aired the place properly the rest of the house should be habitable by now. It never was my idea to have her staying here for the rest of the war. She and Meredith cooked that up between them.'

In his awkward way he'd done his best to comfort Ellen, yet she felt it wasn't enough. He hadn't said that she mustn't dream of leaving, and that left her feeling worried.

What if he really wanted to be rid of her? This had been her home since 1918 and the thought of leaving to make her way in the world was frightening.

'If you go, Mam, then I shall, too,' Mariah assured her. 'I hate the thought of causing so much trouble.'

'If it's anyone's fault, it's mine.' She looked so sad that her daughter's heart went out to her at once. 'If I hadn't given in to Harry in that one weak moment, we shouldn't be in this pickle.'

'Well, Mam, I for one am glad that things happened as they did, or I wouldn't be standing here now.'

'I know, *cariad* and I wouldn't have missed knowing you for the world.'

'Just for the record, Mam, did you just accept Harry's invitation to come here because you loved him, or because it meant a roof over our heads?'

Ellen bit her lip. 'A bit of both, really. I suppose at the back of my mind I hoped that he felt the same about me, and that after he recovered from his wife's death he might turn back to me. Plenty of men remarry quickly when left with an infant to bring up. Of course, I was young and foolish then. Still a teenager with romantic notions. Nothing came of it, as you know.'

'Because he had servants and could afford to hire nannies and governesses,' Mariah agreed. 'He'd have had no trouble finding someone to look after Meredith.'

'Oh, it wasn't just that. Class distinction was even more prevalent than it is now. There would have been no question of a wealthy land owner like Harry Morgan marrying a little shop assistant, because that's what I was, Mariah. Working class. My dad worked down the Cardiff docks, loading and unloading the ships. He was a good man, none better, but the Morgans wouldn't have given him the time of day.'

Mariah was silent, waiting for her mother to speak again. Her heart bled for the young woman who had come into this house, trusting and full of hope, slowly coming to the sad realization that her dreams were crumbling away.

'And I bet that's what sticks in her craw now,' Ellen remarked at last. 'If your mother had been some society beauty it wouldn't have mattered as much. But her precious son-in-law lowered himself to get entangled with a little nobody.'

'Mam!' Mariah put her arms around her mother and they stood entwined for a long moment before Ellen finally broke away.

Down the corridor another sort of soul-searching was taking place.

'How long have you known about this?' Henrietta demanded. She was thoroughly shaken by her encounter with Harry and her new-found knowledge, but it was no good burying her head in the sand. She wanted to get to the bottom of the whole sorry situation.

'About Mariah being my sister, you mean?'

'Half sister!'

'Very well, my half sister. Oh, since just after Chad was killed. It's funny in a way; I felt the same way you did about Mariah being in the house and I wanted to get rid of her, and that's when Dad spilled the beans.'

'Really, child! You know how much I dislike slang!'

'That just about says it all, though, doesn't it? We've sort of opened a Pandora's box, and the nasty little gems of information have come spilling out.'

'Ugh! So everyone knows about this but me? Is that what you're saying?'

'Oh, no. Dad thinks he's managed to keep it quiet.'

'Now that I cannot believe. Servants always know what is going on in a house.'

'Perhaps that was the case in the past, but it's different now. Most of our long-term servants have either died or joined up. Ruth is the only survivor of my young days, apart from Ellen, of course.'

'Oh yes, the wonderful Ellen!'

'There was one servant who found out quite by accident, but he's since been killed. He was a young footman who worked here before he left to join up. He was an orphan whom Ellen took under her wing. It was ironic in a way that he was the one who managed to betray her. He came back here on leave, bringing a friend with him, and he proudly pointed out that photograph she keeps on her mantelpiece as being that of her late husband, who died at Ypres. As luck would have it the friend had been a neighbour of the Richards family back in Cardiff, and he remarked that this Bertie Richards had never been married. In fact, he was Ellen's brother.'

'And knowing he was gone and couldn't speak up for himself, she passed him off as her husband? The nerve of the hussy! Well, Meredith, I'm off home by the first available train in the morning. You couldn't pay me to stay under that man's roof a minute longer. To think how he's pulled the wool over my eyes all these years. I've always looked up to Harry Morgan and been glad that my daughter was married to such a fine man, but not any more!'

'You can't go, Grandmamma!' The words came out in a long wail. 'Please say you'll stay! I'm all alone! I can't manage without you. I'll have a word with Dad, and I know he'll listen to me.'

'You're hardly alone, my dear, in a house full of people.'

'Something's been going on with them upstairs!' The housemaid, Rosie Yeoman, bounced into the kitchen, her eyes sparkling. The cook looked up from her pastry-making with a frown.

'What do you mean, girl?'

'I just bumped into Mrs Richards in the upstairs corridor. She's been crying. Her eyes were all red and swollen.'

'Get on with you! She must have caught a cold or something.'

'And that Mrs Meredith, the old granny, she's locked herself in her room and won't come out. I knocked like I'm supposed to, and asked if I could get in there to dust, and she said not now, thank you, come back later.'

'She's just lost her husband,' the cook reproved. 'Only natural if she wants to be alone now and then, see.'

'And what about Mr Morgan, then? I passed him on the stairs and he growled at me to get out of his way, and that's not like him. He's usually so considerate. No, Mrs Edwards, something's up. If you ask me, there's been a row between Mrs Richards and the old one, that's why they're all worked up.'

'That's Mrs Meredith to you, girl. Show a bit of respect.'

Rosie tossed her head. 'Say what you like, there's something going on. What do you think, Ruth?' This was addressed to the older maid, who had just come in.

'I don't know what you're talking about.'

'There's been a fuss with them upstairs!'

'All I know is, if a house be divided against itself, that house cannot stand; Mark three, twenty-five,' Ruth retorted. 'That's what they tell us in chapel, anyway.'

'Then you do know something,' Rosie breathed.

Ruth gave her a sly look. 'My lips are sealed!'

Chapter Seventeen

'I thought we'd seen the back of her,' Rosie Yeoman grumbled. 'Marched out of here this morning without giving us so much as a penny piece, and now she's back.'

'Don't talk like that about your betters,' the cook said automatically, but privately she agreed with every word the chit had spoken. Everybody knew that when you stayed in a big house you tipped the staff when you were leaving, at least those who had given personal service, which Mrs Edwards certainly had. Making little snacks between meals when the old lady demanded them, feeling sorry for the newly bereaved Mrs Meredith.

'P'raps she left something for us with Mrs Richards,' the young maid had said hopefully, but the cook had been quick to dampen that notion. Ellen Richards would have sent it down to them at once, if that had been the case.

Ruth had already gone up and stripped the bed and turned the mattress, and now everything had to be done in reverse because the room's late occupant was staying on. Mr Morgan had driven her to the station and now they were back, within the hour no less.

'I'm so glad you changed your mind, Grandmamma!' Meredith was delighted.

'If you are, you're the only person in this house who is!' Henrietta retorted. 'And I didn't change my mind, as you put it. I sat in that waiting-room for ages, waiting for a train which never arrived. It was fortunate that your father insisted on staying to see me off, or I'd have been stuck there with no way of getting back to the house.'

'I wonder what made the train late?'

'This wretched war, I expect. The station master muttered something about a problem on the line. I have no idea what that meant. A tree down, perhaps, or a live bomb. How should I know?'

'Never mind; you're back now, and I want you to stay.'

'I have no intention of staying on here, Meredith. I shall try again tomorrow, but this delay has given me an idea. Why don't you come to Hereford and stay with me for a while? I'd enjoy your company, and it would get you away from this untenable situation.'

Meredith considered this. 'Perhaps I should, only I can't leave Henry behind.'

'No reason why you should. Bring him and his nurse with you. My house is big enough, even with the drawing-room shut off. They can have the blue room. His cot can travel in the guard's van. I'm sure we can find someone to put it back together when we reach the other end.'

But when the plan was put to Myfanwy, she squeaked in alarm. 'Oh, no, madam! I couldn't go to England!'

'Nonsense!' Henrietta told her. 'It's hardly the ends of the earth, girl! In fact, if you knew your geography, you'd realize that it's right next door to several Welsh counties.'

'Dada wouldn't like it,' Myfanwy reminded her, which was probably true.

'Very well, then, you can return home to your father, which I gather is what he wants in any case, and we'll find a replacement for you when we return to my home.' But even this threat failed to move the girl and Henrietta had to concede defeat.

It had been some days since Mariah had heard from her husband, and she was beginning to worry.

'Didn't anything come for me this morning?' she asked, but Ruth only shook her head.

'There wasn't any post at all, Miss Mariah.'

'What, nothing at all?' This was most unusual because scarcely a day went by without some official missive coming for Harry.

'Oh, haven't you heard?' the cook remarked, when Ruth mentioned this a bit later. 'Evans the post is on the sick list. Broke his ankle yesterday, see. The Matthews boy told me all about it when he delivered my grocery order.'

'How did he manage that, then?'

'Fell off his bike coming down Heol Dewi Sant. Someone's cow got loose and when he came over the brow of the hill there it was, smack in the middle of the road. He had to swerve to avoid it and he hit a lamp post instead.'

'There's terrible,' Ruth sympathized. 'How will they manage without his money coming in, I wonder?'

'Oh, their Bronwen will tip up her wage packet from the colliery office, I'm sure, but it's the bike that Sioni's worried about. Buckled the front wheel, see, and how's he supposed to get it mended with this old war going on?'

'Take it to the blacksmith, of course,' Ruth told her. 'If he can't straighten it out, nobody can. I'd better go and let Miss Mariah know. She's fretting herself to a shadow worrying that something's happened to Mr Aubrey.'

Mariah poked her head round the door of her mother's linen room. 'Just going down the village, Mam. Do you need anything?'

'I could do with a spool of white cotton, if there's such a thing to be had in the shops. Harry's put his foot through yet another sheet and I'll have to sides to middle it.'

Mariah peered at the sheet. 'Look at the size of that hole! By the time you cut that lot up the middle and sew the sides together you'll end up with a sheet that's only fit for a single bed!'

Harry Morgan still slept in his marriage bed, which was in fact the double bed where he had been born. Ellen was finding it increasingly difficult to replace the worn sheets which went with it; the fine bed linen which had been new in his grandmother's day were now nearing the end of the line.

'Why are you going down the village at this hour of the day?' she asked, as she fumbled in her purse for the necessary coins.

'Sioni Evans came off his bike, and he's in the cottage hospital with a busted ankle. I'm going down to the post office to see if there's anything for us.'

'There's terrible,' Ellen responded automatically. 'Too bad he can't be nursed at home. How is his poor wife supposed to visit him over there, with the bus service cut back?'

'I think he only went there to get the plaster cast on. Then they'll pack him off home. Anyway, that's why there wasn't a delivery this morning.'

Ellen glanced at her daughter. 'He's all right, you know. If he wasn't, we'd have heard.' They both knew that she wasn't talking about the postman.

'I know, Mam. I know.'

'You run along, then, *cariad,* and don't forget my cotton!'

The postmistress beamed at Mariah. 'I know what you've come for,' she said archly. 'A letter from hubby, is it? Funnily enough, you've got two of them today. They must have been held up somewhere.'

The back wall of the tiny post office held an enormous rack of pigeon holes, and she reached into one of these and held out a bundle of assorted envelopes. It was all Mariah could do not to snatch them from the poor woman's hand. As promised there were two addressed in Aubrey's familiar writing. She would tear the latest one open as soon as she got outside and then, as soon as she knew that he was in good health, she would save the other for later, as a treat.

'I'm sorry to hear about Sioni,' she said, as she prepared to leave. 'Who will be taking his place; do you know yet?'

The postmistress shrugged. 'Don't ask me, Mrs Mortimer! All the men from hereabouts are either working down the pit or away at the war. I suppose it will come down to us women, as usual. Good for nothing but housework, we were, until that Hitler got too big for his britches, but now they find they can't do without us. I did ask Sioni's wife if she'd like to take it on, but she said she couldn't ride a bike and was too old to start now. I suppose I'll just have to put a notice up in the window and see if anything comes of it.'

'Um, don't do that just yet, Mrs Crabbe.'

'Why, do you know of someone?'

A rare feeling of excitement had come over Mariah. Did she dare to do it? It might solve all her problems. 'What about me, Mrs

Crabbe?'

Taken aback for a moment, the postmistress nodded. 'I don't see why not, Mrs Mortimer, if you feel you can take it on. It's just temporary, mind, till Sioni gets back.'

'Of course. Won't there be some sort of red tape? Interviews, that sort of thing?'

'No need to worry about all that. It's not as if you want it to be your life's work, is it? By the time that old inspector hears about you, Sioni will be back at work. You've lived here all your life and you must know the place like the back of your hand. No chance you making the wrong deliveries. And we know you're not one of them German spies, coming here in disguise to see what we're all up to! Can you be here at five in the morning to help sort the mail coming in on the train?'

Outside, Mariah began to laugh, and once started she was unable to stop until the tears flowed down her cheeks. Mariah Mortimer, postwoman!

CHAPTER EIGHTEEN

'You'll never believe what's happened now!' Ellen raised her eyes to the ceiling. 'Just when I thought we'd got rid of the old bezom she's decided to stay!'

'Surely not, Mam! Didn't Harry run her to the station this morning? I saw Ruth carrying her suitcases out to the car.'

'Oh, she started out all right, but before you could say Jack Robinson she had turned round and come right back!'

'I wonder who apologized to whom?' Mariah mused.

'Oh, that didn't have anything to do with it. Apparently the train failed to appear — trouble on the line or something — so they had no choice. Then Meredith talked her gran into staying. I know, because she came in and told me so. Meredith, I mean, not the old girl. You could have knocked me sideways with a feather!'

'Does Harry know she's staying?'

'I believe he still has that pleasure to come. But never mind that. Did you hear from Aubrey at last?'

Mariah's shining eyes made a reply unnecessary. 'I have something to tell you, though, Mam. Behold Cwmbran's new postwoman!'

Ellen stared at her daughter in amazement. 'Are you having me on? Because if you are, you can stop that, right now. I've had enough shocks for one week. I doubt if my heart could stand any more!'

'Certainly not. I heard there was a temporary vacancy, so I snapped it up. It's just until Sioni Evans is back on his feet, of course. It'll get me out of the house while all this upheaval is going on, and my pay is going straight into my post office savings account. It'll be a little something to help set us up when Aubrey comes marching home again.'

'People will have to learn to call you Mortimer the post,' Ellen laughed. 'Bit of a mouthful, isn't it? But I hope you haven't taken on too much. Are you sure you can manage it, *cariad?* All that, and the gardens too. When are you going to sleep?'

'It's only mornings, Mam, and I've got the Swansea Six licked into shape. They're quite capable of carrying on while I'm out.'

Ellen was afraid that they were exploiting the six young workers, but it seemed that they regarded it as doing their bit for the war effort. 'We're digging for victory, like Mr Churchill says,' Dafydd explained proudly, when she tentatively suggested that they might be working too hard. 'We're going to beat that old Hitler, see?'

So Mariah pedalled off at dawn each morning to get her instructions from the postmistress, then it was off to meet the milk train at Cwmbran station, where she had to load a heavy mail bag on to a trolley which, with much huffing and puffing, she pulled to the post office.

'I've found muscles I didn't know I had,' she told Mrs Crabbe. 'I thought I was fit from all that hoeing and digging, but I feel like I've just run ten miles, uphill all the way!'

'You'll soon get used to it,' her employer told her. 'Before the war we used the van, of course, but we can't get the petrol now. I save the coupons in case we need to deliver large parcels to outlying districts. You can drive, I suppose.'

'Yes, I can, but I don't get much practice these days. Not that I need to, really. I'm used to walking and cycling everywhere, like everybody else.'

'Have you got your puff back, then? We'll sort the post, and then you must get started on your rounds. People don't like it if the post is late. They come and complain to me about it, they do. I remind them there's a war on, but that won't wash with some of them. Think they own the earth, see!'

'You know what you've done, don't you, Meredith Morgan!' Harry was extremely annoyed with his daughter. 'You've destroyed my peace of mind! Never mind what the pair of you have done to poor Ellen!'

'Don't shout, Dad!'

'I'm not shouting. I'm just speaking firmly.' He gritted his teeth. There were times when he wondered how they could possibly be related to one another, so different was their outlook on life. 'Your grandmother was all set to go back to Hereford, until you stuck your oar in.'

'Come on, Dad! It wasn't my fault that the train didn't arrive!'

'No, but you didn't have to fall on the woman's neck and beg her to stay.'

Meredith's bottom lip quivered. 'I need somebody, Dad! You don't understand what it's like to lose someone you love.'

'I did lose my wife, remember.'

'That was years ago. Grandmamma and I

understand each other. We've both lost our husbands. She knows what I'm going through. All you care about is your precious Mariah!'

'*Cariad!* Nobody could love you more than I do. You must know that. If I've come to Mariah's defence recently it's only because she's been the unfair target of your grand-mother's dislike. I'd do the same for you if need be.'

Meredith ignored this. 'It's not fair!' she grumbled. 'All I wanted was for Grand-mamma to stay with me for a while and I'd have thought you could give me that much. Now you want to get rid of her.'

'If it means that much to you, she can stay, at least for a while,' Harry conceded. 'I must be mad, that's all I can say!'

Meredith hid a smile. Dad was like putty in her hands. She knew how to handle him!

When his daughter had gone, Harry walked around his study, too restless to settle down to any useful work. He realized with a pang of guilt that he should give Meredith more attention, but there were times when he didn't like her very much. Ever since she'd learned that Mariah was in fact her half sister she'd been cool towards the other girl. There was no denying that it had come as a shock, but time had passed and she should have got over it by now. It wasn't as if he'd produced another daughter out of a hat, so to speak. The two girls had been together all their lives. Shouldn't they have been delighted to know that they were related?

He admitted that he had tried to show Mariah some extra affection over the years, to make up for her more difficult start in life. Nobody would ever know how hard it had been for him, being unable to openly acknowledge her as his own flesh and blood. What was the use of trying to explain that to Meredith, though? Her mind was made up. You might as well try to shift the Rock of Gibraltar as to reason with her.

'It's all settled, Grandmamma,' Meredith reported back. 'Dad wants you to stay!'

Henrietta frowned over the top of her spectacles. 'Did he say that, Meredith?'

'Not exactly, but I know he meant it.'

'Humph!'

'Look, Grandmamma; this is a big house. You don't need to come into contact with Dad at all, or Ellen and Mariah, come to that.'

'I have to see your father over the meal table. I really don't think I can face that.'

'Please?' Meredith wheedled. 'I really need

you here. Nobody in this place understands me. I'm so lonely, Grandmamma!'

'Very well, I'll stay, but only for your sake, Meredith. But if things don't go smoothly I shall return home, and if you don't choose to accompany me, why, I'll have done my best for you, and you cannot say I haven't tried.'

In her heart of hearts Meredith knew exactly why she resented Mariah so much. Finding out that Harry had betrayed her mother was one thing, but Antonia was a shadowy figure, known to her only in old studio photographs. It was hard to think of her as a real person. The worst part was that Meredith was somehow diminished by the sudden advent of a sister, and an older sister at that, because Mariah had come into the world some three weeks before her.

All her life Meredith had relished her position as daughter of the house, feeling superior to the housekeeper's daughter, and now she was experiencing what amounted to an identity crisis. This had been overcome when she married Chad Fletcher, especially when she gave birth to their son, but then Chad was killed while helping to rescue men stranded at Dunkirk. In turn, Mariah had married Aubrey Mortimer and the tables had been turned once again.

'A penny for your thoughts, child!'

'I was just thinking about Chad.'

'I know, my darling. Did you love him very much?'

Meredith considered this for a long moment. 'I thought I did, but now I'm not so sure. Sometimes I wonder if I only married him so I could stay in this house for the rest of my life. You know he was meant to inherit the estate after Daddy's death, and I was afraid that if Chad married someone else they wouldn't want me hanging around like the family ghost. It was Daddy's idea for us to marry, you know, and I liked the idea of being a bride, so I agreed to it.'

'Your father wanted what was best for you,' Henrietta remarked. A relic of the Victorian era, she saw nothing wrong with such arrangements, idiotic though they might seem to a modern woman. 'And it's all worked out for the best, hasn't it? You are still here, and Baby Henry will inherit the estate in due course.'

CHAPTER NINETEEN

Mariah was greatly enjoying her new work. While getting on and off her bicycle so often was a bit of a nuisance, it was easier on the back than the constant hoeing she'd been used to. Some days there was more post to be delivered than others. Few of the local women had husbands in the services because most were employed at the colliery, but some had grown children who were away doing their bit, daughters especially.

There was one woman who always waited at her cottage door long before the post was due to arrive, and Mariah hated to see the poor soul's face fall when there was no envelope to put into her hand.

'I do know how that feels, Mrs Griffiths,' she confessed. 'I so look forward to hearing from my husband and I find it quite worrying when I don't hear from him for a week or two.'

'He's in the air force, isn't he, Mrs Mortimer? My Gareth is fighting in Africa, I believe. Imagine, he'd never been farther than Llanelly when all this started, and now look at him. In the middle of a desert somewhere.'

On another occasion Mariah was asked inside to have a look at a little girl's rash.

'For it costs money to get the doctor to come and we don't have it to spare. I thought you might know. You have a kiddie of your own, don't you?'

'No, that's Mr Morgan's daughter, actually. The baby's mother, I mean. Has your little girl got a temperature?'

'I haven't taken it, miss. She won't open her mouth and if I force the thermometer in I'm afraid she'd bite it and break it. And that would be a shame, wouldn't it?'

Mariah agreed that it would. She wasn't sure whether the woman was worried about the loss of her thermometer, or the possible effect on her child's stomach or mouth if she bit on the glass.

'I'll tell you what I'll do, Mrs Stephens. I'll pop a note in at the district nurse's house asking her to call and see Bethan. Will that do? I'm really not qualified to judge what's wrong. In the meantime, it won't hurt to sponge the child down with cool water every once in a while. Can you do that?'

Gradually people came to know Mariah, and she was often the recipient of a piece of news, or a whispered confidence. The most interesting bit of gossip came when she delivered a small package to Bessie Harries, a plump and attractive widow whose miner husband had died some years before with silicosis, or miner's lung.

'You work up at the house with young Myfanwy Prosser, don't you?'

Mariah agreed that she did. It was easier to go along with the mistake than to get involved in a long-winded explanation.

'Well, then, you can tell her from me that her brother is walking out with our Gwyneth, see?'

'Oh, which brother is that, then?'

'The oldest one, him they call Llew. Good-looking boy, black hair, typical Welshman. Lovely voice he has. Sings solo up the chapel.'

'Is it serious, do you think?'

'Early days, yet, Mrs Mortimer. Early days. Why do you want to know? Not got your eye on him yourself, have you?'

'Me? I'm a married woman!' Mariah laughed. 'I just thought it would be lovely for the family if Llew got married and took a wife home. I've heard they're not managing too well in the house now Myfanwy's gone out to work.'

'Our Gwyn won't be taking over any time soon. They have to save up before they can marry see, and the pay's none too good in that shop where she works. Evans the draper, up on Broad Street. The trouble is he can't afford to pay much because he doesn't get the trade like he used to. Not with points for this and points for that. Four coupons required for a pair of ladies knickers, and now we're to get only forty-eight coupons for the whole year. I ask you! How are we supposed to put clothes on our backs when that's all they give us?'

'I'd better push on,' Mariah murmured, anxious to stem the flow, but she might as well have tried to stop the Towy River in spate.

'As everybody says, all Job Prosser's problems would be solved in no time if he'd just take another wife.'

Mariah's ears pricked up then. 'Is he thinking of remarrying, then?'

'He just needs a bit of encouragement,' the woman simpered. 'I was thinking I might try one of them fatless sponges people are talking about, and take it round there as a present. The boys would appreciate it, and that would make Job notice me.'

'It's worth a try, I suppose. Why don't you get your Gwyneth to find out if Job is already seeing anyone? It could be embarrassing if you turned up on the doorstep and found he wasn't interested. Let me know how it turns out.'

On Sunday afternoon Mariah was sitting in her mother's room with her feet up as the pair discussed the events of the past week. Sunday being a day of rest, she was greatly enjoying this hour or two of leisure. She'd already had to take her belt in by a notch as a result of all the extra exercise.

A knock came at the door. 'It's me, Mrs Richards, Ruth. There's a man to see you. He won't say what it's about. I've put him in the morning-room and told him to wait.'

'What sort of man?'

'Begging your pardon, Mrs Richards, it's that Job Prosser. Myfanwy's dada.'

'Oh, no! What does the man want this time? If he's come to try to drag Myfanwy home, he's got another thing coming. She's happy and settled here, and Meredith is pleased with her work. After all the bother we've had here recently I simply will not let him upset the apple cart!'

'I am not here for Myfanwy!' Job announced as soon as Ellen entered the room, thereby taking the wind out of her sails.

'Oh? What is it, then?'

He shuffled his feet. 'I was thinking you might like a walk, Mrs Richards.'

'With you, do you mean?' Taken aback, but intrigued at the same time, she decided that it couldn't do any harm just to spend half an hour in his company. It was a long time since any man had shown an interest in her as a person, and she was curious to know what he had in mind.

'We could go down Farm Lane, if you like.'

This was a pretty walk which local people often took on a summer evening. It was also a place where half the population of Cwmbran might see them together, and comment on it! In fact, when a widower took a widow out walking in public the news spread like wildfire. Ellen wasn't ready for that sort of involvement.

'Perhaps you'd care to see the grounds here, Mr Prosser? There's a fine ornamental pond on the other side of the copse, and a herb garden which I'm told was planted in Mr Morgan's grandmother's day. Of course the rose garden and the perennial borders have all been done away with since the war began. My daughter and her young helpers are growing potatoes and other vegetables as far as the eye can see. And the green-houses are filled with tomatoes nowadays. There used to be some fine orchids in there years ago.'

'Aye, I'd like to see how the vegetables are coming along,' Job responded.

'Right, then! I must go upstairs and change my shoes.' Ellen sped upstairs, not knowing whether to be pleased or annoyed by this turn of events.

Mariah leaned over the bannisters, grin-ning. 'So he didn't bite your head off, then? Where is he now, on his way home with a flea in his ear?'

'If you must know, we're going for a walk, just as soon as I've found my old lace-ups.'

'What, together?'

'No, one behind the other, marching along like good little soldiers. Of course we're go-ing together. Not out in public, mind. I'm going to show him your vegetables.'

'Oh, very romantic, I'm sure! Don't get carried away, will you!' Mariah dodged the playful blow which Ellen aimed in her direc-tion. It was about time that her mother had somebody nice in her life, after living like a cloistered nun all these years. She was still a young woman, and she deserved to be loved and cherished.

But just what did Job Prosser have in

mind? You didn't have to be a genius to work that one out. It was Mam's own business if she wanted to marry the man and go to live in his cramped terraced house to look after his herd of youngsters. If she found love again she might not mind giving up her present luxurious surroundings, because that's what they were, even under the difficulties brought about by the war.

But would she fit in there? Her old friend Megan Jones would be delighted to have Ellen living close by again, but what about the other miners' wives? Wealthy people were not the only ones who practised snobbery. Ellen had lived the greater part of her life in the home of Harry Morgan, the man who employed most of the men of Cwmbran. He owned the very roofs over their heads. And that was not all. Mariah shuddered to think what would happen if it ever came out that Ellen had given birth to Harry Morgan's child. She would be shunned completely.

CHAPTER TWENTY

Harry Morgan felt as if the weight of the world was on his shoulders. All his life he had loved summertime in Cwmbran. As a boy, home from his boarding school, he had spent long, lazy afternoons lying in the long grass, watching the birds and small mammals that abounded in the countryside. He would sometimes ride with his father to visit their tenant farmers; Harry on his sturdy Welsh cob and his father mounted on his great grey gelding, Bucephalus. There was always the annual holiday to look forward to, when they took rooms at Barry and spent the day on the pebble beach at Porthkerry.

All that was nothing but a distant memory now. They would soon be entering the fourth year of the war and it seemed that the conflict was no closer to being resolved than it had been in previous months. Life was getting harder for people on the home front, with all this rationing and shortages, and for people like Harry, who was trying to keep things going, it was fraught with difficulties.

They were trying to improve production levels at the mine, and his manager Llew Roberts was almost working himself into a nervous breakdown. Every time Harry called into the office it was to find the man wringing his hands and going in several directions at once.

'Calm down, man!' Harry would say. 'Worse things happen at sea!' But Roberts was incapable of doing any such thing. Some day Miss Evans would let herself into the office and find her boss stretched out flat on the floor, Harry was convinced of it.

Harry's own temper was becoming frayed. On grumbling to his womenfolk that as far as the war effort was concerned, they seemed to be taking one step forward and two steps back, Mariah attempted to console him.

'Never mind, we're all trying to pull our weight. Our vegetable gardens are the pride of Cwmbran, though I do say it myself.'

'And how will that help if the invasion comes?' he snapped. 'What do you mean to do, slap Hitler with a carrot?'

'Harry, really! There's no call for that!' El-

160

len cried.

He mopped his brow with his pocket handkerchief. 'Sorry! Sorry! I can't think what came over me. Sorry, Mariah. Of course your work is very much appreciated. You do know that, don't you?'

His work as a magistrate did little to soothe his worries. While the miners were working overtime and other people were 'digging for victory' there were one or two villains who saw ways to turn the conflict to their own advantage. Materials mysteriously disappeared from builders' yards, and one or two shops were broken into and tinned food stolen. The Methodist minister thundered his disapproval from the pulpit but it had little effect. The thieves probably didn't attend chapel in any case.

'I want you to keep your eyes and ears open when you're on your delivery rounds,' Harry told Mariah.

'I will, but people are not likely to tell me anything, are they? Half the people are related by marriage and even those who are morally upright themselves wouldn't rat on someone they know, especially to me. I live under your roof, and am therefore on the side of the bosses!'

As it happened, it was a small innocent who let slip the information which led to the arrest of two local ne'er do wells. When Mariah was plodding down one of the rows of terraced houses she noticed a little girl sitting on her front step, blissfully consuming a bar of Cadbury Bourneville. Struggling to push a rolled-up magazine through a letter box, she smiled at the child, whose face was smeared with chocolate.

'What a lucky girl you are, Gwenllian! Is that your sweet ration? You'd better save some for another day, hadn't you?'

'Not my ration!' the child mumbled. 'It fell off a lorry, see!'

Mariah's eyes opened wide. She knew what the euphemism meant, although it appeared that the girl did not, being too young to understand.

'It fell off a lorry, did it? That was lucky, wasn't it?'

The girl nodded. 'It fell down on the street, see, and my dada picked it up and saved it for me.'

The door flew open then, and a harrassed woman with her head in a turban grabbed the child by the arm and dragged her to her feet. 'You get upstairs to bed, Gwenny Phillips! Right now, I say!' She glared at Mariah before shutting the door in her face. The last thing Mariah heard was the child's anguished wail, followed by the sound of a slap. Poor little devil, she thought. That bit of chocolate was dearly bought.

When the case came up before Harry — the two criminals being Gwenllian's father and his younger brother — he gave them the choice between a prison sentence and joining up. They chose the latter.

'And if they get themselves killed it'll be all your fault!' Mrs Phillips screamed at Mariah, the next time she carried her satchel of letters down the street. Mariah made no reply. What was the point of arguing with the woman?

Even the most optimistic person was forced to admit that the war wasn't going well for the Allies. By the spring of that year the German forces had penetrated deep into Russia. The British Eighth Army, serving in North Africa, had been forced back into Egypt. Poor Mrs Griffiths was frantic about her Gareth and every time Mariah turned into her street, the woman was there to greet her.

'Can you tell me anything about what's happening over there?' she cried, wiping her eyes with the hem of her apron. 'Only I thought Mr Morgan might have a bit of news, him being one of the big wigs, see.'

'I'm so sorry, Mrs Griffiths. We're just like everyone else, we only know what we hear on the news.' She wished she had words of comfort to offer, but what was there to say?

'I wish they could tell us more,' Harry complained, when they were seated beside the wireless that night.

'Don't they tell us everything, then?'

'No, Ellen, I don't suppose they do. When things are going badly, they dare not give us the complete picture. It would be no good for morale.'

'Sometimes the news is good, from our point of view.'

'Granted, but how much of that is mere propaganda?' Naturally, there was no answer to that. 'The worst of it is,' he went on, 'that we can't know what's happening behind the scenes. Churchill and the others have it all in hand, but they can't broadcast it because we mustn't allow the enemy to know what our plans are. It's so frustrating, having to sit helplessly by, while others see all the action. At least our troops know they're doing something. Old codgers like me sit helplessly on the sidelines.'

The attack on the port of Dieppe took place on 19 August. An assault force of some six thousand men approached the coast of France in the early hours of the morning. The majority were Canadian soldiers, with the rest being Royal Marine commandos and some American Rangers. The raid was supported by eight Allied destroyers and seventy-four Allied air squadrons. The plan was to attack at three different points along the coast.

The operation was a dismal failure, resulting in great loss of life. In one sector the landing craft were intercepted by a German convoy, and the noise of the resulting fight alerted those manning the coastal defences. In other sectors the Allies met with heavy machine-gun fire and were held back on the beach by the heavily wired sea wall. In other cases tanks were stopped by concrete obstacles which had been erected in the streets and their crews taken prisoner or killed in battle.

Mariah came into her mother's sitting-room just as the evening news broadcast was about to come on. She had been delayed by having to patch up one of the Swansea Six who had fallen out of a tree and scraped his knees. The two women were amazed when Harry burst into the room and switched off Ellen's wireless.

'Here! I was listening to that! You know very well the news is about to start!' she protested.

'You can hear it tomorrow. Come on! It's

time we had an air-raid drill.'

Mystified, they followed him down to the cellars, where, at the outbreak of war, the walls and ceiling of the old wine cellar had been reinforced to form an air-raid shelter.

'What's all this about, Harry?' Henrietta wanted to know when everyone was gathered together. 'There hasn't been an air raid in this part of Wales, as you know.'

'And that has made us complacent, Mother-in-law, something we can't afford to be. That was quite good, all of you, but try to improve on your response time in future. Off you go now, and thank you.'

'What are you up to?' Ellen hissed, when Mariah had shepherded the Swansea Six up the stairs in the wake of Meredith and her little party.

'I didn't want Mariah to hear the news. There was a big attack on Dieppe yesterday, which didn't go well. Thousands dead, or taken prisoner, I understand. I had a phone call from London during which I heard about it, in part.'

'But . . .'

'The fact is, Ellen, that the RAF were involved, trying to protect our troops from attack by the Luftwaffe. I'm sorry to say that more than a hundred of our aircraft have been lost.'

'Aubrey!' Ellen breathed. 'Oh, no! Do you think something might have happened to him? Oh, my poor, poor Mariah!'

Chapter
Twenty-One

They couldn't keep it from her for ever, of course. She had to be taken aside to have the news broken to her, before someone else blurted out the news.

'It might be better coming from you,' Ellen told Harry. 'I'm glad you didn't let her hear it on the wireless, though. That would have come as too much of a shock.'

'You're the girl's mother,' he said.

'And you're her father! She looks up to you, you know she does.'

'I don't see what that has to do with anything,' he grumbled, but he knew she was right. 'We'll tell her together, then. I'll do the talking and you can stand by with the smelling salts, in case.'

But the smelling salts weren't needed. Mariah remained quite calm when they told her. 'Don't worry, Mam. He's not dead. I'd know if he was.'

'Oh, *cariad!*' The final total among members of the RAF was sixty-four dead, as well as numerous other casualties. Ellen suspected that the chances of Aubrey having returned safely to England were slim but naturally she didn't say so.

'I know he'll be in touch soon, to let me know he's all right,' Mariah said firmly, but it was only a brave front. Inside she was a mass of nerves. Her stomach was clenched and she had to fight to prevent herself from vomiting. 'I'm going to ring his camp,' she kept insisting, but Harry held her back.

'I've already been on to the base, *cariad,* and been told they're not giving out any information. You must try to be patient. Aubrey will know how you must be feeling; he'll be in touch as soon as he can.'

'Unless . . .'

'Yes. In that case, someone in authority will contact us very soon.'

But although Mariah hovered within hearing distance of the telephone, refusing to eat or sleep, or even to lie down, Aubrey didn't call. Late in the following afternoon it rang, but when she snatched it up it was only a wrong number. She replaced the earpiece on its stand, blinking back the tears.

Then the duty Boy Scout came tacking up the drive on his ancient bicycle, and handed the dreaded orange envelope to Ellen, who had rushed downstairs to intercept him.

'Any reply, missus?'

'You can send a telegram to that evil devil, Hitler,' she sniffed, 'and tell him from me I hope he rots in hell!'

'Do you know his address, missus?'

'What? No, of course I don't know his address! I was just thinking out loud. Off you go, boyo. No reply.'

Slowly she ripped open the envelope. 'Regret to inform you . . . Pilot Officer Aubrey Mortimer . . . missing in action . . .' She crumpled it up and thrust it into her apron pocket.

'That was the telegraph boy, wasn't it, Mam?'

'I'm afraid it was.'

'Give it here, then. Let me see.'

Wordlessly Ellen handed over the scrap of paper, biting her lip until it bled.

'Missing, Mam! He's only missing. That's good news, isn't it? It doesn't say he's dead, you see.'

The girl was radiant. Ellen couldn't bear to see the hope in her eyes. 'That's right, *cariad*. You know what I always say: while there's life, there's hope.'

In due course a letter came from Aubrey's commanding officer. One of the men in Aubrey's wing had reported having seen the aircraft he was piloting being hit by enemy fire over the sea. 'I'm pretty sure he pranged,' he had concluded. Asked whether he had seen the crew coming down by parachute he said he didn't know. He had been too busy trying to avoid two German planes which were on his tail. The last he had seen was Aubrey's 'kite' disappearing into the water.

Strangely, the person who provided Mariah with the most support in those dark days which followed was Meredith. Somehow all her envy of Mariah had disappeared in the wake of this disaster. 'We're in the same boat now,' she remarked. 'I know how you must be feeling.'

Mariah did her best to respond to this well-meaning solicitude. 'Thank you, Merry. You're very kind.' On the inside she was seething. How could Meredith possibly know how she felt? Yes, she was a war widow, and that was hard to bear. But at least she knew that Chad was gone and would never be coming back. It was the uncertainty of Aubrey's disappearance that was so difficult for Mariah to face. What if he was alive somewhere, badly wounded and not getting the treatment he needed? And if he was already dead, had he suffered?

'I know he's not dead!' she kept reminding herself. 'I'd know if he was!' At night she peered up at the stars, glancing from one to the next as if they somehow held the answer to her anguished questions. Was that where heaven was, up there in the skies, as they were told in the Sunday School hymn?

With a sudden shock she realized that she was no longer sure if she believed in the existence of God. How could a loving creator permit wars and tragedies to happen? Why didn't he send a bolt of lightning to strike down the Nazis and their ilk?

'Are you there, God?' she whispered. 'Please keep my Aubrey safe!' But there was no reply. Like the stars above, God, if he existed at all, preferred to keep silent.

In the days that followed, Mariah tried to keep her spirits up. By this time everyone in Cwmbran knew what had happened, and many of the householders met her on the doorstep with words of sympathy. Occasionally a housewife would press a small packet into her hand, containing a home-made biscuit or a square or two of chocolate, and these small kindnesses did much to cheer her sad heart.

Music of course was the great standby in a Welsh village, and she took to walking back into Cwmbran on Sunday evenings to stand outside the Methodist chapel as the sound of their hymns surged out on to the street.

One weekday evening she had gone down to Megan Jones' home on an errand for Ellen, and had stayed late. Knowing that Megan's husband would soon be coming in, she reluctantly left for home, and then, in the distance, she saw a column of miners approaching, singing as they came. The music of the favourite hymn *'Bryn Calfaria'* (Calvary Hill) filled the twilight, and as each man peeled off on reaching his street he continued to sing, never missing a beat. Mariah's heart seemed to swell as if it would burst out of her breast, so beautiful was the encounter.

Her mother enjoyed the lighter music on the wireless. She always tuned in to *Worker's Playtime* when they were sitting down to their midday meal with the Swansea Six. It was broadcast live from factory canteens and the programme gave her the feeling that they were 'all in it together', as she put it, when talking about the war effort.

'There's that American song again,' Mariah noticed. 'It seems to be very popular. That's the second time I've heard it today.'

' "Praise the Lord and Pass the Ammunition". It's got a jolly tune,' Ellen agreed. 'I read in the paper that an American song writer, Frank Somebody, came up with it after the Japs bombed Pearl Harbour last year. Patriotic of him, wouldn't you say?'

The Swansea Six seemed to think so, too. They took to marching about in single file, with rakes and hoes over their shoulders, pretending to be soldiers. 'Pass the ammunition and we'll all be free!'

Half listening, Mariah thought she heard the youngest member of the crew singing 'and we'll all be three!'

'Haven't you got it wrong, Ceri? There are six of you.'

'Don't know what you mean, miss!'

'Well, that song. The words "we'll all be free" and you are singing "three".'

'That's 'cause I'm not a baby, miss,' he explained, leaving her more confused than ever. Thinking that it didn't really matter she let it go, but later she mentioned it to Ellen, who started to laugh.

'I believe I know what's going on! Poor Ceri gets teased sometimes because he's so much younger and shorter than the rest of them. The other day he was helping me count the eggs, saying one, two, free, four, and Huw heard this and laughed at him. "It's three, boyo, three! Only babies say free!" That could explain it, don't you think?'

Light dawned. Mariah smiled, for the first time in days. Ellen saw this, and was glad.

'I don't know about you, but I'm thankful we took these evacuees. I was a bit upset at the time, wondering how we'd manage, but I must say they've been a godsend.'

'They certainly have, all those hours they put in on the land. I could never manage it all by myself and it doesn't look as though we'll ever be allocated a land girl.'

'It's not just that. For orphans they're cheerful little souls. We could all learn a lesson from them.'

'Mm.'

'Oh, *cariad,* I didn't mean . . .' Ellen's face fell. 'I've put my foot in it, haven't I?'

'It's all right, Mam. It's all right. You don't have to watch your tongue all the time.'

CHAPTER
TWENTY-TWO

'Mrs Mortimer! You got a minute?'

Mariah turned round to find Bessie Harries puffing up behind her. 'Yes, Mrs Harries? Can I help you?'

'I was just wondering, er, how your mam is.'

'Mam? Very well, thank you. I'll let her know you were asking.' The woman's face reddened. Mariah watched, fascinated, as the flush spread over her fat neck. 'What is it, Mrs Harries?'

'It's a bit awkward, like. Um, I just wondered what she thinks of Job Prosser.'

'I rather think that's her business, don't you? But just for the record, she hasn't mentioned him to me. Not lately, anyway.'

'But she has been seeing him, isn't that right? Walking out with him, as it were.'

Mariah hardly knew what to say. Her mother had been going out for walks with Job, but that wasn't the same thing as walking out! She was pretty certain that Ellen liked the man, but was she contemplating a future with him? Prosser seemed to have designs on her, although whether he fancied Ellen, or simply wanted a housekeeper, she couldn't say. With three pay packets coming into the house the man could afford to pay some woman to come in and do basic housework, but he wouldn't have to pay a wife, would he!

Bessie Harries had been watching her with an anxious expression on her face. 'So what I was hoping you could tell me, Mrs Mortimer, is whether there's anything in it. Do they mean to make a go of it? I don't want to make a fool of myself, throwing my hat into the ring, if he's asked her to marry him, and that.'

'I suppose I could find out. I'm not making any promises, mind. Mam can get a bit touchy at times.'

'Only he's a lovely man, see. I wouldn't blame her if she did want to snap him up.'

'I'll see what I can do,' Mariah told her again. And why, oh why, did I just do that? she asked herself. Blithering idiot!

The closer she came to home, the more she felt like kicking herself. She had no right to ask Mam personal questions, and when it came down to it she should side with

Mam rather than Bessie Harries. Not that it was her business to side with anyone. Job Prosser could make up his own mind, and Bessie would just have to take her chances.

She managed to get her mother alone just before bedtime. Ellen was not in good humour. The Swansea Six had just had a pillow fight, and one of the pillows had just about exploded. The feathers had gone everywhere and little Ceri Davies looked like a half-plucked chicken with down sticking to his hair, his pyjamas, and even up his nose.

'You are going to get down on your hands and knees and retrieve every one of those feathers,' she told them sternly. 'I don't mind you having fun, but this is going too far!'

'We were just playing, missus.'

'I can see that, Dai, but we need that pillow. I wouldn't be able to replace it for love nor money. You'll have to stuff those feathers back in the ticking and I'll sew the end in place tomorrow.'

This was easier said than done. As fast as they pushed the feathers in they came out again, floating around the room.

'They keep sticking to me, Mrs Richards,' Trevor complained.

Ellen showed no mercy. 'That's too bad,

Trevor. Perhaps another time you'll think before you act. Don't you know there's a war on?'

'Come on, Mam, and leave them to it. I'll make you a cup of cocoa and you can put your feet up.'

'It had better be a weak one, then. The tin is half empty.'

'I'm sure I can find a spoonful and no, Dai, there's none for you boys. You don't deserve it!'

'Aw!' came the chorus, but Mariah hardened her heart and shut the door firmly on her brood.

'Have you seen Job recently?' she asked, keeping her tone casual.

'Once or twice. Why do you ask?'

'Just curious, that's all.'

'Curiosity killed the cat!'

'And satisfaction brought it back!' They laughed, remembering the nursery patter they'd exchanged in the old days.

'Going out with Job makes me realize how much I've missed,' Ellen said at last. 'I've never really had a man friend before. I was too shy when I was young. I met plenty of lads when I worked at the department store in Cardiff after leaving school, but none of them ever asked me out. I did go to one of the firm's staff dances, but I was a real wallflower and never got up the nerve to go back. Then I had you, and that put paid to any involvement.'

'Oh, Mam!'

'Don't take it like that. All I meant was, I came here and I hardly ever went out, so how could I meet anyone? And if the truth be known, I didn't really want to. Once bitten, twice shy, as they say.'

Ellen stared into the distance. What she knew in her heart, but which wild horses couldn't drag from her, was that she loved Harry Morgan. There are some women who cherish just one love in their lives, and she was among them. Unfortunately he did not reciprocate her feelings, so that was the end of that.

'So what are your intentions now?' Mariah asked, when it became obvious that Ellen had nothing more to say.

Her mother looked at her over the top of her glasses. 'I don't know what you mean.'

'Come on, Mam! What if he proposes marriage? What will you do then? You must have thought about it.'

'I suppose it has crossed my mind, but we're hardly at that stage yet! I rather think he's like myself, just glad of a bit of company.'

'But why you, Mam? Why not one of the

women he knows locally?'

The way that Ellen's chin came up warned Mariah that she had gone too far. 'And why not me, pray? I like to think I'm not exactly past it, you know! And we happened to meet when he came here enquiring after his daughter, and perhaps he liked the look of me then. Why does any man take a liking to a member of the opposite sex? Possibly he fancies ladies with auburn hair!'

'I'm sorry, Mam. I didn't mean it the way it came out. It's just that I met someone on my rounds who happens to have her eye on Job Prosser and I was hoping that she wouldn't make a move in his direction and spoil things for you. But if you don't feel anything other than friendship for the chap, well then, no harm done.'

Ellen narrowed her eyes. 'Who is this person?'

'Her name is Bessie Harries. She's a widow, looking for companionship, if not something more.'

'Bessie Harries? I don't think I know her. How does she know Job?'

'From the chapel, I think. More than that, her daughter Gwyneth is going out with Llew Prosser, Myfanwy's eldest brother. That makes for a bit of a connection already, and if those two make a go of it, Bessie and

Job will become in-laws.'

Ellen's grey eyes flashed. 'As a matter of fact, Job has invited me to go and hear him sing this coming Sunday evening, at his chapel. He has a very fine voice, you know, and he'll be performing a solo. I wasn't meaning to go, but now I think I shall.'

Mariah closed her eyes slowly. She knew she shouldn't have said anything, but Bessie Harries had been so persuasive. There were any number of clichés that could be attached to this situation. The green-eyed monster had raised its ugly head! Mam was being a dog in a manger! Attending the Sunday evening service with Job, and no doubt being seen home by him afterwards, was tantamount to marking her territory, and by Monday morning all of Cwmbran would be aware that the pair were 'courting'.

'Harry may not like it,' she suggested.

'Harry! What's it got to do with him? He has no say in this whatsoever! I'm his housekeeper, not his wife!'

Was she wrong, or had a note of bitterness crept into Ellen's voice when she said that? Mariah could not be sure, but it boded no good. She was seized by a sudden inspiration. 'Can I come, Mam?'

'What?'

'I'd really like to hear Mr Prosser sing.'

'You're not a Methodist, my girl. You've never been inside that chapel in your life!' 'Neither have you, and that isn't going to stop you. Mind, I suppose you'll have to take up Methodist ways if you wed Job.'

'Oh, don't be so silly! I have no more intention of marrying Job Prosser than I have the man in the moon! But come if you like. I can't stop you.'

Aha! Mariah thought. A straight answer at last! But she couldn't pass that on to Bessie Harries, not when Ellen was determined to keep Job to herself.

CHAPTER
TWENTY-THREE

Mariah pulled a face at herself in the mirror. It was always a mistake to look at one's reflection in a full-length looking glass, she decided. She saw a tall, too-thin young woman with her chestnut hair worn in a victory roll. She was wearing a grey flannel skirt — pre-war — and a washed-out blue check blouse. Unfortunately she hadn't been provided with a uniform for work, being a temporary postwoman, and there was no point in wearing her best clothes when she had to be out in all winds and weathers.

'I wish I had a nice new blouse to cheer me up,' she murmured.

'Why don't you treat yourself then?' her mother enquired.

'Because I'm saving my coupons for a new winter coat, that's why. Fourteen coupons for a lady's coat. I ask you!'

'I could let you have some of mine.'

'No, thanks, Mam. There's a jumble sale

in the parish hall on Saturday. I think I'll look in and see what they have. I might get lucky.'

'Ew!' Meredith overheard this and wrinkled her nose. 'How could you, Mariah? Wearing other people's cast-offs?'

'A good wash and a press and you'd never know the difference.'

'I doubt if you'd find anything suitable,' Ellen warned. 'Nowadays people either wear their frocks and blouses until they're coming apart at the seams, or they cut them down to fit their daughters. Things that go to the jumble nowadays are either full of moth holes or outgrown children's wear. Look, I'll go through my cupboards and see if there's anything you might like.'

'Thanks, Mam, but I'll make do.' Mariah hated the thought of robbing her mother of the few garments she possessed. All these years she had seldom gone far from home and so had tended to wear the same few outfits all the time. The old trick of buying skirts, blouses and jumpers in coordinating colours, to be livened up by a pretty scarf or necklace, enabled her to appear in a variety of combinations. This thrifty habit let her down badly now, when items needed to be replaced.

Henrietta, on the other hand, had prudently stocked up as soon as the storm clouds of war had begun to appear. 'You'd better prepare yourself, old girl,' her husband had cautioned. 'Stock up on undies while you have the chance.' She had heeded his advice, and one of the trunks that had come to Cwmbran was filled with silk blouses, cashmere cardigans and thick lisle stockings.

'You must have a pair of these,' she'd offered kindly, when Meredith had complained loudly about a ladder in her last pair of silk stockings. 'We're the same size, I'm sure.'

Meredith had shuddered at the thought of encasing her elegant legs in what she thought of as 'old lady's hose'. She preferred to resort to what every other woman was doing these days, painting a line on the back of her legs with gravy browning, in imitation of a stocking seam.

'No lady would go out with bare legs,' Henrietta had exclaimed in horror, but Meredith had only laughed.

'I think I'll start wearing trousers, Grandmamma.'

This provoked even more cries of distress, but Meredith couldn't see what was wrong with the idea. Women in factories and the armed forces wore trousers while doing their work, and very practical they were, too. Mariah wore britches to do her gardening, and nobody batted an eyelid about that. Come to think of it, they had always worn jodhpurs for riding, and shorts for tennis, so what was the difference? Who made up these silly rules, anyway?

Mariah pushed one last hair pin into her curls before tying a cotton square over her head. There was no point to spending too much time on her appearance; by the time she'd cycled down to the village she'd be windblown and would have to begin again.

'This seems to be for you,' Mrs Crabbe murmured, as she paused in front of the pigeon hole marked 'Morgan'. 'Do you want it now, or will you get it later?'

Mariah always left their post where it was until her rounds were finished and she called in at the post office on her way home, to leave off her satchel.

'Let me see that, please.' She turned it over in her hand, wondering what it was, and where it was from. It was a small, flat packet; too thick to be a letter and the wrong shape, in any case.

'Well, don't keep us in suspense, *bach!* Aren't you going to open it now?'

Seldom the recipient of any letters herself,

Mrs Crabbe always took a great interest in other people's mail. Official rules forbade employees from interfering with letters and parcels, of course, but postcards were fair game. She loved to read the messages on those and tried to puzzle out what was meant. People with any sense put cryptic comments on postcards in case they fell into enemy hands, and this worked two ways. 'Coming home Sunday' could mean what it said, or it might be something more important, having to do with the war. At least, that was Mrs Crabbe's opinion.

Mariah hesitated. Then she ripped off the paper, revealing a letter, folded in four, and a small, flat box. She opened it gingerly. Inside, nestled on a bed of soft blue velvet, was a delicate pendant. She held it up for Mrs Crabbe to see, a rose-pink heart on a thin gold chain.

'Oh, I say!' The postmistress clasped her hands together in delight. 'Where did that come from, then? Not your birthday, is it?'

'No, it's not my birthday.'

Her heart was skipping beats and she hoped she wasn't going to faint. She unfolded the letter and was relieved and disappointed all at the same time to see that it wasn't written in Aubrey's distinctive scrawl but in small, neat handwriting in black ink.

'Go on, then, tell us who it's from!' Mrs Crabbe encouraged.

'It's from a friend of Aubrey's.'

'Your hubby!'

'What I mean is, the letter came from his friend, but the necklace is from Aubrey.'

'Oh, I see.' Mrs Crabbe didn't understand, of course, and it was evident from the look on her face that her boss was dying to know more, but Mariah couldn't explain. She knew she'd break down if she did.

'Just look at the time! I'd better get started, or I'll be in trouble with people all along my route. You know how the older ones look forward to seeing me, even if there's nothing for them.'

'Yes, that's right, *bach.* Off you go, now! TTFN!'

It always amused Mariah to hear the Welsh-speaking postmistress using the current English slang: Ta Ta For Now. What on earth might the Welsh translation be for that? As soon as she was out of sight she stopped her bicycle and pulled the letter out of her pocket. It was from somebody called John Worseley, who wrote that he was a friend of her husband. She frowned for a moment; she had no recollection of Aubrey having mentioned him. Perhaps it was just that this John was among the chaps who shared a Nissen hut with him.

'I came across this when I was clearing out Mortimer's foot locker,' he wrote.

Mariah winced. They only did that when they were sure someone wasn't coming back.

'I know he meant it for you because I was with him when he bought it. It was in the window of a pawn shop down in the town, and he went in and asked the price. He told me he'd save it to give you on his next leave. Anyway, I thought you'd like to have it, so I hope I'm doing the right thing by sending it to you now.'

She thrust the letter back into her pocket and mounted her bicycle. She'd examine her feelings later to see how she felt about this unexpected gift from Aubrey. For now, there was work to be done.

'What a lovely thing!' Ellen remarked, as she examined the pendant later that day. 'It looks to me as if it may be an antique. Where did that chap say it came from?'

'Apparently it was in the window of a pawn shop in the town near their camp. You know how they sell things if they're not reclaimed after a certain period of time.'

'It's too bad this John Wolsey or whatever his name is didn't bring this to you himself,'

Meredith put in.

'I don't know what you mean.'

'Well, don't you remember that when my Chad was killed, his friend came to bring me the news? That was how you met Aubrey and eventually came to marry him. History might have repeated itself, and this time the friend might have fancied me!'

'Really, Meredith! Do you have to be so insensitive?' Ellen frowned at the young woman she had more or less brought up.

Meredith's pale blue eyes opened wide. 'What have I said? I only meant. . . .'

'We know what you meant! And next time, kindly keep your silly ideas to yourself!'

Meredith ran out of the room, upset that her little joke had fallen flat. She'd grasped the fact that Mariah was thoroughly unsettled by the unexpected gift from her missing husband, and had tried to lighten the atmosphere. She was heartbroken for her half sister, but nobody seemed to realize or care that she, too, was grieving for her own lost husband. Why did life have to be so cruel?

CHAPTER
TWENTY-FOUR

'Are you coming to evensong with us, then?'
Henrietta asked, her eyebrows raised.

The four women stood, hatted and gloved,
in the front hall of the house. An observer
versed in local fashion would have known
by their headgear that they were going in
different directions. Henrietta wore a smart
summer hat, embellished with a bow of navy
blue petersham ribbon, while her granddaughter sported a straw boater trimmed
with artificial poppies and cornflowers.

Ellen, on the other hand, wore a shapeless
felt creation, a relic of former days, and the
blue beret perched on the back of Mariah's
curls was the same one she wore when she
felt like a change from wearing a head scarf
to work.

'No, we're going to chapel, Mrs Meredith,'
Ellen told her.

The eyebrows almost disappeared into the
other woman's white fringe. 'I didn't know

you were chapel, Mrs Richards!'

'I expect they're going to hear Myfanwy's father sing,' Meredith explained. 'Isn't that right, Mariah? Myfanwy wanted to go with them, but of course I had to say no, and now she's sulking.'

'Ah, so that's what all the fuss was about!' Henrietta sniffed. 'I thought I heard her answer back, and I was pleased to see that you stood firm. Once you give servants an inch, they'll take a mile.'

Ellen shuffled her feet, well aware that Harry's mother-in-law placed her firmly in the servant category. She'd show her what was what! 'I understand that Mr Prosser has a very fine voice,' she said firmly. 'Myfanwy must be very proud of her father. I can quite understand why she wanted to be present this evening.'

'Well, she can't, Mrs Richards. Mrs Fletcher employs the girl to look after Henry, and she's needed to care for him while we are at church.'

Listening at the top of the stairs, Harry sighed in exasperation. Would these women never stop sniping at each other? Mariah noticed him and turned to Ellen. 'Come on, Mam! We don't want to be late.'

'No, indeed,' Ellen replied. In fact, she hoped to get there early so as to take her seat before too many people arrived. She didn't fancy walking in under the curious eyes of a full house, even though she did have Mariah along for companionship. She need not have worried; Megan Jones and her husband, Merfin, arrived on the steps just as they approached the chapel.

'There's lovely you could come,' Megan began. 'Mind you, I know you didn't come here just to see me. Better fish to fry, you have this evening!'

'That's right!' her husband put in, with a sly grin on his handsome face. 'Come to hear the Reverend Williams, haven't you, *bach?* There will be a good crowd tonight, see.'

Mariah had never been in the Methodist chapel before, and she looked about her with interest. It was packed with people dressed in their sober Sunday best, and she was glad to see that she and Ellen had made the right choice of clothing for the occasion. Even so, all eyes seemed to be on them, and one or two women nudged their husbands and sent knowing looks in Ellen's direction. Evidently they knew about her friendship with their soloist of the evening and had her pegged as the next Mrs Job Prosser!

Embarrassed, Mariah looked down at her

gloved hands. Fortunately, it was time for the service to begin, and all eyes swivelled to the front as a man with a tuning fork announced the first hymn.

Later, Megan explained that the roof had leaked, unfortunately damaging the piano, which was why it wasn't in use that evening. 'Not that that bothered those who used their God-given talent to praise the Lord!'

'Who is that young woman over there?' Ellen hissed. 'Look, over by the wall. Why is she glaring at me like that?'

'Shush! Tell you later!' Mariah whispered. The man the girl was with must be Llew Prosser, who was a younger version of Job; his companion must be Gwyneth Harries. Bessie must have told her daughter about her hopes and now Ellen was getting the evil eye. Sure enough, Bessie was there as well, eyes fixed on her hymn book. A pillar had blocked Mariah's view of her until they all stood up to sing.

All's fair in love and war, Mariah thought, filled with horror the next moment as she realized what the old proverb meant to her.

Then it was Job's turn. He had a truly magnificent voice which raised goose pimples on Ellen's arms. She was about to applaud when she remembered where she was and sat back, hoping that nobody had noticed her sudden movement.

Then it was the turn of the visiting preacher. His sermon was in Welsh, which neither Mariah nor Ellen understood. Ellen wished that they'd been able to leave after hearing Job's solo, but of course that wouldn't have done at all. Apart from anything else they were sitting near the front and everyone present would have seen what was happening. Their departure would have been seen as a grave insult, not only to the congregation but to the Lord Himself.

The man was getting worked up now. Hellfire and brimstone wasn't in it, she suspected. Leaning forward in the pulpit he looked towards Ellen, stabbing an insistent finger in her direction. She cringed. He had obviously picked her out as a sinner and was telling the world about it.

Had he somehow been able to read her mind? Or was he upset because she was church, and not chapel? She looked sideways at Mariah, who was trying to stifle a giggle. Now the minister was jabbing his forefinger at an elderly miner, who sat with his arms folded and a stolid expression on his face. She shifted in her seat. Oh, this hard pew! Why couldn't she have brought a cushion?

At last it was all over. 'Did you enjoy it?'

Merfin asked.

'Job's solo was wonderful, I thought.'

'Of course, you wouldn't have understood what Reverend Williams was saying,' Megan said.

'I think I caught the drift! But why was he pointing at me? Did I do something wrong?'

'Na, na. His text was: "Though your sins be as scarlet", see. He was trying to bring all of us to repentance, not just you!' Megan laughed. 'Here comes Job. I suppose he'll be wanting to walk you home now!'

'I don't think you've met my son Llew,' was Job's opening remark. 'And this is his girlfriend, Gwyneth.'

'I know your mother,' Mariah smiled.

'I know. She said.'

'And this is my mother, Mrs Richards.'

Ellen nodded pleasantly. Gwyneth looked her up and down in an insolent manner before turning her gaze on Mariah once more. 'There's funny, you delivering the post! I didn't know they let women do that, or I'd have gone after the job myself. Better than working in that rotten shop!'

'It's only temporary. Just until Sioni gets back on his feet.'

'If he ever does. No joke that, breaking bones at his age. Still, it's nice for you to have something to do, isn't it? Nothing much for you to do up at the house, with servants to wait on you and that!'

Megan gave a slight shake of her head, as if to say, 'Don't bother.' Her husband had by this time moved away to talk to a work mate and hadn't heard Gwyneth's little speech. 'I've found that knitting pattern you wanted, Ellen. Why not pop round now and pick it up?'

'Yes, I will, thanks. I've just finished pulling down my old red jumper that was gone under the arms. I want to knit it up again into something for the boys.'

The two moved down the street, leaving Mariah to face the lovely Gwyneth. 'So nice to have met you,' she said sweetly.

Llew tipped his cap in her direction, which caused his girlfriend to link her arms with his as she almost dragged him away.

'Will your mam be long round at Jones'?' Job asked. 'I was planning to see her home. Both of you, that is,' he amended hastily.

'I'm not sure, Mr Prosser. Once those two get talking it's hard to prise them apart. I'll go and see, shall I?'

'Not to worry. She should be safe enough walking up to the house with you. Tell her I'll be in touch.' He, too, tipped his cap before taking his leave.

Now what? Should she go in search of

Mam and the mythical knitting pattern, or should she walk home by herself? She decided on the latter course of action. Nothing was likely to happen to Mam on the way and she herself needed some time alone.

Meanwhile, Ellen was enjoying a good gossip with her friend.

'There's spiteful that Harries girl is,' Megan decreed. 'What was the matter with her, anyway? Insolent, that's what I'd call it.'

'Her mother fancies Job,' Ellen explained, 'and I'm standing in her way!'

CHAPTER
TWENTY-FIVE

'Be a love and run up to the nursery with these towels, will you?' Ellen asked. 'Your legs are younger than mine.'

The household washing was still sent out to the Daffodil Laundry but it was her task to check it against her little red book when it came back. The man who collected it and brought it back in his horse-drawn van was stone deaf and it was no good arguing with him if something was lost. On the rare occasions when that happened she wrote a note to the proprietress and it was usually put right.

'I was going up there anyhow, Mam. I wanted to let Myfanwy know how much we enjoyed her father's singing. He's almost good enough to turn professional, wouldn't you say?'

Myfanwy got to her feet when Mariah entered. She'd been kneeling on the rug, playing with Henry and his building bricks. That is to say, she built towers and he knocked them over, with shrieks of glee.

'What did you think of Dada's singing?' she asked.

'He certainly has a wonderful voice, doesn't he? I don't know how he does it, when he's breathing in coal dust every day.'

'He gargles with salt water, Mrs Mortimer. I don't know if all singers do that, but it seems to work for Dada. I'd like to have gone to hear him myself, but I was needed here. What did you think of the Reverend Williams, then? I'm told he preaches a powerful sermon.'

'He does that. Of course, I'm afraid I only understood one word in ten, but I gather he was determined to hunt sinners down and get them to change their ways.'

Myfanwy laughed. 'Did you see my brothers there?'

'Just Llewellyn, I think. He had his girlfriend with him.'

Myfanwy pulled a face. 'Oh, her! I hope our Llew doesn't pop the question any time soon. She's a sharp-tongued cat, and her mam is no better.'

'Bessie Harries, you mean? I've always thought she seemed rather nice.'

'That's because you don't know her as

well as I do. Sweet as honey when she wants you to do something for her, but miserable as sin when things don't go her way.'

Mariah hesitated. Should Myfanwy be warned? Or was it Job who needed warning? She made up her mind and plunged right in.

'I believe that Mrs Harries has designs on your father, Myfanwy.'

'Don't do that, Henry, there's a good boy,' the girl said, seeing that the child was about to hurl a brick at the window. 'Come on, I'll build you another tower, a real castle this time.' Not looking up from what she was doing, she appeared to be mulling over what Mariah had said. 'Do you know that for a fact?' she said at last.

'I'm afraid so. Mrs Harries stopped me in the street the other day and had a word with me about it. She seemed to know that Mam was seeing a bit of your father, and she wanted to know what her intentions are.'

'There's cheek!'

'I couldn't tell her anything. Mam's never been one to talk about her private life, and after all they haven't been going out very long, have they? I think Mam just likes having a bit of companionship.'

'I'd be glad if Dada did marry again. Then I could get on with my life without feeling so guilty about leaving him in the lurch, as he likes to remind me. Your mam's nice; I wouldn't mind if they made a go of it.'

'And what if nothing comes of it? Do you think he'd turn to Bessie then?'

Outside the door, Henrietta paused to listen. She had no compunction about doing so because that was usually the only way you found out what your servants were up to. Naturally she would never listen in to a private conversation between people of her own class. No doubt the nursemaid was complaining because she hadn't been allowed out on Sunday evening!

As it happened the girl said no such thing. However, she and that Mariah did say something far more interesting. She couldn't wait to tell Meredith about it.

'You're lucky they weren't having a good old moan about you, Grandmamma! You know the old saying: eavesdroppers never hear good of themselves!'

'Don't be silly, dear. That miner that your old nanny is walking out with happens to be Mary's father!'

'Mary? Oh, you mean Myfanwy!'

'I call her Mary! Are you listening to me, Meredith? I said that the miner is that girl's father.'

'I know that. Ruth told me weeks ago. What's strange about that? They're both free agents. Myfanwy's mother died years ago, of tuberculosis, I think.'

'Then I hope the girl has been tested, to make sure she isn't carrying the disease. You have Henry to think of. But you're not allowing me to tell you what I heard. There may be a wedding in the offing!'

'Are you sure? Nobody has mentioned that to me.'

'Of course I'm sure. I heard the girl saying something about looking forward to having the Richards woman as a stepmother. What a nuisance! I suppose we'll have to look for a new housekeeper, in that case. The woman can hardly stay on here after she's married. Her husband will expect her to live down in the village with him. Quite a comedown for her, I'd say, after living in the lap of luxury here for so long.'

'Unless Dad allows her to stay on and bring her husband with her.'

Henrietta looked ready to explode, until she saw that her granddaughter was laughing at her. 'Oh, you! You had me believing it for a moment! No, this is excellent news. We'll have the woman out of this house once and for all, and don't tell me you won't be pleased!'

'I really am grateful to Ellen for everything she's done for me, you know.'

'And that does you credit, dear, but you must never forget that she and your father together betrayed your poor mother. When I think of my poor Antonia it makes me want to weep!'

'According to Dad, Mother was never aware of what happened,' Meredith said uncertainly. 'Not that it makes it right, of course.'

'Huh! How does he know what my daughter knew and what she didn't? Men are all the same; they tend to believe that we women are none too bright. Well, I'm about to show Harry Morgan a thing or two. She tossed her head defiantly.

Meredith knew with a sinking feeling that her grandmother was about to make trouble again. 'Don't you think we ought to wait and see what transpires? They haven't actually announced their engagement yet, have they?'

'By what I heard, it's a foregone conclusion, dear. I think I'll go up and see Harry now. I believe I heard him come in a while ago.'

'Grandmamma, I do wish you wouldn't.'

'Listen to me, Meredith. Antonia was my very dear daughter. I've been heartsick over what those two did to her. You must allow me to deal with this. It is my right.'

Out of spite, Meredith thought, but she held her tongue.

'Yes, Mother-in-law. What can I do for you?' Harry had just lit his pipe and was looking forward to a quiet evening with the newspapers before the nine o'clock news came on. He hoped she'd say her piece and leave. What she had to say brought him bolt upright in his leather armchair.

'I suppose you are aware that your housekeeper will be leaving shortly?'

'Why, is she going on holiday or something? She hasn't mentioned it to me.'

'Leaving for good, Harry. The woman is about to marry that coal miner chap she's been dallying with.'

'Good grief!'

'I see that she has not had the grace to inform you of this. Still, she'll have to give in her notice soon, won't she? I explained to Meredith that we should inform you at once, because of the difficulty of finding a replacement for her.'

She'd had her little triumph, but she didn't know that rage was welling up inside Harry Morgan, like a great red dragon rearing its head. He controlled himself with an effort. He had no intention of letting her see how upset he was.

'I don't think we need to replace Mrs Richards, do you, Mother-in-law? You and Meredith spend your days lazing around the house with no notion of doing anything useful. You should be able to cope with the running of the house between you! Meanwhile, thank you for bringing this to my attention.'

She left the room, closing the door none too gently behind her.

Harry put his head in his hands and groaned. Find a replacement for Ellen Richards? He would never be able to do that. But if after taking care of him all these years she had a chance of happiness with this man Prosser, who was he to deny her that? He would wish them well, give them a substantial wedding present, and let her go with a smile.

CHAPTER
TWENTY-SIX

Mariah fingered her pendant. She found herself reaching for it every time her thoughts went to Aubrey, which was a dozen times a day. Someone had told her that the pretty little heart was made of rose quartz, and the chain was perhaps pure gold. Welsh gold, they believed, but that was just guesswork. She didn't care if the piece was valuable or not; to her it was worth a king's ransom.

Imagine finding such a lovely thing in a pawnbroker's window! Who had abandoned it there? Some desperate woman, needing to pay the rent? A thief, who had looted someone's bombed-out home? She would never know.

As the days went by, there was still no news of Aubrey, and she began to lose courage. Each time the telephone rang, or somebody came to the door, her heart stood still. Work was torture to her now, because she both hoped and feared to find some missive in the post bag which would tell her what had become of her husband.

Even the antics of the Swansea Six failed to amuse her as they had in the past. She'd had to reprimand the littlest one, Ceri Davies, for swinging on the wooden gate at the end of the drive.

'It won't do it any good, *bach*. If those hinges fall apart we'll never be able to replace them, and then what shall we do?'

'Why didn't you put better hinges on before the war?' he wondered.

'Oh, we used to have lovely big iron gates here then, and iron fences as well. Beautiful they were.'

'What happened to them, missus?'

'Oh, they came and took them away for the war effort, Ceri.'

He had heard people say that sort of thing so often that it held no meaning for him. 'Will they bring them back, then, after the war stops?'

'I don't think so, *cariad.*'

'You should have kept them,' he told her. 'When the German tanks come we could have locked the gates to stop them getting in.'

She ruffled his hair, not trusting herself to speak. She cursed the unseen enemy who would rob a child of his innocence.

Now that September was here, the boys were all attending the Cwmbran school. One of them was in standard three, and he came home full of excitement because of something his teacher had told her class.

'She's got this big jar of pepper in the stock cupboard, missus.'

'Has she? Why does she keep it in there and not at home?'

'It's in case the invasion comes. There's two doors in our class room. If the enemy comes Miss Probert is going to throw the pepper in their faces while we escape through the other one, see?'

'Oh!' That was all that Mariah could say. She had no doubt that the elderly school teacher would lay down her life for her pupils if necessary, but why on earth give them a song and dance about pepper? Unless it was intended to keep up morale, like Mr Churchill saying we shall fight them in the streets? She shook her head in bewilderment. Ever since this wretched war had started it seemed as if the whole world had gone mad.

Not long after that, however, something happened to upset the inhabitants of Cwmbran House which sent the war news to the back of Harry's mind, not only because he owned the colliery but because he was also the local magistrate. He had a telephone extension upstairs in his study but there was also one on the ground floor, in a booth in the hall. Mariah happened to be nearby one evening when the phone rang. She let it ring several times, expecting Harry to pick up, but when nothing happened she flung back the folding door and grabbed the earpiece off its cradle. 'Cwmbran twenty-two!'

'Is that you, Mrs Richards?' It sounded like Betsi Thomas at the exchange.

'No, it's Mariah. Can I help you?'

'There's a trunk call for Mr Morgan.'

'I'm afraid he's not at home, Miss Thomas. Perhaps I could take a message and ask him to ring the caller later?'

There was a pause while the operator said something in muted tones. Then she was back. 'Caller says it's urgent. She'll speak to you, then.'

The line was appalling. 'Can you speak up, please? I can't hear you.' The static continued. 'I'm so sorry, I can't make out what you're saying.'

'Please hang up, caller, and try again.' That was Betsi, listening in as usual, in case she missed something interesting. The line went dead.

'Blast!'

'Language!' Ellen had come downstairs in time to witness Mariah's frustration. 'Who was that, anyhow?'

'No idea. The line was too bad. According to Betsi it was a matter of urgency, whoever it was.'

'If it was all that urgent they'll ring back later,' Ellen advised. 'So you'd better not rush off.'

'I wouldn't do that, Mam. You never know, it might be word of Aubrey. . . .' Her voice trailed off.

The phone rang again, startling them both.

'Hello? Hello? Is that Cwmbran House?'

'Yes, it is. Mariah Mortimer here.'

'Oh, but I wanted Mr Morgan.'

'I'm afraid he's not at home. Can I take a message and ask him to ring you when he returns?'

'I suppose that will have to do. This is Verona Fletcher speaking. Meredith Fletcher's mother-in-law.'

Mariah forced herself to remain patient. Of course she knew Mrs Fletcher; the woman had no need to explain. If she didn't hurry up and get to the point the pips would go and Betsi would be interrupting again.

'Something dreadful has happened! It's absolutely appalling! I really cannot put it into words!'

'Perhaps if you could just give me a hint?'

'I can't hear you!'

'Have you been bombed out, Mrs Fletcher?'

'What's that? No, of course I haven't. What makes you say that?'

'Look, Mrs Fletcher, I'll tell Mr Morgan that you'd like him to return your call. That's the best I can do, unless you'd like me to bring Meredith to the phone?'

'Oh, no! You mustn't do that! It's unthinkable!' The line went dead. Mariah frowned at the earpiece before replacing it.

'What on earth was all that about? It sounded like a comedy sketch on the wireless! All that squawking coming from the other end, and you pretending you didn't know what was going on.'

'No pretence about it, Mam. As you may have gathered, that was Verona Fletcher, in a right old tizzy. She kept saying that something was awful, but she wouldn't explain what she meant by it.'

'I hope this doesn't mean that something has happened to her house and she's got nowhere to go! We've already got Henrietta Meredith staying here. I don't think I could handle it if Verona Fletcher was billeted on us as well! Putting those two under the same roof would be like putting two fighting cocks in a cage. You know they've never got on.'

'That will be for Harry to decide, Mam. You know that Verona's husband was some sort of distant cousin of his. That's why Chad was supposed to inherit the estate in due course.'

'This place is becoming more like a zoo every day. I'm beginning to think that marrying Job and leaving here might be a good idea.'

So they were back to that again! 'So has Job proposed, then?'

'No, he has not. Mind you, he keeps moaning about how difficult it all is without a woman in the house to see to things. He misses having a hot meal put on the table as soon as he comes through the door.'

'What! You mean he sits down to the table in all his grime!'

'Oh, that's just a figure of speech. I imagine he has a good wash first.'

'But what does he expect you to do about it? Nip down there every day and look after the place?'

Ellen grimaced. 'I've a nasty idea that he's working up to making his proposal. He'll tell me that he's so lonely, surrounded by piles of dirty crockery, that he'd like to put a ring on my finger. I'm holding out for something more romantic. At least a bunch of chrysanths and two ounces of Mintoes to sweeten me up first!'

'Oh, Mam, you are funny!'

'I'm deadly serious,' Ellen retorted.

CHAPTER
TWENTY-SEVEN

Harry listened carefully to what Verona had to say, and interrupted her when she threatened to go into a bout of hysterics.

'I cannot say what ought to be done until I am in possession of all the facts,' he told her, in his best magisterial manner.

'But I already have all the facts,' she bleated.

'Forgive me, but I don't think you do. Please allow me to know, Verona! Unfortunately, this war has brought out a number of people who, instead of choosing to fight for king and country, have decided to use it to their own advantage. I have already seen that in my work here. This young woman is probably attempting to extort money out of you when she doesn't have a leg to stand on.'

'But Harry, I —'

'Not another word. I shall get on the morning train, and with any luck I'll be with you by late evening.'

'Can't you get here any earlier? Can't you bring the car?'

'I don't have enough petrol coupons, Verona. Just sit tight, and I'll be there as soon as I can.'

He could tell that she was close to tears now. 'But what if she comes back, Harry? What am I to do?'

'Lock your doors and windows, and on no account let her inside the house. If necessary, call in the police. Do you promise to do as I say?'

'I'll try,' she sniffed.

After ringing off, Harry went straight to Ellen. 'I have to go down to Wiltshire in the morning. Can you pack a small case for me? I expect I could be away for two or three days.'

'Do you really have to go? It'll be a beast of a journey,' she warned. 'How many times will you have to change trains? You'll be exhausted before you ever get there.'

'It can't be helped. Verona needs me there.'

'Hasn't she got friends there who can help her?'

He shook his head. 'This is a family matter, Ellen, and highly confidential. This must not on any account become public knowledge.'

'I see,' she said, not understanding at all, but extremely curious.

'Of course you don't.' He smiled. 'But remember what it says on the posters!'

' "Is your journey really necessary?" ' she quoted.

'Not that one! "Be like Dad; keep Mum!" '

He obviously wasn't going to tell her what it was all about, so she went to his dressing-room and packed his bag. Then she carefully brushed his homburg hat and checked his dark suit for any spots or wrinkles. He wasn't going to a funeral this time, but she guessed that he'd want to dress in a sober manner. Whatever it was that had him dashing off to Verona's Wiltshire village sounded serious.

'Can you run me down to the station in the morning?' Harry asked Mariah.

'I can if you're prepared to get there early. There won't be time for me to bring the car back home and then go biking back to the post office. I can leave it there and drive it home after work.'

He agreed to this, with the result that she found herself parking his Lanchester in the station yard the next morning. 'Have a good trip, then! I hope the trains aren't too packed out so you get a seat.'

'I hope so, too,' he sighed. 'Remember the days when I had my own private railway coach? No chance of travelling that way now!'

As they got out of the car, he said casually, 'By the way, you won't mention this to Meredith, will you?'

'Meredith? No, of course not, if you don't want me to. But why?'

He tapped the side of his nose, leaving her more puzzled than ever. How could his journey be so hush-hush if it involved Verona Fletcher?

The trip to Wiltshire was even more brutal than Ellen had warned. Stoppages on the line impeded progress on several occasions, and by the time he disembarked at Byrde Halt it was almost dark, and there wasn't a taxi to be found. Verona had given up her car for the duration, so he was left with no choice but to trudge through the uninhabited lanes, wishing he'd brought less baggage.

Verona met him on the doorstep, wringing her hands. 'Thank goodness! I thought you'd never get here!'

'I've done the best I can, Verona. For goodness sake let me get inside before the blackout warden catches me.' He badly needed a stiff drink. 'I don't suppose you have a whisky and soda to hand, do you? I could do with one.' But he was out of luck.

'You know I don't keep that sort of thing in the house,' she reproved him. 'I do have a little sweet sherry left over from Christmas, if that will do.'

He shuddered. 'No, thank you! And before you ask, Ellen has packed my tea and sugar ration for three days, so you can make it good and strong.'

While she twittered off to put the kettle on, he divested himself of his overcoat and loosened his tie. It looked as if they were in for a long night.

After two quick cups of tea and a stale Marie biscuit, he got down to business. 'Now, then, Verona, let's have your story again. Take it slowly, because I don't want to miss anything. First of all, who is this girl?'

'Her name is Dulcie Saunders. She turned up here yesterday afternoon with a little boy. She says that he is Chad's son.'

'I gathered that much from what you said on the phone. If the boy is indeed your grandson, how is it that this is the first you've heard of this woman?'

'Oh, I know who she is, Harry. She came to the village from London, just before the war. Her aunt and uncle kept the local pub, the Green Man, and Dulcie came to help out when her aunt was taken ill.'

'That must be around the time that Chad came to stay with us at Cwmbran.'

'Yes, that's right.'

'So it's quite feasible that she and Chad came to know each other, especially as this Dulcie was staying at the pub.'

'I suppose so, although I don't recall Chad saying anything about that to me. Still, young men don't confide in their mothers about that sort of thing, do they? Then, of course, Chad and Meredith were married, and settled down at Cwmbran House.'

'And this girl remained in the village?'

'I really have no idea, except that she says that she returned to London when her aunt died, and she's been there ever since.'

'Until now.'

'The house her parents rented was destroyed recently in a bombing raid and there was no room for Dulcie in the boarding house where they've gone temporarily. So that's when she arrived here, with her child. She wants to stay with me. She says I owe her that much, since I'm the child's grandmother!' Her voice ended in a wail.

Harry scratched his ear. 'So how old would this child be, then?'

'A bit older than Henry.'

Harry's mouth showed his distaste. 'So conception could have taken place before Chad's marriage to my daughter.'

'I know, and I can't tell you how sorry I am, Harry.'

'No need for that, Verona! These things do happen.' And who should know that better than me? he thought. 'We don't know yet that there is any truth to the girl's story, do we?'

'I'm afraid we do. I have the child's birth certificate here.' She went over to a mahogany bureau and withdrew a folded document, which she handed to him. It recorded the birth in the district of Putney of one Lucas Chad Fletcher, son of Chad Fletcher, gentleman, and Dulcie Mary Fletcher, *née* Saunders.

Harry stared at it glumly. The possibility hadn't yet occurred to Verona that her son might have been married to this woman. In that case he must have committed bigamy, and since he'd been killed at Dunkirk he was no longer here to explain himself. It would kill Meredith when she found out, and a great deal depended on which of the two girls Chad had married first. He'd have to take steps to find out.

'I'll take charge of this,' he murmured,

thrusting it deep into the pocket of his suit. 'Meanwhile, if this girl comes back, as I have no doubt she will, you must on no account give her any money, no matter how hard she begs, or what kind of sob story she gives you.'

'But, Harry, if little Lucas is my grandson, I have a responsibility to help, especially if they have nowhere to go. There are new people at the pub now; I don't know where the uncle went.'

'First let me investigate this girl's story, Verona. And, as I've said, don't get involved. I shall call in at the police station tomorrow and alert them to the possibility that this Dulcie may be a confidence trickster.'

CHAPTER
TWENTY-EIGHT

'Quickly, Ellen! Shut the door and lock it!'

'Lock it?'

'Yes, just do as I say!'

Ellen had never seen Harry in such an agitated state. Bewildered, she turned the key in the lock. They were in her private sitting-room, and even Mariah made a habit of knocking before coming in. She could not imagine what the matter might be. Had he uncovered some secret to do with the war? Perhaps an enemy spy in Cwmbran? It seemed preposterous.

'I've been to see Verona Fletcher,' he began.

Of course he had. She already knew that, so why did he need to tell her again? Now she was even more puzzled. 'Yes, Harry?'

He expelled a long breath. 'This won't be easy, Ellen, but I have to tell someone, and it may as well be you. It's to go no further than this room for the present; do you understand that?'

She nodded, resisting the urge to tell him to spit it out.

'Well, then. Verona has received a visit from a young woman, claiming to be the mother of Chad Fletcher's child.'

Whatever Ellen had expected, it was certainly not this. 'But Chad is dead. And as for Henry . . .'

'Not Henry. This is a boy named Lucas Fletcher.'

Ellen ran her hand through her auburn hair, disarranging it. A lock of hair escaped from her neat bun, brushing her collar. 'I don't understand.'

'This is a young woman who lived at Byrde before the war. Her aunt and uncle kept the local pub. Verona was acquainted with the people. This Dulcie could well have known Chad back then. According to what Verona has been told, she gave birth to Chad's child after returning to London, where she has been living with her own parents ever since. Now they've been bombed out and she has nowhere to go, so she turned up on Verona's doorstep, asking to be taken in.'

'Huh! It's Verona who is being taken in, most likely!'

'That's what I believed at first, but there

is more to the story. Take a look at this.' Ellen took the crumpled certificate from him. She had to read it several times before the significance of it sank in. 'But according to this, she was married to Chad!'

'Except, of course, that we don't know when the marriage took place.'

'Oh, poor little Meredith! Does this mean she wasn't really married to Chad?' Ellen's mind flew back to Meredith's beautiful wedding just before the outbreak of war. The lovely ceremony at the church, followed by the sumptuous reception here in this very house. Had that all been a sham? She looked at the certificate again and did some hasty mental arithmetic. Her hand went to her mouth. 'Harry, according to this, the boy is a bit older than Henry. So this Dulcie must have married Chad before he and Meredith were wed.'

'Not necessarily. The girl may have been pregnant before the marriage took place and he simply married her to give the baby a name. Or, of course, he may have married Meredith first, although at this point it doesn't seem likely.'

'I can understand him wanting to do the honourable thing,' Ellen remarked, 'marrying the girl to save her from disgrace, but then why make it worse by involving Meredith in something so wicked and illegal? Why not confess his mistake and explain why their plans had to be cancelled? Or why not throw himself on her mercy and explain that he'd got this girl into trouble, and beg her to forgive him? I daresay Meredith would have had hysterics, but sooner or later she'd have come to terms with the problem, one way or another.'

'And risk losing everything? No, Ellen, I suppose that young man took a chance, hoping he'd get away with it.'

She thought about it for a moment or two, and then she shook her head decisively. 'I didn't like Chad very much, especially after he started pestering Mariah, but I can't believe he'd be that foolish. Just consider the options. He leaves the poor girl in the lurch, or he marries both Dulcie and Meredith for reasons of his own. He must have known that the girl would turn up eventually, and then there would be an uproar. No, none of this makes sense.'

'Sense or not, she's come forward now, and there's nothing we can do about that.'

'Then what are you going to do? You can't just leave it at that. And what if she writes to Meredith with a tissue of lies? I really do think that Meredith has to be put in the picture before anything else happens.'

'Eventually, but not just yet. My first move is to find out if a marriage between Chad and Dulcie Saunders actually took place. I've contacted an acquaintance in London and asked him to conduct a search of the records there. I was thinking of doing it myself but the way things are in London just now, with the Blitz and so on, I decided it was best to leave it to someone who knows his way about. He's promised to ring as soon as he has any news. In the meantime, I suppose we'll just have to wait and see!'

'You're right, of course. I can see that. There is no point in getting poor Meredith all worked up until we know the full story. At the very least she is going to be very distressed, knowing that her husband fathered a child by another woman. I fervently hope that her marriage turns out to be the legal one. Bad enough to learn that your husband was a bigamist, without finding out that you gave birth to his child out of wedlock.'

'And don't forget Henrietta! She'll go mad when she hears about this.'

Ellen's head drooped. His mother-in-law was already — quite naturally — in a state after learning that he was Mariah's father. She had a low opinion of him now, and believed that Ellen had trapped him into taking her and their daughter into his home after Antonia died. It was only one step from there to accusing him of engineering a marriage between her beloved granddaughter and this Chad Fletcher, who had turned out to be a rogue.

Ellen got up to unfasten the door. It was almost time for Ruth to bring up the hot milk which she always had at bedtime, and she had no wish for her to find the housekeeper and her employer together in a locked room! There was enough trouble in the house without setting the servants talking.

She caught Harry looking at her strangely.

'What is it, Harry? Don't you feel well?' He looked so white and strained that she wondered if he was about to have some sort of attack.

'I feel as well as can be expected, under the circumstances, Ellen. But I've talked this over with you because I couldn't keep it all bottled up inside me. The thing is, don't you see what this could mean for Meredith and my grandson?'

'Of course I do. It's all most unfortunate, but they'll survive, somehow.'

'It's more than unfortunate. Don't you see? If Chad married this Dulcie before he wed Meredith, then this little Lucas could be heir to the Cwmbran estates, not Henry. And if I die before the boy reaches the age of majority, which could well happen, then what is to stop Dulcie from moving in here and taking over? What will become of my poor Meredith then?'

Ellen sat down again abruptly. Cwmbran House and the estates that went with it were entailed, which meant that with each generation they had to be passed on to the nearest male relative. Meredith was Harry's only child, so his heir had been a distant cousin, Chad Fletcher. He had invited Chad to stay with them, ostensibly to train him in the management of the colliery and the outlying farms, but also because he hoped that he and Meredith might fall in love and marry.

Unlike her half sister, Mariah, Meredith had been a shy child, lacking in confidence. When it was too late to change anything, Harry had realized his mistake in having his daughter educated at home, under the care of a governess, instead of sending her to school. When she was older there had been tennis parties and birthday outings, all carefully supervised by Ellen, but that wasn't the same as mingling with other young people in the give and take of the outside world. Harry had liked the idea of what amounted to an arranged marriage, which would provide for his daughter after he was gone. Now that security had come crashing down around them.

From down the hall the distant ringing of the telephone could be heard. Harry leaped to his feet. 'That could be Purvis, ringing from London. It's a bit early for there to be any news, but you never know.' He made off with a surprising turn of speed for a man of his age.

Moments later, he was back, his face alight with joy and relief.

'It's all right then, is it?' she asked, thinking that his fears had been laid to rest.

'It's more than all right!' he shouted. 'That was my solicitor, apologizing for disturbing me at this hour of the night, if you please! He's heard from the Red Cross, Ellen! Wonderful news! We've got to tell Mariah. Aubrey Mortimer is alive! He's a prisoner of war in Germany.'

CHAPTER
TWENTY-NINE

'I told you he wasn't dead, I told you!' Mariah cried, oblivious to the tears which were flooding down her face.

'I know, *cariad*.' Harry patted her on the back, his mouth working with emotion. Others had come running when they heard the noise, wondering what was going on. Meredith stood nearby, shedding a few tears of her own, and even Henrietta managed a frosty smile.

'Break out the champagne!' Harry whooped. 'This calls for a celebration!'

'Begging your pardon, sir, but there isn't any,' Ruth told him, thinking that the good news must have turned him mental, because they hadn't had anything like that in the cellar since the outbreak of war.

'Fetch tea, then, or something, woman! And bring a cup for yourself.'

'Oh, no, sir, I couldn't do that!' Ruth was shocked. A servant of the old school, she knew her place, even if nobody else did. She would, though, summon the other servants and they'd have a little celebration of their own. That's if they weren't already awake from all the commotion.

She met Cook on the stairs. Mrs Edwards was a portly woman and her moon face appeared even larger because of the rags sticking out in all directions, like a sun in a child's drawing. Every evening she painstakingly tied strands of her hair in those rags in a vain effort to curl it, although there was never any visible difference in the morning.

'It's the invasion, isn't it?' she quavered. 'It's come at last. What are we going to do? Where are we supposed to go?'

'Nowhere, dressed like that!' Ruth snapped. Mrs Edwards should at least have put some decent clothes on. If they had to go on the roads as refugees she herself was going to be properly dressed. She kept a packed suitcase beside her bed in case they had to get away at a moments' notice. 'If it was the invasion we'd have heard something on the wireless before they got this far inland.'

'That's all you know, Ruth! That's the first thing them Huns would do, knock out the wireless and the newspapers so nobody would know what they were up to!'

'Don't be silly. We were all down in the kitchen listening to ITMA this evening, and then you had that silly mystery play. Not knocked out then, was it? But do stop going on about the invasion. There's good news for once in a while. The master had a call from London. Mister Aubrey's been found alive. They've taken him prisoner, but he's not dead!'

'Praise the Lord! Is he all right? Is he wounded? Did he crash that aeroplane of his?'

'I know no more than you do, Mrs Edwards.'

Mariah was asking much the same questions, but Harry had no answers.

'We'll hear more in due course, I have no doubt. As of now, I have only the basic facts.'

'But it's been weeks now. Why has it taken so long to contact us?'

'Your guess is as good as mine, Mariah. I expect we were notified as soon as the Red Cross received word. I don't suppose that the Germans were falling over themselves to let our side know. The main thing is that Aubrey is alive, and relatively safe.'

'Yes, Mariah,' Meredith piped up. 'He won't have to go on any more of those dangerous missions, will he? You'll get him back when the war is over.'

'Yes, *cariad;* she has a point there,' Ellen smiled.

'I know, Mam. But I know Aubrey. He won't like it, having to sit out the rest of the war on the sidelines. Still, I know what Meredith means. He has a better chance of surviving locked up in some camp back behind the lines.'

Word of Aubrey's miraculous survival spread around Cwmbran like wildfire. Mariah was well liked in the community, and better known now that she was delivering the post to people's homes. Everywhere she went she was congratulated. Women beamed at her in the streets and men came up to shake her by the hand.

'There's lovely for you,' they kept saying, and indeed it was. There were times in the middle of the night when she was besieged by doubts. Was he being starved or ill treated? Was he in some sort of barracks with other Allied prisoners, or being kept in solitary confinement? What if he'd been shot at or wounded when his plane came down? Her imagination ran riot at times and she had to take herself in hand so that fear would not overcome her.

'I'm told that you can write to Aubrey, and send him parcels,' Ellen beamed one day.

'But how? We don't know where he is!'

'That's what the Red Cross is for. They'll see that it reaches him.'

'I'll make up a parcel right away. I wonder what's best to put in it?'

'Cigarettes, I expect, and chocolate. You can have my ration.'

'You know Aubrey doesn't smoke, Mam.'

Ellen shook her head in exasperation. 'Don't be silly, *cariad*. Ciggies will be worth their weight in gold. He can use them to trade for things he wants. Or for bribing the guards, or something.' She had a sad recollection of her late brother, Bertie, writing home during the Great War, saying how important smokes were to the fighting men.

Mariah got a fit of the giggles when Henrietta presented her with a pair of socks she'd knitted, explaining diffidently that there might be room in the parcel and that Aubrey might find a use for them. Henrietta glared at her in annoyance. 'What's the matter, miss? Aren't they the right size for that husband of yours?'

'Yes, I'm sure they are, and I'm very grateful. Thank you very much indeed, Mrs Meredith.'

'Then what are you laughing at? Nothing wrong with them, is there?'

Mariah studied the socks, which had been

knitted in stripes of all colours of the rainbow. The older woman had obviously been using up oddments of wool, which was the right thing to do since large quantities of new yarn were virtually unobtainable. 'They're lovely, Mrs Meredith, and beautifully knitted. It's just that, well, I'm not sure if he'd be able to wear them with his air force uniform, that's all.'

'Stuff and nonsense! If all else fails he can wear them as bed socks. Winter isn't far away, and a German prison camp is hardly Buckingham Palace. He'll be glad of them then.'

Mariah was sorry that she hadn't been able to help laughing. All things considered, it was very good of the woman to have made this contribution to Aubrey's welfare, particularl as she hadn't a good word to say about Mariah herself. 'Of course he will, Mrs Meredith. I know he'll appreciate them.'

So the parcel was packed with much love, and dispatched to the address they were given. There was no guarantee that Aubrey would ever see it, but Mariah hoped that if it didn't reach him, the contents would bring comfort to some other lonely serviceman far from home.

She continued to hold on to the hope that

one day she and Aubrey would be reunited, and they could pick up the pieces of their lives again. When it came right down to it, their marriage, and indeed the time they had spent together since their first meeting, could be measured in days rather than months or years. They had met during wartime and most of their courtship had been conducted through letters. Their honeymoon had consisted of a single week-end in a cottage on the Cwmbran estate, and after that a couple of forty-eight hour passes were all that Aubrey had managed to wangle. Even that time had been mostly taken up with travelling in order for them to spend a few hours together.

She poured out her feelings in the letters she wrote to Aubrey now. At least she had a few little tales to tell of her delivery rounds. Even though he had never lived in Cwmbran and hadn't met the people involved, it was news from home.

I dread meeting Bessie Harries. I try to avoid her whenever possible but she lies in wait for me behind her lace curtains, and pops up like a jack in a box when I try to dash past her front door. She's all agog for the latest news of Mam and Job Prosser, and I know she doesn't believe me when I say I haven't a clue.

Then there's poor Mrs Griffiths. She's the one whose boy is with the army in North Africa. The news from there isn't good, and of course she's worried sick about her Gareth. She will keep asking me if I've heard anything about what's really happening there, and when I say I've no idea, she begs me to find out. For some reason she's got the idea that Harry has the ear of the Prime Minister and knows more than he's telling. I've tried to disabuse her of the notion, but she won't have it. 'You can tell me, Mrs Mortimer,' she says. 'I promise I won't breathe a word to a living soul.' I really think that this war has turned her brain. If Gareth doesn't come safely home again, I don't know what she'll do.

Reading this over, she suddenly realized that it wouldn't do at all. Some German officer might read it and glean something useful from it. Smothering a word she wouldn't want Ellen to hear her using, she crumpled the page and began again.

At long last she heard from Aubrey. It wasn't the fat, newsy letter she'd been hoping for, but a poorly printed card on which the writer was supposed to cross out the choices which did not apply: 'I am well/I am not well' being one such section.

Despite the drawbacks of this system, the little communication that had come from Aubrey meant the world to Mariah. His hands had touched it, and very possibly his lips had kissed it. She slept with it under her pillow.

CHAPTER THIRTY

'What would you like me to read to you tonight?' The Swansea Six were tucked up in bed in what had once been known as the Blue Bedroom, but which was now their dormitory. 'One of your Enid Blytons, perhaps?'

Two of the boys voted for *Mr Galliano's Circus,* and three for *The Secret Island.* Young Ceri Davis, who usually begged to hear the *Adventures of the Wishing Chair,* was unaccountably silent. Just as well, she thought, because the older boys would no doubt have dismissed it as babyish, preferring something a bit more thrilling.

She was halfway through the story when Ceri leaned over the side of his bed and was horribly sick, all over the rush matting.

'Oh, dear! We'll have to finish this tomorrow night, boys. Dafydd, run and fetch me a basin of water and a towel, will you? And one of you bring the mop and bucket, please.' She turned to Ceri. 'Don't worry, boyo, we'll have you tidied up in a minute. What brought this on, I wonder? You haven't been eating green apples again, have you? Does your tummy hurt?' The child managed to shake his head. 'Can you tell me what's wrong? Open your mouth and let me have a look. Put out your tongue, please.'

When she had attended to the child, and mopped up the floor, Mariah went in search of her mother.

'We've got trouble, Mam. It's young Ceri. He's been sick in his bed and he's burning up!'

'Have you taken his temperature?'

'Yes, and it's 102, I hope it isn't something awful that can be passed on to the rest of them.'

'I shouldn't worry too much. Children do catch things once they start school, but they tend to bounce back in no time.'

'But what if it's something ghastly, like diphtheria, or infantile paralysis?'

'There's no need to go off the deep end, *cariad.* I'll tell you what we'll do. We'll move the child into the Rose Room for now, and call the doctor in the morning. There are two beds in there, and I can spend the night with him in case he needs anything.'

'But what if —'

'What if, nothing! I've seen you and Meredith through all the childhood complaints so I'm quite capable of dealing with this. And if something did happen, I know that Dr Lawson would turn out.'

Much relieved, Mariah returned to the boys' room. 'You're going to sleep in another room tonight, Ceri. Auntie Ellen will look after you. You'll have a good night's rest and the doctor will come and take a look at you in the morning. No school for you tomorrow!'

A chorus of groans greeted this statement. 'Lucky duck! Wish I could stay home! It's the maths test tomorrow and I can't do decimals!'

Ceri struggled to sit up. 'Got to go to school!' He croaked. 'Tomorrow's Friday!'

'Yes, I know, and the day after that is Saturday and you'll have all weekend to recover.'

'Must go to school. It's the hundred smells! The others won't like me if I don't go!'

'Don't worry, Ceri. Come on, swing your legs over the side and I'll help you up. Auntie Ellen will have your bed all ready for you by the time we get to the Rose Room.'

'I wish I'd known about this sooner,' Ellen grumbled. 'There hasn't been time to air the bed, so I've stripped it and made it up again with sheets straight from the airing cupboard. I could have put a pig in the bed but for the fact that he's got a temperature.'

Ceri began to moan and protest. 'It's all right, Ceri,' Mariah reassured him. 'Did you think Auntie Ellen meant a real pig?' Perhaps the child didn't know that this was what local people called the stone hot-water bottles that were found in every home.

'It's the smells!' he mumbled again.

Ellen sniffed. 'I can't smell anything. Can you, Mariah?'

'He keeps saying that. He can't be delirious, can he, Mam?'

'I shouldn't think so. It's probably just him getting mixed up again, the way he does. Why don't you go on and tuck the others in? I can manage here.'

Still puzzled, Mariah went back to the remaining five boys. 'Ceri keeps saying something about a smell at school. A hundred of them, in fact. Have you any idea what he's talking about?' Five heads moved from side to side.

The following morning Mariah looked in on her mother before she left for work. 'How is he, Mam?'

'Still not well. I've been sponging him

down all night but his temperature's going up even more. As soon as it's a decent hour I'll call Dr Lawson.'

'Yes, that would be best. Listen, Mam, I think I'll drop in and see his teacher when I've finished my rounds, see if she can shed any light on what might be troubling him. You can tell him that if he mentions it again.'

'Right! Off you go, then. You don't want to be late.'

'So long, Mam!'

'So long!'

Mariah cycled off, unaware that before the day was out she would have made a new friend.

While she was surrounded by people who cared for her, she felt the need for a woman of her own age to confide in, now that Aubrey was so far away. She and Meredith weren't on the same wavelength these days, thanks to Henrietta's interference, and there was no one else. Megan Jones was always ready to lend a sympathetic ear, but she was Mam's friend, really, and of a different generation.

Mariah arrived at the Cwmbran school during playtime. The two yards — one for girls and the other for boys — were filled with shrieking children. She made her way past two older girls who were twirling a long skipping rope while others stood in line, awaiting their turn.

'Salt! Mustard! Vinegar! Pepper!' The child in the middle managed several hops before tripping up.

'You're out, Gaynor! Your turn, Derys!'

Mariah smiled at the luckless Gaynor and received a gap-toothed grin in response.

'Can you show me the way to standard one, please?'

'Yes, miss!' She trotted off, not looking back to see if Mariah was following.

The teacher looked up from her work in response to Mariah's knock on the open door. She was a pleasant-looking girl of about Mariah's own age, neatly dressed in a jumper and skirt.

'Do come in. Are you one of the parents?'

'No, not exactly. I suppose I'm a sort of foster parent, in a way. I've come about Ceri Davies, one of our evacuees.'

'Oh, the little chap from Swansea! I wondered why he wasn't in school today. Look, won't you sit down? I'm Lucy Adams, by the way.'

'Mariah Mortimer.' She perched herself gingerly on the edge of a child-sized chair, with her knees almost up to her chin. 'He's not at all well and we've had to send for the doctor. Naturally we couldn't let him out of the house this morning.'

'I understand. Is that the only reason you've come?'

'No, something rather odd has happened. He keeps saying that he must be here because of the smells.'

'Smells?'

'Yes, something about how he must be here because it's Friday, and the others won't like him if he lets them down.'

A wide grin suddenly crossed the young teacher's face. 'I think I know! Do you think he means scents?'

Mariah held up her hands in mystification. 'Smells, scents, who knows?'

'We are trying to encourage punctuality and good attendance at the school, and some of the first-timers tend to miss a day or two now and then, after managing to convince their mothers that they have a tummy ache.'

'Yes?'

'So whenever we have perfect attendance all week, these young ones are allowed to parade into all the other classrooms carrying a placard which says: "100 per cent". Then they get a story read to them during the last period on Friday afternoon. They look forward to that, and woe betide anyone who spoils their perfect record!' She grinned again. 'I see I have some explaining to do! Cent, you see; not scent. One hundred smells!'

'Oh, it's good to laugh!' Mariah gulped, wiping the tears from her eyes. 'I've had such an anxious time lately. My husband was shot down some time ago and we've just heard that he's alive, a prisoner of war. Do you have someone in the forces?'

'I've a brother in the merchant navy. He's all right so far, but my mother worries.'

'She would. Look, why don't we get together some weekend? I could show you the countryside. There are some pretty walks in these parts.'

'I'd like that. I'm sorry, Mrs Mortimer, I must fly. The bell will be going any minute and I have to see the children in. I'll be in touch and we can make a plan.'

CHAPTER
THIRTY-ONE

Harry came to see Ellen, his face grim. 'No joy, I'm afraid. Somerset House has no record of a marriage between Chad Fletcher and a Dulcie Saunders.'

Ellen's face lit up. 'That's good then, isn't it? It proves that their supposed marriage never existed.'

'I'm afraid that isn't the case. With all the bombing going on, especially in London, there are always breakdowns in the system. The clergyman, or more likely the registrar in this case may not have had time to forward the appropriate paperwork to the proper authorities. The place where the wedding took place may even have been bombed since then, and the records destroyed, so even if we could trace it to the source we might not be able to find proof.'

'Then I don't know what you're worrying about. If Dulcie wants to make some claim on you, the onus is on her to prove that she was Chad's wife, not the other way about.'

'What I want is peace of mind, Ellen. I need documentary proof.'

'You can't get documentary proof of something that never happened.'

'My point exactly!'

They were interrupted by a knock at the door. The creases in Harry's forehead disappeared when he recognized his old friend, Doctor Lawson.

'James! What are you doing here?'

'Just came to take a look at one of your evacuees.' He turned to Ellen. 'Nothing to worry about, Mrs Richards! Just a bout of tonsillitis. I'll leave you a prescription for a bottle of something which should help, and you can keep on with what you've been doing; sponge baths and plenty of fluids.'

'I'm so glad, doctor! We were afraid it might be something serious.'

'Nothing that can't be mended. His temperature's coming down already, thanks to your good efforts. Anyone else in the house that needs looking at, while I'm here? What about you, Harry? I think perhaps I should give you the once over.'

'What! There's nothing wrong with me, man!'

'On the contrary, you look as if you have the whole world on your shoulders. I think

I will have a look at you, if you don't mind. Prevention is better than cure, and all that. Would you excuse us, please, Mrs Richards?'

'Certainly, doctor.'

'I really don't know why you're making all this fuss, James,' Harry grumbled, unbuttoning his shirt.

'Because I don't like the look of you, that's why. Neither of us are getting any younger, old man, and you're looking a bit grey. Are you sure there's nothing bothering you?'

'Apart from the war, you mean? The colliery, the Home Guard, my duties on the bench?'

'You're trying to do too much, man. It's time you thought of slowing down. Turn over some of these responsibilities to someone else.'

'Like you are, you mean! Coming out of retirement to take on the duties of that young partner of yours who's away in the army. We've all got to pull our weight if we're to win this war, James. And as for handing over my responsibilities, who do you suggest they should be given to? There just isn't anybody, and well you know it.'

Lawson sighed. 'I know, but you must try to manage something. Your blood pressure is higher than it should be, and someone needs to help you shoulder the burden here.

It's a great pity that Chad died when he did. I know you were grooming him to take over the running of the mine in due course.'

Harry bit back a sharp retort with an effort. Although James had been his friend since they were young, he did not feel able to share this latest problem with him. The fewer people who knew about it, the better.

'I'll be all right, James. I want to keep going as long as possible. It's my duty to keep things running on the home front while younger men are actively engaged in the fighting.'

'That's the damned thing about war! It's not just the men and women in the services who feel the pinch. It's all those who are left behind, struggling to keep their heads above water. Casualties come in all shapes and sizes. How's that daughter of yours managing without her husband?'

Harry stared at the doctor. How had he found out that Mariah was his child? Then he realized and pulled himself together. 'Meredith? Oh, she's all right. Her grandmother is staying with us for the duration; that keeps the girl busy. And then there's young Henry, of course. We have a nursemaid for him, but Meredith still likes to spend time with him.'

'Of course, the baby! Better tell those

women to keep the child away from the boy with the sore throat. As far as I can tell it's plain old tonsillitis, but you never know. Well, I must be on my way. Don't work too hard!'

If only it *was* work that was the problem, Harry thought.

Ellen came back in, looking worried. 'All clear?'

'Yes, he's gone. He could tell I was fretting about something and he tried to get it out me. It would have done me good to get it off my chest, but I didn't dare say a word.'

'James is a doctor. He wouldn't have told anyone,' Ellen reminded him.

'Oh, Ellen! What am I going to do?'

Her heart went out to him. He looked so pale and worn; it was no wonder that the doctor had picked up on his friend's anxiety. 'Meredith has to be told,' she said firmly.

'No! I can't have that! I'm her father. I have to protect her. That's what fathers are for.'

'And what if this comes out and she's the last to know? She'll never forgive you, Harry. When Dulcie doesn't get anywhere with Verona, what comes next? She could write a letter to Meredith, telling her the whole story. That would be ten times worse! Or what if she goes to the newspapers with her tale? You're a prominent person. I can just see the headlines! Magistrate's daughter in love triangle! War hero a secret bigamist!'

'Chad Fletcher was not a war hero, Ellen, as you know quite well. He refused to join up and he'd be with us now if Aubrey Mortimer hadn't talked him into taking that boat to Dunkirk to help rescue the soldiers stranded on the beaches.'

'But he did go to Dunkirk, Harry, and he was killed there. That makes him a hero in the eyes of some people, Meredith included. But never mind all that! Meredith must be told, and the longer you leave it, the more difficult it will be.'

On returning from work, Mariah went upstairs to see Ceri. She found him sitting up in bed, engrossed in a tattered copy of the *Dandy.*

'Here's a *Beano* for you, Ceri. Somebody left it on the station platform and nobody knows who it belongs to. It's last week's but I don't think you've seen it.'

'Cor! Thanks, missus. What's this word here?' He pointed to the open page. He loved the cartoons but his reading skills had not yet caught up with his intelligence.

'Zowee,' she told him. 'It's a sort of nonsense word, I think. Now listen, Ceri.

I've been to see Miss Adams and we've got it all straightened out. You were a bit mixed up when you were talking about scents, or smells. When your class parade around the school with a poster that says: "100 per cent" that's just a way of saying that standard one has one hundred per cent attendance for the week.'

'I don't get it!' He frowned.

'You were all present,' she amended. 'But never mind that. Miss Adams said to tell you it's not your fault if you can't go to school because you're ill in bed, so although your friends won't be able to parade around the school, they won't have to do without their story, because she'll read it to them anyway.'

'That's no good!' he wailed. 'I'll miss it! I won't know what happens next!'

'Ah, but I have a lovely surprise for you, Ceri. Miss Adams is coming to have tea with me on Sunday, and she says she'll bring the book with her, and read this week's chapter to you. How will you like that?'

'Cor!' he croaked again.

'Why don't you tuck down and have a little rest? I'll come back and see you later.'

Obediently he snuggled down, a happy smile on his little monkey face.

'Everything all right?' Ellen enquired, as Mariah quietly shut the door behind her.

'He seems happier now I've had a word with his teacher. Incidentally, I've invited her to tea on Sunday. All right?'

'Of course. I'll ask Mrs Edwards to try to make something nice, although goodness knows what it will be.'

'I don't suppose she'll mind what we serve, Mam. She's looking forward to the outing. She's not from round here and she hasn't made many friends yet.'

'We'll do our best to make her feel at home, *cariad,* and as it happens it may be just as well. Harry has some rather unwelcome news for Meredith and she's less likely to throw a fit if she knows she could be overheard by an outsider.'

CHAPTER
THIRTY-TWO

'Will you excuse us, please, Henrietta?' She looked up from her knitting, while her granddaughter paused in her tapestry work. 'I need to have a word with Meredith.'

'Certainly, Harry. Do you wish me to leave?'

'No, no, Mother-in-law. You stay here in the sitting-room. I'd like Meredith to come upstairs with me.'

'It's not Henry, is it, Dad? He hasn't caught something from that wretched boy?'

'Henry is quite well. Do come along when I ask you!'

She rose to her feet, frowning. It wasn't like Dad to be so snappy. Something must have upset him, but she had no idea what it could be. She said as much.

'Just come with me, girl, and you'll find out.'

He led the way to his study, where Ellen was waiting. She had prudently brought along a bottle of smelling salts in her apron pocket, just in case the poor girl passed out from the shock of what she was about to hear.

'Please sit down, both of you,' Harry commanded.

'But what is this all about?' Meredith wanted to know.

'Sit!' he roared.

'I'm not a dog, Dad!' she protested.

'If you were, I might not have as much difficulty in getting you to listen!'

'You'd better do as your father asks, Meredith.' Ellen spoke softly, trying to soften the tension. 'He has something rather unpleasant to tell you, and this won't be easy for him. Try to listen to what has to be said, and wait until you've had time to absorb it before you say anything in response.'

'You're worrying me, Nanny.' In time of stress Meredith always reverted to her old way of addressing Ellen, as if going back into the safety of her childhood years would make things all right. But this problem could not be smoothed over with a hug and a kiss, and something from the sweetie tin, Ellen knew.

Harry cleared his throat several times. 'Verona — your mother-in-law — has been contacted by a young woman, who has a little boy. She maintains that he is Chad's son.'

'Chad? You mean my Chad?'

'That's what she says.'

'That's rubbish, Dad, utter nonsense!'

'I certainly hope so, for all our sakes. However, the problem is that she has made this claim, and it has to be looked into.'

'Who is she, this woman?'

'Her name is Dulcie Saunders.'

Meredith shrugged. 'I've never heard of her. Where is she from? How is she supposed to have known Chad?'

'It seems she's from London originally but she did live at Byrde for some years before the war. She may well have come across Chad then. According to her she returned to London to have her child and has lived there with her parents until now. They were recently bombed out and she has nowhere to go.'

'There you are, then!' Meredith's expression was scornful, as if any fool could have seen what the girl was up to, everyone except Verona and Harry, that was!

Harry swallowed hard. 'There is something I have to show you, *cariad.*'

Here it comes! Ellen thought, fumbling in her pocket for the smelling salts.

Meredith frowned at the birth certificate. 'This doesn't prove anything, Dad! Fletcher is a common enough name, and there must be tons of other Chads in the world. This Dulcie is married to one of them. This is just coincidence, that's all.'

'And is it a coincidence that Dulcie Saunders lived within shouting distance of our Fletchers, and later married a totally different man of the same name?'

'Oh, I don't know, Dad! All I know is that Chad is dead, and I won't have you blackening his name. I don't want to hear another word about this fantastic story! I'm going downstairs now, and I'll thank you not to mention this again!' She flounced out of the room, leaving Ellen and Harry with their mouths open.

'It's the shock, of course. She can't be expected to take it all in at once, Harry.'

'But we can't just leave it like this.'

'It looks as though you'll have to. The worst is over now. If Dulcie does try to contact her, at least it won't come out of the blue. Why not wait until we know more. and then try talking to her again? When she's had time to calm down she may be in a more reasonable frame of mind. She may recall something which may be of use.'

'Such as?'

'Such as some remark Chad made, which passed over her head at the time, or the memory of some unexplained absence of his.'

In the main sitting-room, Henrietta was still knitting away placidly. 'Is everything all right, dear? What was it your father wanted?'

'What? Oh, sorry, I was far away, Grandmamma. It was just something about Chad's mother. Dad went to see her the other day. She was in a bit of a flap.'

'Poor old thing,' Henrietta murmured, ignoring the fact that she herself was some years older than Verona. 'She misses her son, of course. What mother wouldn't? My Antonia has been gone for years but I still think of her every day.'

Meredith bent over her stitchery, carefully choosing another colour.

'I've some more blue bits you can have,' Henrietta told her.

'Thank you, Grandmamma.' Embroidery wool was hard to find in the shops but Henrietta saved all the leftover bits from her knitting to pass on to Meredith. Even with her ingenuity at weaving stripes and patterns into the scarves and mittens she was making for charity there were still some strands that were too short to be of use.

Meredith stitched away as if she hadn't a

care in the world, but inside she was in turmoil. Chad, with a child? Could there be any truth in such a preposterous tale? Why had she no intimation of this before? If only she'd paid closer attention to the birth certificate. If the boy — Lucas — was much older than Henry then Chad's relationship with Dulcie could have blossomed and died before he and Meredith even met. It was still a shock, of course, but hardly a betrayal of their marriage.

He should have told me, though! she thought, forgetting for a moment that she had refused to believe that any of this had happened. People were supposed to start married life with a clean slate, weren't they? If he had confessed anything like this to her she would have expressed shock, refused to discuss it for a while in order to make him suffer, and then graciously forgiven him for past shortcomings. He, of course, would then have told her that this Dulcie meant nothing to him compared with what he now felt for Meredith, the love of his life! At least, that was the sort of thing that happened in the romance novels she brought home from the library!

Pausing to thread her needle, she looked at her tapestry, which depicted a vase of flowers, and uttered a groan. She had somehow managed to fill in a whole spray of leaves in bright scarlet wool instead of the apple green she'd reserved for the purpose.

'Damn!' she shouted.

'Language, dear! Have you pricked your finger?'

'No, Grandmamma. Just my heart!'

'I think you need some fresh air,' Henrietta remarked. 'Why don't you go for a nice walk? You've been cooped up inside all day. Better still, why not take Henry with you? That Mary doesn't have him outside often enough. When your mother was a baby I made sure that she was outside for at least an hour a day, even in winter. Well wrapped up, of course, so she didn't catch cold.'

'Myfanwy, Grandmamma. Her name is Myfanwy.'

'I call her Mary. I don't believe in fancy names for servants, Meredith. It gives them inflated ideas of themselves. It only leads to trouble in the long run, you mark my words.'

'Don't call her Mary! I won't have it!'

'Don't you raise your voice to me, my girl! I can't imagine what has come over you today. You've been like a cat on hot bricks all afternoon!'

She was amazed when, instead of apologizing prettily, Meredith rushed out of the room, letting the door swing shut behind her.

The flowers had long ago been dug up to be replaced by useful herbs which would spice up the bland wartime diet they were forced to eat, but the old sundial was still in the centre of the herb garden. Meredith ran up to it and was suddenly brought to a standstill by the message inscribed on it.

'Remember only the happy hours.' Leaning her arms on its bronzed face she began to cry. She'd tried so hard to do just that, blocking out all the unpleasantness that the war had brought her way. Trying to present to the world the appearance of a brave little widow, whose husband had died for a cause. Trying not to think about her father's confession, that Mariah Richards, the housekeeper's girl who had been her childhood companion, was in reality her own half sister. Trying to rejoice in her only child, who was a spoilt little imp.

'Why me?' she howled. 'What did I ever do to deserve this?'

CHAPTER
THIRTY-THREE

'Horsey, Mummy!' The little boy twisted around, wriggling and pointing.

'Do keep still. You'll have me over in a minute!' The young woman, trudging wearily along the dusty lane, hefted the child higher on her hip and turned to see what he was looking at.

An old-fashioned canvas-topped wagon was inching up the road, pulled by a sturdy chestnut horse. She thought at first that it was a gypsy van, but then she saw the faded lettering on the side: Daffodil Laundry. Letting her shabby grip fall to the ground she held out her free arm with her thumb up.

'Whoa, Twm!' The old chap holding the reins said something she couldn't understand.

'Sorry, I don't speak Welsh!'

'There's lucky it is I speak English, then,' he cackled, exposing a mouth with half the teeth gone. 'Need a ride?'

'Yes, please.' She handed the boy to the driver and scrambled up behind him, tossing her bag in the back as she came.

'Where are you going, *bach?*'

'I'm looking for Cwmbran House. Do you know it?' He held one hand behind his ear and she gathered that he was deaf. 'Cwmbran House!' she yelled.

'No need to shout, *bach.* Just speak clearly. I'll be calling at the house after a while, so just sit tight until we get there. All right?'

She nodded, too exhausted to respond. Presently, lulled by the rhythmic clopping of the horse's hooves and the swaying of the wagon, she dozed off. The child leaned into her shoulder, sucking his thumb. Soon he, too, was fast asleep.

'Who might you be, then?' The cook looked the woman up and down, making no move to allow her over the doorstep.

'I'm Dulcie, and this is Lucas.'

'Oh, yes, and who might you be when you're at home?'

'None of your beeswax! I want to see Mr Morgan, or Mrs Fletcher.'

'Is that so! Folks that want to see the gentry use the front door.'

'We came round the back because I hitched a ride in the laundry cart.'

'Do you know anything about this, Mr Fredericks?' She turned to the laundryman who was manhandling the cotton bags into the kitchen.

'Eh?'

'Them two. She says they've come to see old Morgan.'

'Met them coming up Towy Lane. Said they were coming by here. Gave them a ride. That's all I know.'

'Rosie!' the cook bawled. The young housemaid looked into the room, her eyes narrowing when she saw the visitors. More evacuees by the look of them, which meant more work for her!

'You wanted me, Mrs Edwards?'

'Well, I wasn't exercising my voice for the fun of it, girl! Run upstairs and find Mrs Richards. Tell her there's a person here asking for the Morgans.'

'I don't want to see no Mrs Richards!'

'You'll see her and like it, young woman! Mr Morgan is an important man. Nobody gets to see him without her say-so. Well, Rosie Yeoman? What you waiting for, then? Get yourself up them stairs and be quick about it!'

Rosie fled.

'You may as well sit down then, take the weight off your feet,' the cook went on grudgingly. 'But whatever your business is, you'd best be quick about it, or Mr Fredericks will be gone and you'll have to leave on shanks's pony.'

'Oh, I'm not going anywhere. I've come to stay,' Dulcie said, with more confidence than she felt.

Ellen was about to have a bath when the maid came panting up the stairs. 'Please, Mrs Richards, can you come down to the kitchen?'

'What's the matter, Rosie? Can't it wait? I'm about to have my bath.'

'There's a woman down there asking to see Mr Morgan, or Mrs Fletcher. She came with Fredericks the laundry, see? There's a little boy with her as well. Dulcie, she calls herself.'

Ellen's heart skipped a beat. This would happen when Harry was out! She had to think fast. 'I can't come down in my dressing-gown. I'll have to go and get dressed again. Please show them into the morning-room, and fetch them a drink. A glass of milk, or something. Can you manage that?'

'Yes, Mrs Richards.' She sped off, wondering what it was all about.

Pulling her girdle up over her hips with an

effort, Ellen considered various alternatives. Should she call Meredith, and let her deal with it? Better not, or Harry would fly off the handle when he found out what she'd done. Send the girl away with a flea in her ear? Not a good idea. There wasn't another train for hours and she might hang around the neighbourhood, blurting out her story. Where could Harry be?

Fully dressed again, but this time in her Sunday best, Ellen peeped into the boys' dormitory, where she found Dafydd stretched out on his bed, engrossed in a comic.

'Dafydd, I need you to do something very important. Can you do that?'

'Expect so, missus.'

'I want you to take my old bike and go searching for Mr Morgan. When you've found him, ask him to come back here at once. You're to say it's urgent.'

'Where do you think he'll be, missus?'

'It's hard to say. Try the colliery office first, and if he's not there, ask Mr Roberts if he knows where Mr Morgan has gone. If that doesn't help, you'll need to do the rounds of the farms. You may spot his car as you're going by. Don't forget, it's urgent.'

'Yes, missus!' He slid down the bannisters on his way out, and she didn't have the heart to scold him. The quicker he found Harry, the better.

The first thing that struck her when she entered the morning-room was that the boy, Lucas, might have been Henry's twin. He was a little taller, to be sure, but he had the same fairish hair, and the same trick of frowning when he met someone he didn't know. If Ellen had ever doubted that Chad had fathered this child, she was convinced now.

The girl, Dulcie, did not stand up when Ellen came in. No manners! Ellen felt herself at a disadvantage standing there, so she sat down at the table and waited for the girl to speak. An explanation wasn't long in coming.

'I suppose you know why I'm here?'

'I know what this is about, yes, but I don't know why you've come. You certainly were not invited.'

'I've come here because that other old bat wouldn't let me stay. I told her I had a right, but she kept saying that this Mr Morgan had told her not to let me in. I ask you!'

'If by that you mean Mrs Fletcher senior, then you should not have gone there. She's an elderly woman, and not at all well, as I understand it.'

'I've got rights!' Dulcie repeated. 'And

now I've seen all this I know I should have come here a long time ago. Anyhow, I told that cook I didn't want to speak to you. I want Mr Morgan, or the other Mrs Fletcher.'

'Mr Morgan is not at home, but I've sent someone to fetch him. There's nothing more I can do until he returns.'

Little Lucas began to cry. Rubbing his eyes with his fists he presented an unlovely sight, with his nose running.

'I think you'd better bring your little boy upstairs, Miss Saunders. You can give him a wash and put him down for a nap.' Fortunately there was an extra cot in the nursery, a relic of the days when Ellen had two babies to care for.

'I'm not Miss Saunders. Mrs Fletcher, my name is!'

Ellen ignored this remark. Luckily the child now began to cry so loudly that anything more that his mother might have said was drowned out.

'What's going on in here? Is it Henry?' Mariah poked her head round the door but stopped in confusion. Ellen gave a warning shake of her head.

'Run up and get the baby bath out of the nursery, will you, Mariah? Bring it to my room right away.' She snatched up little Lucas and marched out of the room. Dulcie whatever her name was was forced to follow.

Dafydd ran Harry to earth at the sweet shop, where he had just finished paying for his pipe tobacco. Fortunately the boy had gone there straight from the colliery office and had not been obliged to peddle for miles around the farms.

'Mr Morgan, sir! You have to come home at once. Mrs Richards said!'

'What's the matter, boy? Is there trouble?'

'Don't know, sir. She said it was urgent.'

'All right, I'm on my way.' He picked up his package, tipped his hat to the woman behind the counter, and dashed out to the car. Something must really be up. It wasn't like Ellen to panic, and if it had been a case of fire or illness, she would have telephoned for help. It crossed his mind that his lawyer might have rung up from London, with news of the Fletcher mess. He prayed that the news was good.

CHAPTER
THIRTY-FOUR

Harry rushed into the house to find Ellen hovering near the door.

'It's Dulcie! She turned up here a little while ago, and she's brought the boy with her. Oh, Harry! He looks just like Henry! They could almost be twins!'

'Where is she now?'

'Upstairs. We had to put the little boy to bed, he was completely worn out with all the travelling.'

'Where did they come from; do you know?'

'I can't get a word out of her, except that she wants to speak to you or to Meredith. They arrived in the laundry wagon, of all things!'

'Does Meredith know?'

'Not yet. She was out somewhere with her gran when all this was going on. I didn't think you'd want her told just yet.'

'Good! I'll go up and see Dulcie now.' He

took the stairs two at a time. Ellen followed more slowly. Little Lucas wasn't the only one who needed his bed. She would have given anything just to lie down and drift off into oblivion, hoping that when she woke up the trouble would have resolved itself.

'Good afternoon, Miss Saunders. It is Miss Saunders, isn't it?' Harry held himself very upright and his expression was stern. Many a person who had appeared before him in court had quailed under that look, even when their crimes were much less grave than the one he suspected the girl was trying to perpetrate here.

Dulcie looked at him defiantly. 'It's Fletcher, if you must know.'

'Yes, I gather that you've been calling yourself that, but I don't know what you hope to achieve by it. Nonetheless, we'll let that go for the present. Be so kind as to explain why you've insinuated yourself into my house without so much as a by your leave.'

'I don't know what you mean.'

'Come now, Miss Saunders! You turn up here, totally unexpected, dragging that poor child with you, with some story about my daughter's late husband being the father. My daughter is still very upset over his death and your sudden appearance will

274

cause her even more distress. I must warn you that I am a magistrate, and the consequences of your actions could be most serious. Now, if you leave this house at once we'll try to forget that this ever happened.'

'You'd like that, wouldn't you, mister! Well, I'll tell you this for nothing. I'm not going anywhere until I've seen Mrs Fletcher and heard what she's going to do for me. It isn't right that her brat's got all this, and my boy's got nothing. And if you don't let me see her, I'm going straight to the newspapers. We'll soon see what they think about that, Mr fancy Harry Morgan!'

Harry turned his back on her and left the room, with Ellen hard on his heels. 'If I'd stayed there a minute longer she'd have felt the weight of my hand!' he growled. 'And imagine how that would sound to the world at large.'

'What do you mean to do, Harry?'

'Nothing tonight. She'll have to be given a meal and a bed. There aren't any more trains, even if she could be persuaded to leave. I'll deal with this in the morning.'

'Should I lock her in her room, then?'

'To stop her running away? No point in that. Obviously I wish she would melt into thin air.'

'But what if she wanders round the house

and bursts in on Meredith?'

'You leave Meredith to me.'

Meredith was highly indignant when she heard that Dulcie was actually in the house. 'How dare she, Dad! How dare she!'

'She certainly seems determined to get something out of us. My first priority is to find out what it is.'

'Isn't it obvious? She's out for all she can get. She'll spin us some yarn about her relationship with my husband, knowing he isn't here to defend himself, and she won't go away until we've paid her off!'

'We'll see about that!' Harry said, his expression grim. 'This smacks of fraud and blackmail, two very serious crimes, Meredith. This will have to be dealt with, but not tonight.'

'Where is she? I'm going to have it out with her, right now.'

'No, *cariad,* you are not. Look at it this way, she'll have a sleepless night, wondering what's going to happen to her, and she'll be easier to deal with in the morning, when her defences are down.'

'That sounds cruel, Dad!'

'Perhaps it does, but we cannot let her get away with this. Either I deal with this in my own way, or she gets handed over to the police.'

'I want to be there when you question her, Dad.'

'I don't think that would be wise.'

Meredith tossed her head. 'I don't care. This is about Chad, and I have a right to know. Otherwise this will haunt me for the rest of my life.'

'I understand, but not a word to your grandmother. I shall ask Ellen to be present, as a witness. If this does lead to a court case later on, with someone other than myself on the bench, then there should be an independent witness.'

'All right. I don't mind Ellen being there, since she's already in the picture.'

'And then there's the child, Lucas. He mustn't be there, possibly interrupting the proceedings, or being frightened by raised voices. I'm sure Myfanwy can manage him for an hour or so.'

'Oh, no! That . . . that changeling is not setting foot in my nursery, and that's my last word on the subject.'

'An innocent child, *cariad.*'

' "The sins of the fathers shall be visited upon the children",' she quoted.

Harry sighed. He could hardly blame his daughter for feeling spiteful. 'Perhaps Mariah will look after him,' he conceded. 'I want all this kept from the servants for as long as possible.'

The following morning a tense little group met in Harry's study. Ellen and Dulcie looking as if they hadn't had a wink of sleep between them; Meredith with her lips tightly compressed. She was neatly dressed in a twin set and pearls, very much the lady of the manor. Ellen was reminded of a knight who donned his armour before riding into battle.

Harry went straight for the jugular. 'State your full name, please.'

'Dulcie Mary Saunders.'

'Aha! Not Fletcher, then!' Out of the corner of his eye he saw Meredith relax slightly. So it had occurred to her, then, that Chad might have made a bigamous marriage, either with her or this interloper. He picked up the birth certificate that had shown her as a married woman. 'Are you aware that it's an offence to give false information when registering a birth?'

'They didn't ask me for a marriage certificate, did they? And if it hadn't been for her,' she shot a look of pure venom at Meredith, 'if it hadn't been for her Chad would've married me.' Meredith glanced at her coldly and looked away.

'Now that is settled, perhaps we can begin at the beginning,' Harry suggested. 'How did you meet Chad Fletcher?'

'I've known him for years. I came from up London to help out my auntie. She was sick for a long time and needed someone to fetch and carry. Chad used to come into the pub with some other blokes and he asked me out a few times. One thing led to another; you know how it is.'

'Go on.'

'Auntie died, and I went back home. I no sooner got there when I found I was in the club. So back to Byrde I go, asking Chad what he's going to do about it. He'll have to marry me, I tell him, and give the baby a name. Sorry, Dulse, he says. That's what he use to call me, sort of like the seaweed, see? Sorry, I can't marry you, cos I'm already engaged. It's all fixed and the invitations have been sent out. Then you'll have to un-fix it, I tell him. It's too bad about her. I'm sorry if she's upset but I came first, and that's how it's got to be. Then he just sneers at me and says how do I know it's his? It could be anybody's. That's what they all say, isn't it? Only no matter what you think of me now, I was a good girl, see. Never had nothing to do with a man until Chad come along.'

There was silence in the room, each person deep in their own thoughts. Ellen remembering her despair when she found herself pregnant with Mariah. She, too, had been an innocent young girl prior to that one mistake with Harry Morgan.

Meredith was lost in memories of her total happiness as she planned her wedding to the man of her dreams, and the wonder of her bridal day as she walked down the aisle on her father's arm. And Dulcie Saunders; who knew what she was thinking now, and what her hopes and dreams for the future might be.

CHAPTER
THIRTY-FIVE

'That was cruel,' Ellen murmured, noticing the tear rolling down Dulcie's face. Perhaps the girl wasn't as hard boiled as she'd believed at first. Harry and Meredith weren't saying anything in response and where was the harm in offering her a crumb of comfort?

Harry, however, was not convinced. 'I suggest that this is a made up story, Miss Saunders. Oh, I believe that you were known to Chad Fletcher; that is not in dispute here. But whether he was indeed the father is something else again.' He held up his hand as she started to protest. 'I accept your statement that you were, let us say, monogamous, but there is always the possibility that your lover was someone quite different. Perhaps he refused to accept responsibility, causing you to think of claiming Chad as the father, since he is no longer here to refute it.'

'That's not what happened! I swear on my baby's head! Chad Fletcher was the father. There was never anybody else!'

Meredith spoke up suddenly. 'Chad was in love with me. Did he ever tell you he loved you?'

'Only when he wanted to have his own way!' Dulcie sounded bitter. 'Afterwards it was a different story. And if you must know, he didn't love you, either!' Meredith recoiled as if bitten by a wasp.

'There is no need for that!' Harry reproved. 'My daughter has done nothing to hurt you, so please keep such comments to yourself.'

'It's true, though!' Dulcie burst out. 'It was this place he loved, not her!' She turned to face Meredith. 'He married you so he could get all this!'

Some unspoken words passed between Harry and Meredith.

'What is it? What's going on?' Dulcie demanded.

'Is that what he told you?' Ellen asked gently.

'Yes, it is. I'm telling you the truth. Honestly.'

'I'm sorry to have to spoil your illusions, Miss Saunders, but that simply is not the case. Whether or not Chad Fletcher loved my daughter is one thing, but he would have inherited the estate after my death anyway because it is entailed.'

'I don't know what you mean.'

'It's a legal term, meaning that Cwmbran House and all the land surrounding it cannot be disposed of as I see fit. It must go to the nearest male heir. I have no sons, so Chad, a distant cousin, was next in line. He had no ulterior motive in marrying Meredith as far as the estate went.'

Except that he knew Meredith would be a wealthy woman in her own right, Ellen thought. Harry's wealth extended far beyond the Cwmbran estate and naturally he would use some of it to provide for his daughter.

'What happens to it now, then?'

'In due course it passes to Henry, my grandson.'

'But my Lucas is older than him. Won't it come to him?'

'Your son is not a blood relative,' Meredith sneered.

'How can you say that? Chad was your cousin, and Lucas is his son!'

'Except that you weren't married!'

Dulcie and Meredith glared at each other, like two cats preparing for a fight.

'That will do!' Harry snapped. 'It appears

that Lucas does have some relationship to this family, even though he cannot inherit my estate. My solicitor must be consulted to determine whether he is entitled to anything under the law. Long ago, Welsh law gave rights of inheritance to sons born out of wedlock, but that has long since been superseded by English law, I'm afraid.'

Now it was Dulcie's turn to sneer. 'So if anything, we'll be fobbed off with a few shillings! I haven't come all this way for charity, Mr Morgan. I want what is rightfully mine.'

Harry spread his hands wide. 'I'm sorry, Miss Saunders, but that's the way it is.'

'But what am I to do?' she wailed. 'I've no money, no home, and no husband!'

'Surely you can get a job of some sort,' Meredith told her. 'With so many men away at the war they're crying out for women to fill their places here.'

'You'd know about that, then, would you? Sitting here doing nothing, waited on hand and foot by servants! You can't even look after your own child! What about my boy, then, eh? What do I do with him while I'm working twelve hours a day in some factory?'

'There must be crèches, surely?'

Ellen couldn't bear any more. She could sympathize with Dulcie, and she recognized

284

that Meredith's unkind manner was a front to cover up her distress. Having a stand-up row wouldn't get them anywhere.

'I think that enough has been said for the moment, Harry. Perhaps we could discuss this again after you've had a word with your solicitor?'

'I shall ring him later on. Meanwhile, feel free to make yourself at home, Miss Saunders. I'll speak to you again later.'

Dulcie stood up abruptly and stalked out.

'Really, Dad! Is that the best you can do? Make yourself at home, indeed! I know her type! You'd better lock up the silver, Nanny, or she'll help herself to that before we know where we are.' Meredith, too, left the room, her head held high.

'That went well!' Harry groaned. 'Dulcie determined to grab everything she can, and my daughter behaving like a scold! When I allowed Meredith to be present at this interview I had no idea she'd go off the deep end like this!'

'You can't blame the girl, Harry. She's just found out that her husband wasn't the man she thought he was. Since his death she's built up a picture of him as the perfect husband, cut off in his prime. Now she's learned that her idol had feet of clay. Naturally she's distressed and confused, and since he isn't here to answer for his mistakes, hitting out at Dulcie is the next best thing.'

'I still can't believe this of Chad, Ellen. I know he was a bit of a shirker, didn't want to join up to serve his country, that sort of thing, but he redeemed himself in the end. He was a fine young man. I'm forced to accept that he did indeed father this child, but as for the other accusations made by this young woman, well, that's all exaggeration.'

Ellen looked him straight in the eye. 'I'm afraid you're wrong there, Harry.'

'What? What do you mean?'

'I mean that from what I could see, Chad Fletcher was inclined to be a bit too interested in the opposite sex.'

'A bit of a ladies man? We all have an eye for a pretty girl, Ellen, and if he was inclined to flirt at times, so what? That's what makes the world go round.'

'That wasn't how Mariah felt when Chad made a nuisance of himself with her. Following her around, trying to kiss her, and worse. He even suggested that she should carry on an illicit relationship with him, even after he was married to Meredith.'

'She must have mistaken his intentions.'

'No, Harry! She came to me on more than one occasion, in great distress. Go and ask her if you don't believe me!'

'It's not that I don't believe you, but I find it hard to credit that Chad could have been such a bounder. Why on earth didn't you say something to me when all this was happening?'

'Isn't it obvious? Meredith was so besotted with the man, and so taken up with all the wedding plans, that we didn't want to spoil things for her. Would she have believed us if we'd tried? And even if she had, what then? The atmosphere in this house would have been unbearable, especially if Chad had stayed on, as you wanted.'

'You should have warned me,' he repeated. 'Now see what has happened. My poor little girl is in agony over this.'

Ellen could hardly believe her ears. 'I hope you're not blaming me for this muddle, Harry Morgan! Because if you are, I simply will not accept it! All this is down to Chad, and if his chickens have come home to roost, that is not my problem! May I remind you that, according to your sainted mother-in-law at least, I'm just a servant in this house! It's not my place to tell my betters things they'd rather not hear.'

He looked at her in surprise. 'I'm sorry, *cariad*. You know you mean much more to me than that, but try to understand. It

287

breaks my heart to see Meredith in such distress. I just don't know what to do for the best.'

Ellen was not mollified. 'Do go and ring your solicitor, and let him advise you. I've gone over this in my mind until my head is spinning. If it was me, I'd pay the girl off and tell her to go away, but that's only my opinion. I'm sure she isn't entitled to anything from the estate, but Chad was your cousin, and now he's dead. Surely she should have some kind of compensation?'

'I'll have another word with her tomorrow, and see what can be worked out,' Harry promised.

But when morning came, and Ellen went to rouse Dulcie with a cup of tea, the girl was nowhere to be found.

CHAPTER
THIRTY-SIX

'Mariah! have you seen Dulcie about the place? Her little boy is crying for her and I think she ought to come.'

'Dulcie? No, Mam. Not since last night. Ask Ruth; she might have seen her.'

Ruth knew no more than Mariah did. 'You mean that Mrs Fletcher? I don't believe she's in the house, unless she's up in the east wing with our own Mrs Fletcher. I've been all over the house this morning, seeing to the grates and I haven't set eyes on her.'

'Thank you, Ruth. See if you can catch up with Mariah, will you, and ask her to come back here?'

Mariah returned, tying a head square over her hair. 'What is it, Mam? I have to set off right away if I'm not going to be late.'

'It's that Dulcie. I think she's done a bunk!'

'She's bound to be around the place somewhere. She'd hardly run off and leave

Lucas behind.'

'I'm not so sure about that!'

'I bet she'll be walking round the grounds somewhere. Having a good old snoop. Look, send the Swansea Six out as a search party. They'll love it, and there's lots of time before they need to start for school.'

The boys turned out with enthusiasm, but one by one they returned with nothing to report.

'Have you looked in the greenhouses, and the stables? Did you try the hay loft? And what about the old dairy? Did you think of looking there?'

But the answer to her frantic questions was always the same. Dulcie was nowhere to be found.

'She might have got lost, missus,' Dafydd offered hopefully. 'We'd better give school a miss and search the farms.'

'No, never mind. I expect she's gone down to the village to look at the shops.' Ellen didn't want the boys to know what was going on, and in any case there was no point in panicking just yet. The girl might come strolling in at any minute. If she hadn't returned by lunchtime Harry would have to be told.

She flew up to the room which had been allocated to mother and child. Lucas was standing up in his cot, holding on to the rails as if his life depended on it. His face was tear stained and his nose was running. There was an ominous smell in the room. Ellen sighed.

'At nearly three years old you really should be potty trained, my lad!' she told him. He beamed at her, displaying a row of even white teeth. 'I suppose it's not your fault, though. You did try to call Mummy, didn't you, and Mummy didn't come. Never mind. We'll give you a nice bath, and then see about your breakfast. I wonder what you like to eat?'

When all that was taken care of, and Lucas was happily playing with a set of picture puzzle blocks, Ellen went to take a closer look at Dulcie's room. There was no sign of her battered case, or any discarded garment. Had she left a note explaining her actions? Ellen pulled back the bed covers, searched under the pillow, and even checked underneath the cot mattress, but there was nothing to be seen.

'Old fool!' she chided herself. 'If she'd left a note she'd hardly have put it where nobody could find it!' No, it was as she had first suspected. The girl had taken flight. Hoisting the boy on to her hip she went to knock on the door of Harry's study.

'Come in!'

She put Lucas down on the carpet and he at once crawled over to Harry and began fiddling with his shoelaces. Ellen pointed to the boy, and then put her finger to her lips. 'Done a moonlight flit!' she mumbled, out of the side of her mouth.

'What! Are you sure?'

She nodded. 'I can't swear to it, of course, but you-know-who isn't in the house, and the Swansea Six have searched the grounds. I'd say we've been left holding the baby — literally!'

'I'll be damned!' He mulled this over for a few moments. 'Is anything missing?'

'Probably not. Mind you, I haven't checked my purse, but whatever else she is, the girl doesn't strike me as a sneak thief.'

'Ornaments, then?'

'Most valuables have been sent to the bank for the duration, Harry. You instructed me to do that when it looked as if this place might be taken over by some government department. As for the rest of the bits and pieces, most of those were packed away in the attic when the evacuees came. I didn't think they'd last long with six boys racketing around the place.'

Meredith appeared in the doorway. 'Sorry, Dad. I didn't know you weren't alone. I wanted a word with you about something. It can wait till later, though, if you're busy.' She looked down at Lucas, who was now tearing at the edge of the rug, trying to bring the fringe up to his mouth. 'What's he doing here? Where's his mother?'

Ellen resorted to the back slang she had taught the girls in their youth.

'Ulcieday's un'day an unkbay.'

'What on earth? Oh! Now I get it. Has she really? Gone for good, I mean.'

'We don't know what else to think,' Harry told her. 'We'll wait until tonight, in case there's some other explanation, but if she's not back by morning we must call in the police. Abandoning a child is a serious matter.'

'Good! That's what you should have done in the first place!' Meredith turned to go.

'Just a minute!' Ellen told her. 'What am I supposed to do with this one, then? I don't have time to keep an eye on him all day. We've far fewer servants in the house now than we did before the war but the work still has to get done somehow.'

'That's no problem. Give him to Myfanwy to look after.'

'No, Dad! I told you before, I won't have him near Henry.'

'And I've told you before that I'm still

master in this house, my girl!' It wasn't often that Harry put his foot down where his daughter was concerned, but when he did she knew it wasn't wise to defy him. Not that he ever completely lost his temper with her, but he could be very cold and distant when he was in a mood.

'But what can I tell Myfanwy? I haven't even said anything to Grandmamma about all this, and I won't lie to either of them.'

'There's no need for that. Tell her the truth. He's the child of a distant cousin and we're taking care of him because his mother has been called away.'

'Huh!' Meredith grunted, but she stooped down and picked the child off the floor and bore him away.

'That settles that, Ellen! Now, if there's nothing more, I've this pile of paperwork to see to.' She took the hint.

Two days passed, at the end of which Harry was out of patience. 'I've rung Emrys Williams. He'll be here as soon as he's had his breakfast.'

'Oh, not the police,' Ellen moaned, but it was too late. Eager to obey the great Mr Morgan, Williams had hopped on his bicycle without finishing his meal, and had pedalled up from the village at great speed.

Harry chose his words with care. 'We are

anxious about a missing person,' he began.

'Yes, sir? Is it one of the evacuees?' He licked his pencil in preparation for taking notes.

'It's a young woman who came to visit us recently, Williams.'

'Yes, Mr Morgan. That would be the young Mrs Fletcher, who came in on the train earlier in the week and took a ride with Fredericks the laundry.'

'How the devil?'

'Nothing much goes on in Cwmbran that I don't know about, sir. As it happens, my wife's sister is married to Fredericks's cousin, and that's how the news got about. Now, the young lady has disappeared, you say? Is foul play suspected, sir?'

Harry thought fast. 'I'm sure there's nothing really wrong, constable. The girl has been upset ever since the family was bombed out recently. She's not sure what the future holds and she's inclined to have attacks of nerves.'

'Ah, this old war is getting everybody down, sir.'

'Er, Mrs Fletcher — a distant cousin — was thinking about taking up some sort of war work, but she's been fretting over finding proper care for her little boy. She hoped we'd take him on, but as we told her, we've already got six evacuees as it is, and it can't be done.'

Williams made another note in his book. 'Let me get this straight, sir. The young woman has gone, leaving her child here, without your permission?'

'Got in one, constable.'

'Then, begging your pardon, sir, no crime has been committed, has it? She hasn't actually abandoned the boy, not in the sense of leaving him on the church steps, or the like. I'm not saying it's convenient for you, sir, but he is with family, isn't that so?'

'Then what are we to do, constable?'

'You could always leave him in charge of Myfanway Prosser, sir. She's a good girl. Brought up six younger brothers, she did, like she was born to the job. Yes, that's what you could do, sir. She'll see you right!'

Harry knew when he was beaten. If he tried to take this further it would be all over Cwmbran by nightfall that he had refused to give house room to an infant cousin. It didn't bear thinking about.

CHAPTER
THIRTY-SEVEN

'You mean he's not going to do a thing about it? Really, Harry! How could you let him get away with it?' Ellen was appalled.

'Well, if there's any chance you'd have better luck, run after him and have a go! As he so rightly pointed out, the girl is over twenty-one, and she can go where she pleases. She hasn't committed any crime.'

'She certainly had a good try!'

'Williams is not aware of that, and I wasn't about to tell him.'

'There must be something we can do. How about putting one of those missing persons alerts on the wireless? Or something in the personal column of the newspapers?'

'And what would you suggest we put in it? Come home, Dulcie, all is forgiven?'

'There's no need to be sarcastic, Harry! I was only trying to help.'

'I know you were, *cariad.* I'm sorry. All this is getting me down. And advertising for her would be a waste of time and effort. Even if she came to hear about it, I doubt she'd come back. No, it looks like we're stuck with young master Lucas for the duration.'

'Until he's grown up, you mean?'

'Let's not jump to any conclusions, Ellen. When the girl has had time to mull things over she may come running back to claim the child.'

'And pigs might fly!' Ellen muttered. 'Meredith isn't going to like this, you know.'

'Meredith will have to lump it. You leave her to me. Meanwhile, I shall go and have a word with Myfanwy. She's the one most affected by this.'

Myfanwy was delighted. 'Oh, yes, Mr Morgan. He's a dear little chap, and Henry has quite taken to him.'

'If you're sure he won't be too much trouble.'

'Na, na. I'm used to looking after little boys, see. I had my six little brothers on my hands after our mam died. Just like the Swansea Six they were, and twice as lively.'

'That's all right, then. And you'll be given an increase in your wages, of course, so you won't lose by it.'

'*Diolch yn fawr,* sir!' she thanked him.

Predictably, Meredith had another point

of view. 'Who does this Dulcie think she is?' she fumed. 'If Chad was alive, that might be different. He'd have to live up to his responsibilities then. But Lucas is nothing to me, Dad, and I don't want him here.'

'Calm down, *cariad*. If you were living in a small flat with nobody to help you, then I'd say yes, you couldn't be expected to take him on. But in a place this size, with Myfanwy to do the day to day donkey work, surely there isn't a problem.'

'You don't understand, Dad!'

When she found that Harry wasn't about to give way to her, Meredith went to find Ellen. 'You talk to him, nanny! He'll listen to you!'

'You're wrong there, my girl. When he has his mind made up it would take a bomb to shift him. He's decided that we'll have to keep Lucas, and I'm afraid you'll just have to learn to live with it.'

'What can't be cured must be endured,' Meredith sneered, quoting the proverb on a framed sampler that had hung in the upstairs hall for many years. It had been worked by some long departed female ancestor of Harry's and the sentiment had often been quoted by her and Mariah over the years, usually in jest.

'Exactly,' Ellen remarked. 'I've often

wondered what on earth possessed the woman to choose that for a motto. She must have been very unhappy at the time, unless of course she was ill with some incurable disease, like consumption.'

'What Dad can't get into his thick skull is that every time I look at that boy I see Chad and how he betrayed me. I know he's an innocent child, but he's a constant reminder of what his father did.'

Ellen took Meredith's face in her hands. 'I know this is hard for you, *cariad,* but you are not the one who was betrayed. As we now know, he knew Dulcie long before he met you, and if anyone was betrayed it was her. I admit it's a blow to find out that the man you trusted and believed in could behave so badly, but you were the one he married, after all.'

'Only because I'm Harry Morgan's daughter!' Dulcie's accusation had cut deeply into Meredith's confidence.

'You know that isn't true. The Cwmbran estates would have been his whether he married you or not. He married you because he loved you.'

Unfortunately for Meredith's peace of mind, the scales had dropped from her eyes with a vengeance and she could see clearly, or thought she could, what sort of man

Chad Fletcher had been.

'I suppose it's just as well I married him, nanny. If he'd married somebody else, and brought her here, what would have happened to me when Dad died, I wonder?'

'There is absolutely no point in thinking like that. Chad is dead, and if you were unmarried, who would have inherited this place then, unless your father has some other relative tucked away somewhere? As it is you have Henry, and your future is assured.'

'I've had more than enough of this doom and gloom,' Ellen announced later, when Mariah came home from work and Meredith had gone to weep on her grandmother's shoulder. Henrietta had been put in the picture at last and was quite willing to console her with indignant remarks and Victorian platitudes. 'If I don't get away from this house soon I swear I'll go stark, staring mad!'

'Lucy and I are going to a concert in the village hall on Saturday, Mam. Why don't you come with us? It's in aid of the Red Cross.'

'You know, I might just do that. It would make a change.'

'That's what I told Lucy. It will give her

the chance to meet some people. She's lonely and homesick, I know and that's why she loves to come up here with me.'

'What about the other members of staff at the school? Haven't they made her welcome?'

'They've all been very nice, according to her, but most of them have been brought back out of retirement because of the war, and they have little in common with someone of Lucy's age. And when they get together during their tea break they all start nattering in Welsh, which she doesn't understand.'

'It's good that you've taken her under your wing, then. Now, what's this concert all about? Music, I suppose.'

'A good mixture, I think. Singing, and monologues, and people performing on various instruments. Nothing too heavy or highbrow.'

'Good. I'll look forward to it.'

When they arrived in the village on Saturday evening, having collected Lucy from her digs, the hall was already filling up. Somebody was in the small room behind the stage, tuning up a violin, and there was an animated buzz of conversation as people prepared to enjoy themselves. One or two people — parents of her pupils, Ellen supposed — stopped to have a word with Lucy, while Mariah nodded to various people whom she had come to know on her rounds.

'Ellen! Over here!' It was her old friend Megan, signalling wildly.

'I might have known you'd be here. Merfin not with you?'

'He'll be along later. I'm saving him a seat, but this one's free.' She patted the chair beside her. 'There's glad I was to hear about Mariah's husband being found alive. She's a different girl since the news came.'

They looked across the room to where Mariah was chatting animatedly to an elderly couple seated in the front row.

'I can't think where Merf's got to,' Megan murmured, twisting round to get a better view of the door. 'O, duw!' Her hand flew to her mouth as she stared, eyes wide, at Ellen.

'What's the matter? Is something wrong?' She turned around to see what her friend was looking at. There, framed in the doorway, was Job Prosser and, clinging to his arm, was Bessie Harries wearing a triumphant look on her fat face.

Ellen turned to face the stage, pretending she hadn't noticed. Unfortunately the only seats left empty were two rows in front of where she was sitting, and, short of getting up and leaving the hall, she could not avoid seeing the pair.

Had Job noticed her? It was hard to tell, but Bessie was certainly aware of her presence, looking back slyly once or twice, like the cat that got the cream.

'Wasn't that Job Prosser I saw with Bessie Harries?' Mariah enquired on the way home. 'I couldn't believe my eyes! Are you very upset, Mam?'

Ellen shrugged her off. 'It's a free country. I suppose he can take whoever he likes to some old concert. It doesn't matter to me one bit. Now, do you mind if we don't talk about it?' Everything about the performance had been very good, but afterwards, when Harry asked her how she had enjoyed the evening, Ellen could not recall a single thing about it.

CHAPTER
THIRTY-EIGHT

Mariah was accosted by Ruth as she stacked the dumb waiter with the remains of the evacuees' Sunday dinner. Not that there was a crumb of food left over, apart from cubed beetroot, which most of them detested, but the plates still had to be scraped and stacked. Until recently this job had been undertaken by each boy in turn, but now they were not allowed anywhere near the dumb waiter since the day Harry found two of them joy riding up and down between floors, crouched inside, with Ceri Davies shouting 'make it go faster!'

'Come out of there at once!' Harry had bawled, reducing Ceri to tears. 'Don't you know how dangerous it is? It wasn't built to carry anything like the combined weight of the pair of you! If that rope was to break the thing would go hurtling down to the ground floor, and you with it!'

It was anxiety that made him so cross. It

wasn't one of those lifts that worked at the touch of a button, but the old-fashioned kind where you hauled on a rope to bring it up or send it down. Harry had decreed that no boy should henceforth go anywhere near the thing, supervised or not.

'Yes, Ruth, what is it?'

'What's wrong with your mam, Mrs Mortimer?'

'I beg your pardon?' If Ruth had come carrying tales of some imagined injustice, she had chosen the wrong person! Ellen could be awkward at times, but Mariah would never dream of admitting that to an outsider, much less one of the staff.

'Only she's just told me something funny.' Ruth seemed unaware that she had come close to giving offence. 'She said when that Mr Prosser comes calling, I'm to say she's not at home.'

'Well, if that's what she wants, then do as she says, Ruth.'

'But ain't they walking out together? If she don't want no more to do with him she should tell him herself, not leave it all to me. That's why I asked what was wrong, in case they had a falling out, see?'

'Don't worry about it, Ruth. I'll have a word with Mam.'

'The cheek of it!' Ellen huffed, when Mariah asked what was going on. 'It's nobody else's business who I see or don't see, much less Ruth's! But if you must know, I don't like being made a fool of, that's what!'

'You haven't been made a fool, Mam.'

'Haven't I just! You saw that Job Prosser walking into the village hall with that hussy on his arm! And wasn't she pleased with herself when she saw me! Smirking all over her fat face, she was, like a Cheshire cat. Job was supposed to be going out with me, Mariah. If I had him here right now I'd give him what for, I can tell you! Men are all the same. We've only just come to grips with what Chad got up to, and now I've been insulted by the likes of Job Prosser!'

'There may be some perfectly logical explanation, Mam. At least give the man a chance to explain, won't you? For your own satisfaction, if nothing else.'

'Leave it will you? I don't want you to mention it to me again.'

So Mariah had no choice but to drop the subject, but that didn't mean that everyone else would. As she found out when she went to work on Monday morning. The whole of Cwmbran seemed agog over the little drama.

'There's awful,' the postmistress laughed. 'Imagine that Job doing the dirty on your mam like that. I thought I'd die when he marched in there with that Bessie Harries hanging on his arm, and poor Mrs Richards sat there with everybody gawping! I never heard anything like it. Him a widower with seven children, running around with two women at the same time. Dreadful, just!'

Mariah said nothing, which intrigued Mrs Crabbe even more.

'Unless Mrs Richards already told him to sling his hook, that is. As I said to my next-door neighbour, if they weren't seeing each other any more that left Job free to please himself, though it didn't take him long to find a replacement.'

She waited, obviously hoping for fresh gossip with which to regale her friend. Mariah didn't want to antagonize her employer, but neither did she want the whole community laughing at Mam.

'I don't think Mam is too bothered by it, Mrs Crabbe. I'm telling you this in the strictest confidence, mind, but Mam never expected anything to come of it. She just went out with Job a few times, for companionship.' She paused, knowing that this bit of information would go round Cwmbran like wildfire.

'Ah, that's how I thought it would be. Too

bad, though. I thought they'd make a lovely couple.'

'Mam's never got over losing Bertie Richards,' Mariah said now, tongue in cheek. 'He was killed at Ypres, you know, in the last war.'

'And she's kept his memory green all these years,' said Mrs Crabbe, clasping her hands beneath her chin. 'A Cardiff man, I've heard.'

'Yes, that's right, born and bred. Now I suppose we'd better get the post sorted, or people will be looking out for it, wondering why I'm late.'

People were watching for Mariah, all right, but only because they wanted their share of the drama. Women just happened to be coming to the door to take in the milk or to scrub the steps as Mariah turned the corner into the street.

'Sorry to hear about your poor Mam and Job Prosser,' one of them grimaced. 'That Bessie Harries coming forward and snapping him up from right under her nose. Criminal, that is.'

'Not to worry, Mrs Pugh. Mam's all right. She can't forget Bertie Richards, you see. He died in the last war, you know.'

Variations on this little scene were played out throughout the morning, and by the end of it Mariah was tired out, not to mention feeling guilty. She hadn't actually told any lies, but she'd led the curiosity seekers into drawing the wrong conclusions. It wasn't really awful of her, though, not when she'd done it to prevent Mam from being made a laughing stock. They weren't really unkind women, but they had very little to enliven their dull lives so a bit of juicy gossip was always welcome.

Juicy gossip! Mariah shuddered so hard she almost fell off her bike.

'Look where you're going, *bach!*' She came to with a start, realizing that she'd almost run a man down.

'Sorry!' she called, pedalling away as fast as she could. If people ever found out that Ellen had had a brief encounter with Harry Morgan, and that Mariah herself was the result of their coming together, the fat would be in the fire!

'You'll have to see him, Mam!' she told Ellen. 'The whole place is full of gossip. Everybody had to stop and say something to me about it.'

'It'll be a nine days' wonder, *cariad.* They'll soon find something else to talk about.'

'Not if you can't get this resolved. You'll

never feel comfortable going down the village for fear of people nudging each other and whispering about you. You must see that up here at the house we're news. Like the doings of royalty, if you like.'

'Piffle! Who do you think I am; Mrs Simpson?'

'I did my best today. I kept telling people that you've never got over Uncle Bertie's death. Not that I called him uncle, of course.'

'Quite right too. I haven't, and this war has brought it all back to mind, believe you me.'

'But they've got the idea now that Job proposed marriage to you, and that's why you turned him down. He hasn't, has he? Proposed, I mean?'

'He has not, and that's one good thing about him taking up with that Bessie. I won't have to run the risk of him saying anything, and me having to say no.'

'I don't get it, Mam. If you don't want to marry Job, why are you so put out about him and Bessie?'

'Use your loaf, Mariah! I've explained all that before. Don't fuss over me. I'll be all right in a week or two. I may even go and dance at their wedding.'

'Do Methodists believe in dancing?'

'How do I know? It's only a figure of speech. Do go away and write to Aubrey or something. I've had enough of this silly talk.'

'Not until I've finished what I came to say. Right now they all think that Job proposed. When his friends start twitting him he's bound to say he did no such thing. Then we'll be back to square one. You'll be poor jilted Ellen Richards, up on the hill!'

'Don't be so dramatic, girl.'

'Just see him, Mam, and have it out with him. If nothing else, think of me. I don't want people saying I've gone round telling lies.'

'Oh, very well! I'll speak to the fool. But only if he comes to see me. I'm not chasing after him like a lovesick schoolgirl.'

'Good. Shall I tell Ruth you've changed your mind, and you'll speak to him after all?'

'I suppose so. I only hope I shan't regret this idiotic notion of yours, that's all.'

'Take it from me, Ma, it's all for the best.'

CHAPTER
THIRTY-NINE

'He's here, Mrs Richards!' Ruth was trembling with excitement. 'I've put him in the morning-room, like you said.'

'Thank you, Ruth. I'll come down shortly.'

'Should I offer him a cup of tea while he's waiting?'

'Has he brought his ration with him?'

'No, Mrs Richards, I don't think so.' Ruth was confused. 'Shall I go and ask him?'

'Don't be so silly. Of course not!' Ellen regretted her sarcasm but she had enough on her plate without the staff treating Job like an honoured guest. She stared at herself in the long looking glass and ripped off her old red jumper. It was one thing not giving the man any special treatment but quite enough to go down looking like a scullery maid. She picked up a green blouse, looked it over, and threw it down again. Perhaps the blue one, instead?

'She's in a fine state up there,' Ruth told

the cook. 'Can't make up her mind what she wants. I asked should I get him a cup of tea and she wants to know has he brought his ration. What's got into her?'

'She's expecting him to propose, that's what!'

'Na, na. Haven't you heard? He turned up at the concert with Bessie Harries, and Mrs Richards, she didn't know nothing about it. A proper shock she got, that's what I heard. Went all white and faint looking.'

'That was all a mistake, see. Myfanwy told me when she came down for the babies' milk. Old Job, he had nothing to do with Bessie being there.'

'Pooh! How would she know? She wasn't even at the concert that night. She was right here, looking after them babies.'

'Their Llew sent a note up with Jones the milk. Caused quite an upset, it did, and the whole family taking sides. Trouble is, Llew is walking out with Bessie's girl Gwyneth, see, and she won't hear a word said against her mam.'

Job Prosser sprang to his feet when Ellen sailed into the room, dressed up to the nines.

'Do sit down, Job.' Ellen chose an upright chair with a padded seat and carefully arranged her skirt to cover her knees. He remained standing, twisting his flat cap in his gnarled hands.

'I hope you'll let me explain what happened the other night,' he began.

She raised an eyebrow, and waited.

'I was a bit late coming to the hall, see, and most people were already there by the time I turned up. How was I to know that Bessie Harries was lying in wait around the corner? As soon as I got to the door she leaped forward and grabbed me by the arm. "O, Job", she says, "fancy meeting you here! Shall we go in together?" and there was nothing for it but to do what she wanted.'

'Making a fool of me in the process!' Ellen's tone was icy.

'Wait a minute! I don't see how that was possible. Did you tell me you'd be there? Na, you did not. I was as surprised as the next man to see you sitting there by Megan Jones!'

'And why didn't you mention that you would be there, Job Prosser? Never mind, don't answer that! We're not married so you're free to come and go as you will.'

'I didn't invite you because I had no thought of attending myself. Then, at the last minute, the pianist was taken bad, and our Samuel was asked to fill in, since it was a bit of an emergency. I decided to go to back him up, that's all.'

'Oh, was that one of your sons? I thought he looked familiar.'

'So now you know what really happened, am I forgiven?'

'Nothing to forgive, if Bessie trapped you into it, but you might have come to sit with me and let her go somewhere else.'

'I would not shame the woman,' he said simply. 'She may be a flighty piece but she has her feelings, like anybody else.'

'And what about my feelings, Job? The whole of Cwmbran is abuzz with gossip about us, and don't tell me I'm imagining things. People keep stopping Mariah on her rounds to give her a dig or two. I'm humiliated, Job.'

'Not to worry, *bach*! Come to chapel with me next Sunday and we'll show them all how we feel about each other!'

He moved a chair close beside her, and smiled down beguilingly. How handsome he was! Typically Welsh, with hair as black as the coal he worked with every day. A good, upstanding man, too, as far as she could tell, with a fine family, including the delightful young Myfanwy. If she had any sense she'd marry the chap and count herself fortunate. Why, then, was she suddenly so uncomfortable with the gleam in his eye? She had to stop him before he said what he had come to say and she was forced to turn him down. She cleared her throat.

'Mariah has told me something in confidence about Bessie Harries, Job.'

He frowned. 'Bessie? What about her?'

'She's in love with you, Job. She told Mariah that.'

'There's silly,' he spluttered. 'She tends to come on a bit strong at times, does Bessie, but there's no harm in her. We both hope that Llew and Gwyneth will make a match of it, and that will make us in-laws, see? She's doing all she can to make us one big happy family. Nothing more than that.'

'You're wrong, Job. She's wild about you, man. If you asked her to marry you she'd snap you up in a heartbeat.'

'But I thought that you and I . . .'

Ellen could see the confusion in his eyes. Pressing home her advantage she continued her train of thought. 'I'm sure Bessie would make you a wonderful wife, Job. She's everything that I'm not. She's a local girl, known to everyone; she belongs to your chapel, and she speaks Welsh, which I don't. She'd fit in so well with your family, as I never could. I don't even know how to cook properly, Job, because I've never had to do it. What sort of wife would I make?'

'You could learn, *bach.*'

'I think I'm better off as I am. I've lived here for a quarter of a century doing work I enjoy. You know you don't love me, Job; not as a woman yearns to be loved.'

'I have the greatest respect for you, Ellen, I do indeed.'

'I appreciate that, but I'm afraid it's not enough. Whereas Bessie will be getting her heart's desire if she becomes your wife.'

She was ashamed of herself for talking in this way, like a story in some cheap magazine. Really, I should be on the stage, she told herself. Luckily he seemed not to notice anything amiss.

'If this is how you feel, I'm grateful to you for steering me in the right direction,' he remarked. 'I take it we can still be friends?'

'Certainly we can. Come along, I'll see you to the door.'

Almost before he knew it he was marching off down the drive, leaving Ellen staring after him.

'So much for that!' she muttered.

'I say, Ellen!' Harry called after her as she disappeared into her bedroom, where he could not follow. Mariah came up behind him and took him by the elbow.

'I think she'd want to be left alone for a while. Did you have anything important to say to her? Can it wait?'

'Why, what's the matter with her? Has something happened?'

'Job Prosser was here. I passed him on my way up the drive, and he didn't reply when I spoke to him. He seemed like a man in a trance. I'm guessing that he's been working up to proposing to her, and now she's turned him down.'

'Oh!' Harry turned away with a smile.

Mariah knocked on Ellen's door. 'It's me, Mam! Can I come in?'

'If you must.'

Mariah found her in floods of tears. She put a comforting arm around her mother's shoulders. 'I met Job on my way home. Has anything been said?'

'You could say that. He came to tell me that he hadn't invited Bessie to the concert at all. She waylaid him on his way in, and he had no choice but to sit with her. Anyhow, you know what they say about fools rushing in where angels fear to tread? I let slip that Bessie is in love with him, and told him she'd make him a wonderful wife.'

'Mam!'

'So now he's off to propose to her instead of me, strange though it seems. I always did understand that he wanted a housekeeper rather than a love interest, and I was certain that after doing that sort of job here for so long, I wasn't prepared to settle for so little.'

'Why are you weeping, then?'

Ellen looked so sad that Mariah could have cried. 'I've enjoyed the companionship, child. All these years I've been lonely in a house full of people. It was wonderful to go out and about with a pleasant man to escort me. I'm still in my forties, Mariah. It grieves me to think that I shall go into old age with nobody to care for me in that way.'

CHAPTER FORTY

Christmas was not far off and the Swansea Six were wild with excitement. The teachers at the Cwmbran school were doing everything within their means to make the season bright for their pupils. Not even Herr Hitler could stop the traditional activities they were planning. There was to be a Christmas play with well known carols, and there was great competition between the youngsters as the teachers tried to choose those who were to take part. Naturally it was the sons of real-life shepherds, clad in dressing-gowns, with tea towels on their heads, who would be chosen to gather round the manger in the stable scene.

'Because they can borrow their fathers' shepherd's crooks,' Lucy explained.

The classrooms were a hive of activity as bits and pieces were turned into greeting cards and acceptable gifts. The older girls were even knitting dish cloths out of bits of string, and these would be highly valued by the lucky recipients.

'My landlady has found a book of wallpaper samples for me,' Lucy gloated. 'I'm going to give each child a sheet and we'll make paper lanterns to decorate the classroom. I suppose you're all very busy up at the house?'

Mariah studied her fingernails. 'I'm having a hard time getting into the Christmas spirit this year,' she admitted.

'Of course. You must be worried about your husband in that prison camp. Sorry, Mariah. I didn't mean to upset you.'

'It's not your fault, Lucy. And to answer your question, yes, we're all very busy up there. The boys have been scouring the countryside for holly and ivy, and on the day we'll be opening up the main hall so there can be a roaring fire to cheer us all up. Mrs Edwards is planning a feast of some kind, although she keeps moaning about how it won't be anything like it was before the war. What about you, Lucy? You're going home to Pontardulais, I take it, otherwise you could come to us.'

'That's so kind of you, but yes, I'm going to spend Christmas with my parents. Mum would never forgive me if I didn't! We'll get together when I come back, though, and exchange all our news.'

Christmas, when it came, met everyone's expectations. With the exception of the two toddlers, the whole family went to the midnight service at the church. Myfanwy gladly stayed to look after the little ones, having been promised the next day off, so she could spend Christmas Day with her family.

'Me and Gwyneth will cook the dinner between us,' she confided to Mariah. 'We've invited her mam to join us. I hope your mam won't be too upset if she finds out.'

'Don't worry about that. She'd have wanted to be here with us, even if things had worked out differently with her and your father.'

'I suppose so,' Myfanwy sighed. 'Bessie is all right, but I wish it was your mam that Dada is going to marry. I'd have liked her for a stepmother, and you and me would be sort of sisters then. No good wishing, though, is it?'

'It's all for the best, Myfanwy. Your father needs someone, and I don't suppose you'll ever be going back home to live, will you? You have a career now, and some day you'll meet the right man and you'll be getting married yourself.'

'Pigs might fly!' the girl laughed, but her

eyes showed that her head was filled with dreams.

Harry had ordered a magnificent fir tree from one of the farms, and this was delivered two days before Christmas and set up in the hall. Ellen produced a box of ornaments which had been used as far back as Mariah could remember.

'Don't put any of those glittery ones too near the bottom,' Meredith ordered the Swansea Six, 'or the babies will get hold of them and put them in their mouths.'

'I want all of you to declare a truce on Christmas Day,' Harry ordered.

'I assume you're referring to me,' Henrietta said, primming her mouth.

'Since you put it that way, Mother-in-law, yes, I am. Verona is feeling rather fragile these days and that is why I invited her to spend the holiday with us. As for you, Meredith, I ask you to remember that she is Chad's mother, and as such is deserving of respect. She has lost her only son, and this latest trouble with Dulcie has hit her hard. We are all the family she has now.'

'She's not the only one in that position,' Henrietta complained. 'I am recently widowed, or have you forgotten that, Harry? And since I arrived here it's been one unpleasant surprise after another.'

'No, that hasn't escaped my notice. All I'm asking is that we all pull together to make this a happy time for everyone. *Everyone*, Meredith,' he continued, to forestall the interruption that his daughter was about to make. 'There are to be no nasty remarks about Chad or Lucas in Verona's hearing. No doubt she will wish to spend time with both her grandsons.'

'I was only going to ask about the evacuees, Dad! Usually they stay in their own part of the house for meals. Will they be joining us for Christmas dinner?'

'Not just for dinner, *cariad*. I want all of us to spend the day in the main hall, around the tree. That means all eight of the children, as well as we grown-ups.'

Christmas morning saw the household assembled in front of the fire, opening their gifts. The children had come off best because Harry had scoured the shops in the nearest town to buy what toys and books were available, at least one for each boy and several more to share. To supplement this rather scanty array he had gone through the attics and produced several playthings which had survived from his own childhood.

Little Ceri Davies was overwhelmed. 'Are these all for us, sir? All for us to keep?'

'The football and the paint box and the

Beano annual are yours, Ceri. The train set and the old *Boy's Own* annuals and so on belong to me, but you can play with them. All right?'

'Yes, sir. Cor! This is miles better than the orphanage!'

'So I should hope, child, and we still have dinner to come! I've had two chickens sent up from the farm, and thanks to all those vegetables you lot have managed to grow, we'll have a splendid meal.'

'Apart for the pudding,' Ellen mourned. 'We couldn't get the fruit, so Mrs Edwards has made something which seems to be mostly carrot!'

'Covered with custard it shouldn't be too bad,' Meredith assured her. 'And we did manage to find a few silver threepenny bits to hide in it.'

When the meal was over, and the elderly ladies had retired to their rooms for what Verona called 'a nice lie down', Ellen and Mariah had time to talk over the doings of the day. The Swansea Six had been sent out of doors to try out their new footballs and Meredith was keeping watch over the toddlers, who had collapsed on the Turkey carpet and gone to sleep.

Ellen had noticed the wistful expression on Mariah's face. 'Thinking of Aubrey, are you, *cariad?*'

'It's so hard, Mam! If only I knew if he'd received the parcel we sent! Do you think they'll manage to celebrate Christmas where he is?'

'I'm sure the men will have planned something to keep their spirits up, *cariad.*'

'This has been a rotten year, hasn't it, Mam? The war seems to have gone on for ever, and why does everything keep going wrong when we're trying so hard to soldier on? Aubrey is a prisoner of war, Meredith has learned more than she wanted to know about Chad, and you've been disappointed over Job Prosser.'

'Sand against the wind, my girl.'

A puzzled look crossed Mariah's face. 'I don't know what you mean, Mam.'

'Yes, you do. Don't you recall that governess you girls had, and how she had a thing about William Blake and kept quoting him?'

'I remember "Tyger, Tyger, burning bright", but what was the one you just said?' Ellen stood in front of the fireplace with her hands folded over her stomach, like a good child about to recite. 'You throw the sand against the wind, and the wind blows it back again.'

'What is that supposed to mean?'

'I'm not sure what the poet meant, but

what it says to me is that protesting against things we can't control is a useless occupation. We have to begin by taking action, like our country is doing to win the war, and after that we just have to trust to providence.'

'Why, Mam! I didn't know you were such a philosopher!'

'Ah, well, that's enough for one day. I wonder what's happened to Harry. I didn't see him leave, did you?'

'Perhaps he's gone for a nap, too. I can't decided whether to do the same thing myself, or to go out and get some fresh air.'

'Fresh air would do you good, *cariad*. I'll go and track Harry down. He may fancy a cup of tea while it's all quiet down here. Come to that, I could do with one myself.'

She knocked on the door of Harry's study, and then, receiving no reply, she put her head around the door in case he was napping in his armchair. He was leaning on the mantelpiece and she was horrified to see how ill he looked.

CHAPTER
FORTY-ONE

'Harry, are you all right?' Ellen went to him but he brushed her off.

'Sick!' he mumbled.

'Come and sit down. You've eaten too much, I suppose. That's the trouble; we're not used to so much rich food these days. I told Mrs Edwards that suet and carrots would be an unfortunate combination in a pudding, but I suppose that was the best she could do.'

He clung to the mantelpiece, trying to say something.

'What is it, Harry? What are you trying to tell me?' To her horror he slumped to the floor. He looked up at her piteously. 'I'll go and ring the doctor. I shan't be a moment. You stay right there until I get back!'

And if ever there was a silly thing to say, that was it, she told herself. Then it occurred to her that she need not go all the way downstairs to the phone booth in the hall; there was an extension in this very room.

'Doctor Lawson? Thank goodness I found you at home!'

'Where else would I be on Christmas Day?' he grumbled.

'I'm so sorry to bother you, but this is Mrs Richards up at the house. It's Mr Morgan. He's just collapsed on the floor!'

'Is he conscious?'

'Yes, but he can't seem to talk very well, doctor.'

'Stay calm, and reassure the patient, Mrs Richards. I'm on my way.'

With a sigh of relief she hung up the phone. She snatched up a cushion, intending to put it under his head, and then changed her mind. Would it do more harm than good? She tried to remember what she'd learned in her Red Cross first aid course, but her mind was a blank. There was a world of difference between treating a real live patient and a fellow trainee who was only acting the part.

'It looks like a slight stroke, Mrs Richards. He'll have to go to the cottage hospital. You go and pack one or two things in a bag for him while I call for an ambulance. And I shall want to speak to Meredith, please?'

'Meredith?'

'Of course. As next of kin, she must be told, and I'm sure she'll wish to accompany him to the hospital and stay with him there.'

'Oh!' A number of things went through her mind in that moment. James Lawson had no idea of the connection between her and Harry. Legally Meredith was in fact her father's next of kin so she would be given the privilege of staying with him. Did that mean that Harry was going to die?

Biting her lip, she stumbled downstairs to the hall, where she found Meredith gazing into the fire.

'Can you come?' she whispered, afraid of disturbing the babies. 'Your father has been taken ill, I'm afraid. The doctor is with him now.'

'I thought I heard a car. What's the matter with Dad?'

'A slight stroke, Dr Lawson says. You'd better go up, my dear. The doctor wishes to speak to you.'

'The boys . . .'

'I'll ring for Ruth. She can keep an eye on them for a minute or two.'

By the time Ellen returned to the study it was to find Meredith in a pitiable condition, arms crossed over her stomach and swaying back and forth.

'I can't bear it! I can't bear seeing him like this!'

'Buck up, now, Meredith!' The doctor spoke kindly. He had known her all her life, even brought her into the world, and he knew that she was likely to go to pieces if she wasn't handled with firmness. 'Your father needs you now, so run along and get ready to go with him in the ambulance. Change that flimsy frock you've got on. Hospital wards can be draughty.'

'I can't, Doctor Lawson! I hate hospitals! All the horrid smells, and people vomiting! You mustn't ask me to do it!'

'Couldn't I go instead?' Ellen ventured, desperately willing him to agree. 'I've had more experience of illness than Meredith has, and I shouldn't mind at all.'

'That's right, nanny! You go with Dad!' Meredith told her, before the doctor could reply. 'He'll be all right, won't he, doctor?'

'The next forty-eight hours will be critical, my dear. A stroke like this is often followed by another one a short time later, and then the outlook can be poor. On the other hand, if he survives this he may well make a complete recovery. Only time will tell. Off you go, Mrs Richards, and gather up what you need. The ambulance should be here in a minute.'

Ellen had no idea what might be required of her at the hospital, but she was only too glad to be going with Harry. She gave no thought as to how she might get back home when she was no longer needed there. She refused to think about a less than happy outcome.

Harry was strapped to a stretcher and loaded into the ambulance while a tearful Meredith hovered nearby. Mariah came up as the doors were slammed shut.

'What's happened? Is it one of the boys?'

'It's Dad. He's had a stroke. They're sending him to the cottage hospital. Your mother is going with him.'

'And you'll land in the next bed if you don't simmer down, Meredith,' Dr Lawson warned. 'I'll give you some tablets to help you cope. Mariah will see that you take them.' He climbed into his car and drove away, as the two girls watched speechlessly.

'We'd better go in,' Mariah said. 'Look at you with no coat on! We don't want you catching cold on top of everything else.'

Meredith was shivering violently, but not only from the December chill. 'I should have gone with him, Mariah, but I just couldn't. What if he dies?'

'Of course he's not going to die, and Mam's with him. She'll make sure he's all right. Come along, now; no nonsense!' She spoke to her half sister as she would to the Swansea Six, but it worked. Biting her lip, Meredith allowed herself to be propelled towards the front door, where the two old ladies, roused from slumber, had come down to see what was going on. They spoke simultaneously.

'What is all the commotion about?'

'Did I see an ambulance leaving?'

'Let's get inside and shut the door,' Mariah directed. 'You run along and get into bed, Meredith. I'll be up shortly with some hot milk, and you can have one of these tablets. I'm afraid that Mr Morgan has been taken ill,' she said to the older women. 'He's had a stroke and is being taken to the cottage hospital. That's all we know at present.'

Henrietta's hand flew to her mouth. It was Verona who seemed to take it in her stride, but then she was not as closely related to Harry as the other woman was.

'Perhaps I can look after the little boys,' she suggested. 'I understand that Myfanwy won't be back until late this evening.'

'If you're sure . . .'

'No need to look so doubtful, Meredith! I'm quite capable of taking care of my grandsons for an hour or two.'

Henrietta snorted. 'Grandsons!'

Verona turned on her. 'Yes, Mrs Meredith, like it or not, they are both my grandsons. And don't think I haven't heard your unkind remarks about me and my son ever since I arrived. Chad may have made mistakes in his life, but he was my son, and I will not have his name blackened by you or anyone else.'

'Well!' Henrietta was about to say more, but apparently thought better of it. She turned on her heel and followed Meredith upstairs.

Mariah smiled at the little woman, liking her very much for her dignified stand in front of the long-nosed Henrietta.

'The boys are still in the hall, Mrs Fletcher. I expect they'll be waking up soon, and Ruth will want to get back downstairs to join the others in their jollifications. So if you'd like to get started, I'm sure she'll be happy to see you.'

'Yes, of course. How bad is Cousin Harry, do you think?'

'I'm sorry, I have no idea. I've been out for a walk and I just arrived back in time to see the ambulance doors being closed. My mother has gone with him, so I'm sure she'll let us know as soon as there's any news.'

'That poor little boy!'

'I beg your pardon? Did you mean Lucas?'

'I'm sorry. I was thinking of Henry. Left without a father, poor little mite, and now he may be about to lose his grandfather as well. What's to become of him, Mrs Mortimer, will you tell me that?'

'Time to cross that bridge when we come to it, Mrs Fletcher.'

Mariah was badly in need of reassurance herself, but with her mother gone she had nowhere to turn. Harry Morgan was the only father she had ever known, and now his life was in danger.

'Sand against the wind,' she murmured, half to herself. 'Sand against the wind.'

CHAPTER
FORTY-TWO

'I don't want Dad to die!' Meredith sobbed.

'Of course you don't, darling. And there's no question of that at the moment. Do try not to think about it until news comes from the hospital.'

'I know you're right, Grandmamma, but what if he doesn't recover? I don't know what I'd do!'

Henrietta sighed. 'When something like that happens we just have to try to accept it and move on. Death is so very final, Meredith.'

Meredith was aghast at her own insensitivity. 'I'm so sorry, Grandmamma! I wasn't thinking. You've only just lost Grandpa. This must be bringing it all back to you.'

'I'm afraid it is. I've only been able to cope because of Harry's kind assistance, and now . . .'

Meredith stared with distaste at her soaking handkerchief and got up to replace it with another from her drawer. 'I must think about the future, Grandmamma. What on earth shall I do if Dad does go? I need to make some plan! I wish I could be strong, like Mariah. She's had all this worry about Aubrey, yet she's not falling apart.'

'That's all you know,' Mariah felt like saying. She had been walking past when she heard her name spoken. She paused.

'In the event that the worst happens, the first thing you must do is give notice to her and her mother. Just because the Richards woman had a regrettable interlude with my son-in-law is no reason to keep the pair of them living in luxury for the rest of their days. They won't like it, of course, but they'll have to go.'

Outside the door, Mariah swallowed a gasp. She wasn't sure if either of them would want to stay on when Harry had gone, and they were quite capable of providing for themselves elsewhere. It was the sheer nastiness of this which got her down.

'I told you the last time you brought this up, Grandmamma! Ellen has been like a second mother to me. I couldn't send her away just like that.'

'She did what any paid nanny would do, my girl! When children grow up, the nanny moves on to a new family. Yes, yes; I know she's stayed on here as housekeeper since then. Whether she wants to work as a nanny, or to take charge of another household, I'm prepared to swallow my pride and give her an excellent reference. She won't get far without that.'

'I'm only sorry she turned Job Prosser down,' Meredith remarked. 'Then she could have left without all this fuss and bother.'

'It may not be too late,' Henrietta mused. 'Have a word with that Fanny, or whatever she calls herself. Let her go down to the village and find out.'

'I can't let Mariah go, though.'

'Why on earth not, pray? She's a married woman. If we win this war I expect to see her husband being released from prison and coming home to claim her.'

'And until that happens, she's needed here, as I've said before. She looks after the evacuees, as well as the gardens.'

'A minor detail! Here's what we'll do,' Henrietta proposed. 'I shall give up my house, and make my home here permanently. You'll do well enough with me here to advise you. Verona can take Lucas back to Wiltshire with her, and we'll bring in another girl from the village to look after those evacuees. When the war ends, we'll pack them off back to Swansea. That cannot be far off now. In a matter of days it will be 1943. We'll shut off more of the rooms, and we'll manage very nicely.'

Who did the woman think she was; Hitler's secret weapon? It was all Mariah could do to stop herself rushing into the room and giving vent to her feelings. Instead, she tiptoed down the hall towards her own bedroom.

Meredith, too, was feeling uneasy. It was one thing for her grandmother to offer to help, and if the worst happened, of course it would be good to have her to lean on for a while. But as for her virtually taking over the household, no that would never do.

'Throwing her weight around!' Meredith whispered to herself. 'That's what it amounts to, and how dare she treat me like a child? And it's for me to say who stays and who goes, and Lucas is nothing to do with her. It's Verona who should help me decide what happens to him. Oh, Dad! Dad! Don't you dare die. I need you here!'

The tears came thick and fast now, until her woollen jumper was soaked beneath the chin and she had to fetch a towel to mop herself off.

'What a Christmas!' Ruth told the others down in the kitchen. 'I never thought it would turn out like this, and that's a fact!'

'I thought it was lovely,' Rosie beamed, ' 'specially when Mr Morgan gave us a bottle of wine all to ourselves.'

'You'd better not get used to it, my girl. I thought you'd have signed the pledge by now, that's what.'

'I'll get around to it, Mrs Edwards, only I don't see the harm in having a little sip. If it was so bad the master wouldn't have given it to us.'

'Oh, that poor man!' The cook wiped her eye with a corner of her apron. 'Think of him lying in that hospital, at death's door! He might have passed on already for all we know.'

'Don't say that, Mrs Edwards. If anything happens to him we could all be out on our ears,' Ruth warned.

'Why? What have you heard?'

'I was in the ante room,' she began. The others knew what that meant. Meredith's suite was composed of three adjoining rooms: sitting-room, bedroom and dressing-room. That arrangement had been made long ago and nobody now living knew why it had been done, or by whom. What was known was that there were two ways in and out of what amounted to a small flat. The main door led into the sitting-room, and the bedroom was beyond that. The second

341

door opened into a tiny hallway, with a dressing-room beyond.

'I was taking the clean towels up, like I was supposed to, and I couldn't help hearing what was being said. The old lady was doing all the talking and young Mrs Fletcher was trying to get a word in edgeways.'

'Eavesdroppers never hear good of themselves. That's what my mam always says.'

'None of your cheek, young Rosie!'

'They weren't talking about me,' Ruth explained. 'What shall I do if my father pegs out? Miss Meredith says. The old girl told her not to worry, she'd sell her house and move up here from Hereford.'

'Never!'

'She did indeed,' Ruth nodded. 'But I haven't told you the worst bit, Cook! The first thing you oughter do is get rid of that housekeeper, she says, her and that daughter of hers. That's as true as I'm standing here. And she's to get a girl from the village to look after them evacuees, because they've got to stop on till war's over.'

'Oh, good! My cousin Ida would love a job up here. I'll have to let her know what's going on!' Rosie grinned.

'You'll do nothing of the sort, my girl! Another word out of you and I'll fetch you a clip round the ear! Miss Mariah's been good to you, and her mam as well, come to that! And if that one thinks I'll stay on with her in charge, she's got another think coming! She's driven me half crazy with her complaints ever since she turned up here. There were lumps in the white sauce. The fishcakes needed more flavour. Her morning tea was fifteen minutes late! You wouldn't know she's just a guest in this house. More like an inspector from the Ministry of Food!'

'Where's Mr Morgan?' Ceri wanted to know when Mariah called the boys in to get ready for bed.

'He's not very well, I'm afraid.'

'Can I go and tell him good night, then?'

'He's not here, Ceri. He's had to go to hospital. The ambulance came for him when you were out playing.'

'Is he going to die, missus? That's what happens to people when they go there. I know, because my mam died in a hospital'

'People also go there to be made better. There are lots of doctors and nurses there, who all know what to do. We're all hoping that he'll get better soon, and come home again. You can say a little prayer for him before you go to sleep tonight.'

'What'll I say, missus?'

Mariah smiled. 'Just ask Jesus if he can send him home.'

'I'll tell Jesus he can have my new football if he does.'

Mariah was greatly touched. She knew how much that ball meant to the child. He'd been asking for one of his very own ever since he'd first arrived in Cwmbran.

'I'm sure Jesus will appreciate the offer,' she said gently, but I don't think he needs a football. Run along now, like a good boy. And don't forget to brush your teeth.'

She wished that some word would come from the cottage hospital, but she knew it was too soon.

'Please, please let Harry come through this,' she begged. 'Amen.'

CHAPTER
FORTY-THREE

'I can feed myself. I'm not a baby!'

Harry waved the spoon away, frowning at Ellen as she tried to give him some porridge.

'I see you're on the mend, Mr Morgan!' Ellen looked up to find the ward sister framed in the doorway.

'He won't let me help him, sister! He's making such a fuss!'

The sister, resplendent in a navy blue uniform, with a frilly white cap perched on her head, looked as if she would stand no nonsense from anyone, Harry Morgan included!

'You'll do as you're told, Mr Morgan. Nobody argues on my ward! When the doctor comes to see you this morning he may have something different to tell us, but until then you will do as I say!' She bustled out, confident that in her small world she reigned supreme. Ellen picked up the spoon and

Harry opened his mouth like a baby bird, waiting for its mother to feed it.

They had been here for two days now. After the first few hours it had seemed that all was well, but Ellen understood that he was being kept under observation, in case of further trouble. He wasn't allowed out of bed and, used to being constantly on the go, he was becoming bored.

The main ward, known as male medical, had two long rows of beds which were filled with men in various states of consciousness. Harry had been put in a small private room with large windows that overlooked the sister's domain. She had explained to Ellen that it was mostly used as an isolation room, but in this case it had been allocated to Harry because of his position in society.

'Lot of nonsense!' he grumbled. 'At least I'd have someone to talk to out there!'

'You've got me, haven't you?'

'I can talk to you any time! I need something new to take my mind off things.'

Ellen got up and left the room. She hadn't left his bedside for more than a few minutes at a time, and although she had the use of a comfortable recliner chair to rest on, it wasn't like sleeping in her own bed. More than anything she longed for a nice hot bath and a change of clothes.

'Why don't you go outside for a while, Mrs Richards? A brisk walk will blow the cobwebs away.'

'Perhaps I will. I'm not doing much good in there, sister. He's so cross this morning!'

'That's probably a good sign, my dear. The doctor may have some good news for you both when he makes his rounds this morning.'

'You mean that Harry can come home?'

'Not just yet, but you may as well go soon. We shall have to see what Dr Rowan has to say.'

The cold air brought some colour to Ellen's cheeks. At least it wasn't raining. She settled herself on a wooden bench to survey the passing scene. Two nurses, well wrapped up in red-lined navy blue cloaks, marched past her, laughing at some private joke. She wondered what she was doing here. Harry didn't seem to need her, and everyone at home would be wondering what was happening. She would have to ring the house after the doctor had made his pronouncement. She stood up again, stretching.

'Ellen, *cariad!* I'm sorry I was grumpy! I shouldn't have snapped at you like that.'

'It's all right. You can't help feeling ill.'

'That's no excuse. Ellen, there is something I want to say.' But before he could finish his sentence the doctor was there, with sister standing behind him, her hands folded. Ellen had no choice but to leave the room.

The main ward was quiet and unnaturally tidy. Only two hours earlier it had been a hive of activity as the nurses scurried about with basins of water and cloth-covered bedpans, singing in unison as they went. Only in Wales! Ellen mused.

All that changed when it was time for the doctor to appear! Sheets and blankets were neatly tucked in, personal belongings had been hidden away in the bedside lockers, and the staff had changed into clean aprons. There would hardly have been more spit and polish if royalty had been expected!

'Mrs Richards, isn't it? Can I have a word?'

'Yes, doctor. How is Harry?'

'He's doing better than expected, and if nothing happens to alter that, we may be able to send him home in time for New Year. But no noisy celebrations, mind! I shall write to his own physician and recommend that Mr Morgan must cut back on some of his obligations in the community. This cerebral accident has been brought on by stress, Mrs Richards. It's a warning which must on no account be ignored.'

'Yes, I see.'

'And there is no need for you to stay on any longer. Sister here will keep an eye on him, won't you, sister?'

'Certainly, doctor!'

Ellen found Harry sitting in her chair. 'You're up!'

'Yes, I can sit out for an hour a day, the medico says.'

'And you may be home by the end of the week! That's good news, isn't it?'

'I have to have one or two tests first. He thinks I've lost part of the sight in my right eye. I can't say I notice any difference, myself. There's not a black spot or anything.'

'I'm being shipped home myself, Harry. There's a bus this afternoon I can catch. Apparently it goes up hill and down dale but it eventually makes a stop in Cwmbran! If you've any messages to send you'd better let me write them down. They'll all want to know how you are.'

'Never mind that now, *cariad*. I have something to say to you. I tried to get it out before, but we were interrupted.'

'Yes, Harry?'

'Will you marry me, Ellen?'

She experienced a curious sensation as if the room was spinning around her. She looked around for a place to sit down, but Harry had the only chair. She perched on the end of the bed, which in this place was an unforgivable sin.

'Marry you?' she squeaked.

'You heard me! I should have asked you years ago, but somehow I never quite got around to it, and now the years have gone by without my realizing it. This stroke or whatever it was has brought me to my senses, and I know I don't want to spend the rest of my life without you as my wife.'

'I see.'

'And when I thought you were going off with Job Prosser, that really hit home!'

'You didn't tell me.'

'No. If that was what you really wanted, I would not have tried to stand in your way. You didn't want Job, did you, Ellen?'

'No. no. I was a bit lonely, and Job was good company. When it came right down to it, though, I knew that Bessie Harries was the right one for him.'

'And you, Ellen? Who is the right one for you?'

'I think you know the answer to that, Harry. I've loved you ever since we first met on Barry Island during the last war.'

'Come here, *cariad!*'

She stepped forward and took his outstretched hand, almost afraid to touch him, as if he were made of precious china which could shatter at any second. But he was made of flesh and blood.

'You haven't given me your answer yet, *cariad!*'

'Well, if you're sure,' she faltered. His kiss left her in no doubt.

Jolted along in the rickety old bus, Ellen couldn't stop beaming.

'There's happy you look!'

Ellen turned to the little old woman sitting beside her, with a huge wicker basket on her lap. 'This is one of the happiest days of my life!'

'Oh, aye? Your man coming home on leave from the war, is he?'

'Something like that.'

'I've a son in the navy. He'll be having leave soon, they tell me.'

'Lovely! I expect you'll be glad to see him.'

Ellen tried to look out of the window but the rain made it impossible to see the passing scenery. She leaned back in her seat, thinking of what had passed between herself and Harry. For a whole quarter century they had resided in the same house, almost, but not quite, a couple. The outside world had seen them as employer and housekeeper;

the pair of them had shared a secret, and a daughter! If it had become known that Mariah was their child, people would have thought the worst. Living under the same roof, they must be lovers! Yet apart from that one coupling at Wenvoe they had never shared that sort of relationship.

What would Cwmbran say when news of their engagement leaked out? That would not be for some time yet. She and Harry had agreed to keep it quiet until he came home, and they could tell the family together.

CHAPTER
FORTY-FOUR

'She's coming! She's coming!' Young Evan had spotted Ellen trudging up the drive, and had rushed to notify the waiting family. When she reached the front door it flew open to reveal a large reception committee: Henrietta, Verona, Meredith, Mariah and the Swansea Six!

'How is he?'

'When will he be coming home?'

'What did the doctors say?'

She laughed. 'Let me catch my breath, do! Harry is doing well. I tell you what; let me go up and change out of these wet clothes first and then I'll meet you all in the morning-room. And somebody ask Ruth to bring me a cup of tea, please. I'm gasping for one after tramping all the way up from the square.'

It felt good to get into her nightie and dressing gown. 'Find me my slippers, will you, Mariah? My feet are like blocks of ice, and I'm sure I'm starting a blister.'

'You ought to get straight into a hot bath, Mam!' Mariah scolded.

'And that's what I intend to do before I'm very much older. I must hold this press conference first, though.'

'Now tell us all about Dad,' Meredith begged when Ellen was seated in front of a roaring fire with a cup of tea in her hand. There might be a war on, but at least coal was not in short supply in Cwmbran, not when the master of the house owned a colliery!

'Dr Rowan is very pleased with him. He did say quite firmly, however, that this is a warning. Your father must give up some of his activities and try to lead a less stressful life. He'll have to give up his work on the bench, for instance.'

'But physically he's not too badly off, then? No paralysis, for instance?'

'No, Mrs Fletcher. He was fortunate there. His right eye has been affected, though, he's partially blind on that side.'

Meredith's hand flew to her mouth. 'Poor Dad! Will he regain his sight?'

'Dr Rowan didn't say, but perhaps not.'

'Coo!' Ceri found something to say, as usual. 'Will he have to wear a black patch, like a pirate?'

'No, it isn't that sort of injury, dear. Well, that's about it, everyone. Once he comes home we'll all have to see that he gets plenty of rest, but he mustn't be mollycoddled. He won't like that, and I'm told that he may be bad tempered at times while he's convalescing. He has to come to terms with the fact that he's not as strong as he used to be.'

As the others left the room, Ellen heard Henrietta complaining to Meredith in an undertone something about 'only the housekeeper'. She hid a smile. It would be good to have a camera on hand when Harry broke the news of his forthcoming marriage. Henrietta's face would be a study!

'Come on, Mam! Let's get you upstairs. You look all in!'

'Actually I feel as if I could run a mile!' Ellen smiled at the bewildered look on her daughter's face. She longed to let her in on the secret, but she had given her word not to say anything and that had to be honoured.

'I wish you could have seen that hospital,' she remarked instead. 'I expected it to be a gloomy sort of place with everybody in pain or on their last legs, but no. It was cheerful, with the nurses going about their duties singing songs they've heard on the wireless!'

'I'm thinking of going in for nursing, Mam.'

'Yes, I remember that before the war you had the idea of training as a children's nurse.'

'Only now I want to take a general nursing course.'

'It's a wonderful career, Mariah, but they don't allow married women to nurse in peacetime, do they? So is it worth it? This war could come to an end at any time and then Aubrey will be coming home.'

'And it may go on for years. I just thought I'd let you know my plans before I write off for application forms.'

'But why now, suddenly? You've got your job with the post office, not to mention everything you're doing on the home front. You've told me you love all that. I do wish you wouldn't, Mariah. You're needed here.'

'Oh, Mam!'

'What on earth's the matter? Something has happened while I've been away, hasn't it? You haven't heard of something to do with Aubrey, have you?'

'It's just that I heard Henrietta and Meredith talking. Wondering what they'd do if something happened to Harry. Henrietta was encouraging Meredith to get rid of the pair of us, have a clean sweep!'

'Oh, that again!'

'I gather that she has plans to sell up in Hereford and move here permanently, to more or less become mistress of Cwmbran House. Meredith would have to take a back seat if that happened.'

'Not to worry, *cariad*. Harry is rapidly recovering and will be back with us in a few days. The Wicked Witch of the West can plan all she likes, it won't affect us.'

'But what if he has another stroke, a more serious one next time? No, Ma, I don't want to be caught on the hop, having to make decisions in a hurry. I'd rather move out with dignity before I'm thrown out.'

A mischievous little smile played about Ellen's lips. 'Take it from me, *cariad;* if anyone has to move out of here it won't be you or me. If anyone leaves it's more likely to be Henrietta Meredith.'

'Mam! Do you know something I don't? Come on, spill the beans!'

'As a matter of fact I do have something on my mind, but I'm not in a position to discuss it yet. You'll just have to wait and see.'

'Mam!'

'It's no use your pleading with me, for I'm not going to tell. You'll just have to wait patiently.'

Harry came home on New Year's Eve. As soon as he was settled he summoned the household to his bedroom saying that he had an announcement to make.

'What, me as well?' the cook squeaked. 'I've never been up to that floor of the house in my life.'

'Now's your chance to have a good snoop round, then,' Ruth told her.

'What do you think it's about, Ruth? P'raps we're all getting a raise in pay on account of the new year coming in.'

'You've got a great imagination, Rosie Yeoman! More likely he means to shut this house up and go into a nursing home, and then we'll all get the push.'

'I don't care,' Rosie grinned. 'I'll go and join the Wrens. I'm old enough now.'

They all crowded into Harry's bedroom. The sheets were turned down, ready for him to pop into bed when he became tired, but for the moment he was sitting in his bedside chair, tucked up in a tartan rug. Ellen was standing beside him, waiting for him to speak.

'I've asked you all here to share a piece of wonderful news!' He took Ellen's hand in his. 'I have asked Ellen to be my wife, and she has kindly agreed.'

There was utter silence for a moment as

those present digested the news. It was left to young Evan to break the tension. 'Aw, is that all? I fort it would be somefin' good!'

Ellen laughed. 'Some of us do feel it's somefin' good, Evan! All right, boys, off you go. The grown-ups have some talking to do now.'

Henrietta stalked out of the room without saying a word. After a moment's hesitation Meredith ran after her.

'Oh, Mam! Harry! I'm so happy for you!' Mariah kissed each of them in turn.

'Yes, sir, madam! It's wonderful news. Congratulations to you both!'

'Thank you, Mrs Edwards.'

'When is the wedding to be?' Rosie had to ask. 'I hope it's in June when all the flowers are coming out.'

'We don't want to wait that long,' Harry said. 'There's no point at all in hanging about, now that we've finally made up our minds to do it. When the vicar comes to call on me, as no doubt he will, considering what I've just been through, I'll ask him to call the banns. We can be married within the month; if that's all right with you, Ellen?'

'Begging your pardon, sir, but that don't give us much time to prepare,' the cook remarked. 'We'll have to put on some sort of spread for the guests, rationing or no rationing!'

'We'll have a little talk about it later,' Ellen told her. 'Mr Morgan needs to rest, now, so off you go, everyone.'

When they had gone, she helped him into bed, but his face was grim and he refused to lie down. 'Not until I've seen Meredith!' he insisted. 'I want you to send her to me!'

CHAPTER
FORTY-FIVE

Harry's tone was icy. 'Well, and what do you have to say for yourself this time, my girl?'

Meredith knew she had gone too far. 'It wasn't what it looked like, Dad! Gradmamma is terribly upset. I had to go after her in case something happened to her.'

'In case she hurled herself off the roof, I suppose!' he grumbled.

'I didn't mean anything like that. If she was crying she mightn't have watched where she was going and ended up by tripping.'

'Crying tears of fury, I daresay!'

Dad had never been so cross with her since the time she locked herself in the lavatory and wouldn't come out, fearing punishment for some long-forgotten crime.

'Please don't blame her. This is a shock to her. My mother was her only child, and now you want to remarry. She feels it's an insult to her daughter's memory.'

'Rubbish! Your poor mother died twenty-five years ago, Meredith. If that isn't long enough to respect her memory, I don't know what is! And ever since she passed on I've devoted myself to you, and to my work. Now it's time to start living again.'

'I don't know what you mean.'

'Don't you? Suffering this attack has brought me to my senses. I don't know how long I may have left, but I mean to make the most of it.'

'Don't talk that way, Dad!'

'Facts must be faced, *cariad!* And this applies to you, too. You can't shut yourself away forever mourning Chad. You're still a young woman. You'll wish to remarry some day.'

'To one of the long line of men beating a path to my door, I suppose.'

'Try not to be bitter, *cariad.* When the war is over you'll get to know other men, and you'll forget we ever had this conversation.'

Meredith went to the window and stood there for a long time, gazing out at the rain. 'Aren't you rushing into this marriage, Dad?' she asked, without turning around. 'I can understand that you're shaken up by your stroke, but you mustn't let that push you into making a mistake you'll always regret. Wait six months, say, and see how you feel then.'

'Regret! I tell you this, my girl, the only mistake I've made is not to have married Ellen Richards years ago. Lying in that hospital bed I had time to examine my conscience, and it came to me that I've been using her all these years. She brought you up, she's run my home efficiently, and she provided me with companionship when I needed it. What has she had in return?'

'She was well paid, like all our servants!'

'Is that all she is to you, Meredith? A servant?'

Meredith shrugged.

'Then I'll say this, and listen well. If you cannot accept Ellen as my wife, then possibly it's time you went elsewhere.'

'Dad! You wouldn't send me away!'

'Now don't start crying again! I've seen enough tears this past month to last me a lifetime! You're my daughter, Meredith. I'm not talking about disowning you. However, you've led too sheltered a life in Cwmbran and you don't know what's important when it comes to relationships between men and women. Why not go away for a while, until you can get things in perspective? Then, when you return you'll be able to see things in a new light.'

'But I don't know where I could go, Dad!'

'That's the trouble, isn't it? Living here has robbed you of your initiative. If nothing else you could stay with Henrietta for a time; I've no doubt that she is packing her bags even as we speak, and when she leaves the house this time, there will be no turning back! Or you could accompany your mother-in-law back to Wiltshire. She's a kind old soul, and she's lonely. Never forget that while you and Dulcie have had a low blow, Verona was Chad's mother and she's had to face the fact that her son was a cad. Take Henry with you, and let her have the pleasure of getting to know the boy a bit better. But this is for you to decide. I won't force you out of the house, and I hope you'll stay for the wedding.'

Knowing that it would cause a rift between them if she boycotted the ceremony, Meredith agreed to stay on, at least until that had taken place. It was to be a small, intimate occasion in the parish church, but Ellen did invite the two girls to serve as joint matrons of honour.

Mariah agreed at once, but Meredith refused. Ellen was secretly pleased. 'I felt I had to make the offer,' she told Mariah later, 'but really! Did I want her pouting all the way down the aisle?'

'Don't worry, Mam. She'll come to terms

with it in time. And this leaves you free to ask Megan Jones instead.'

'Megan! Now why didn't I think of her? She's my oldest friend in Cwmbran. The one problem is Harry. Who on earth can he get to be best man? He doesn't have any suitable male relatives that I know of.'

'What about Megan's husband, Mam?'

'Merfin? He's a lovely chap, but he's one of Harry's employees. It would smack of favouritism somehow.'

'I know! I know! He can ask Job Prosser! He'd be the perfect choice!'

'Oh, you! In any case, he's one of Harry's miners, too.'

Harry, however, needed none of their suggestions. 'I've asked James Lawson and he's agreed to serve. We've known each other since the year dot! And if I collapse at the altar I'll have a doctor right there beside me.'

'Very funny, I'm sure! Now all we have to do is decide what to wear, and at my age I am not about to put on white satin and a veil! If I can find a pretty suit and a smart hat I'll be well satisfied. I may go down to the village in the morning and see that little dressmaker who made the suit that Megan wore to her daughter's wedding. I'm sure she could run something up for me.'

'In three weeks, Mam?'

'She will if we invite her to the wedding. The whole of Cwmbran is going to be watching this one and if she's actually present inside the church she'll be able to boast about it to all her friends.'

'It's too bad that you won't be having a honeymoon, though.'

'Who says we're not? Harry has it all planned.'

'Where on earth can you go in the dead of winter, when there's a war on?'

'He knows someone who keeps a very nice guest house up near the Brecon Beacons. She usually closes for the winter and goes abroad, but because of the war she's been forced to stay home. She says she'll be delighted to welcome us there.'

'Really, Mam! Some honeymoon that will be, with your landlady playing gooseberry!'

'If you must know she's going next door to stay with her married daughter, so we'll have the place to ourselves. Any more silly questions?'

'No, that will do for now!'

With Henrietta gone, there was a much lighter atmosphere in the house. The servants were thrilled with their invitations to the wedding, and couldn't stop talking about it.

'Too bad about Myfanwy, though,' Rosie remarked. 'She'll have to stay here with the kiddies and she'll miss it all.'

Verona heard about this, and she approached Meredith. 'Isn't there some way we can allow the child to go? She's so good with the boys, and all the others will be there. Couldn't we bring in someone from the village just for that day? I hate to think of her being left here all alone feeling sorry for herself.'

'Oh, she can go,' Meredith shrugged. 'I'll look after the babies.'

'What on earth are you talking about? You mean to tell me you won't be attending your own father's wedding? That won't do at all! I'm very much looking forward to it, but I'd stay with my grandsons sooner than see you stay behind. I know I'm only your mother-in-law, and I suppose I can't even claim that now that Chad is gone, but my goodness! You need a good talking to, and no mistake!'

Meredith said nothing.

'And don't you flare your nostrils like that at me! You're not a horse. Well, what do you have to say for yourself, eh?'

'I suppose I'll go if I have to.'

'Not the most gracious of responses, but I'll hold you to that. Shall I let Myfanwy know that she can go? We'll take the babies with us and look after them between us. If they start to squirm we can always take them outside.'

So in the end the whole household was there to watch Harry Morgan and Ellen Richards exchange their vows. Mariah had issued warnings to the Swansea Six as to the dire punishment which would befall them if they made a noise or ran up and down the aisle at inappropriate moments. Perhaps it was fortunate that she had invited her friend Lucy Adams to be present. As Ceri Davies said, they had to behave themselves when 'Miss Adams from up the school' had her eagle eye on them.

The only disappointment of the day came when the bridal couple left the church without the bells being rung. That was forbidden for the duration of the war, being reserved as a warning if the invasion came. Ellen didn't much care. Nothing could spoil her happiness now.

CHAPTER
FORTY-SIX

January, 1943. Mariah had been left in charge of the house. Harry and Ellen were away on their honeymoon; Verona and Meredith had gone to Wiltshire, leaving the babies behind in Myfanwy's care. The Swansea Six were still very much in evidence at evenings and on weekends but in between times Mariah found herself at a loose end. There was, of course, no gardening to be done at this time of year, although there were still cabbages to be seen in the garden, sometimes covered with a drift of snow. She still made her deliveries in Cwmbran and to the outlying farms, but Sioni Evans was recovering well and would soon be taking his old job back.

She wandered upstairs and into the comfortably appointed room which had been her mother's sitting-room for so many years. Bertie Richards' photo still held pride of place on the mantelpiece, and beside it lay the antique love spoon which Harry had given Ellen as a wedding present.

'I do not have the talent to make one for you myself, but this is the next best thing, *cariad*,' he had told her.

Mariah picked it up and ran her finger around the inside of the hearts carved in the polished wood. She wondered about the identity of the young man, now long dead, who had made it as a token of love for his own sweetheart. What had become of them? Had they married and produced a family whose descendants possibly worked the coal face at Cwmbran today?

She sighed, filled with sorrow for herself and Meredith, whom war had separated from the men they loved. Chad was gone for good and Aubrey was held prisoner, far away. The pain was almost too much for her to bear.

'Miss Mariah! Are you up there?'

'In here, Ruth.'

'I think you should come. There's a man out in the drive. Just standing there at the gate, he is, looking all round. We can't make him out at all. Cook's worried in case he's a German spy. You'd better come and see. We might have to call the police.'

Mariah dodged into Harry's study and snatched up the binoculars he used for bird

370

watching. 'Make sure all the doors are locked, Ruth, just in case.'

'Yes, miss.' She hurried away to check all the entrances. Mariah went into the little room over the front door. From there she would have a view of the drive without going outside.

The man was still there. Why didn't he come to the door if he had legitimate business here? She adjusted the eyepieces to get a better look. To her horror she saw that the man was wearing RAF uniform.

'I've done what you said, miss. Locked all the doors and closed the windows. What's the chap doing now? Is it someone we know?'

'Oh, Ruth! I think he's in the air force. Something must have happened to Aubrey in that prison camp, and this man has come to tell us about it.'

'Now don't you jump to no conclusions, miss. It could be a friend of Mr Mortimer having leave in the district, and now he's calling in to say hello. That could be it, see?'

'Then why is he dawdling around down there? I can't stand this, Ruth. I'm going out to meet him.'

'Miss, wait! What if he's dangerous? You mustn't go out there by yourself! And take your coat; you'll catch your death!' But her words were lost on the wind as Mariah wrenched open the front door and hurtled down the drive.

The man turned round at the sound of her shoes crunching on the gravel. Mariah faltered and looked at him in disbelief. 'Aubrey? Is that you?'

He ran to her, just in time to catch her as, for the first time in her life, she fainted.

'You! Come and help me with her, please!' he called, seeing Ruth dancing on the doorstep with her hands tucked into her armpits. Between them they got Mariah into the house, still half dazed.

'Shall I make her a cup of tea, sir?' By now Ruth had recognized Aubrey, although she wasn't entirely sure that it truly was him. They did say that everyone had a double.

'Something stronger seems to be in order, if there is such a thing in the house. For Mariah, I mean, although I could use a dram myself. It's perishing out there!'

'Yes, sir. I'll see what I can find.'

'Aubrey, what . . .' Mariah was still dazed.

'Don't try to talk, darling. You'll be all right in a minute. The maid has gone to fetch us a nip of something. Is your mother at home, or Harry? They should be told that I'm here.'

'They're away in the Brecon Beacons, sir,' Ruth announced, pushing a tray under his nose. 'On their honeymoon, see?'

'On their honeymoon? You mean, together?' Now it was his turn to feel confused.

'Of course together. That's what usually happens when people get married!'

'OK, let's just start again. I don't know what's been going on here, but we can sort it out later. I don't mean to be rude, but I'm here to see my wife, so if you'd like to leave us alone for a bit I'd be grateful. All right?'

'Yes, sir.' Ruth was not at all put out by this abrupt dismissal. Because they were down in the kitchen the drama had passed Mrs Edwards and Rosie by, and she had a story to tell!

'Who was that chap?' the cook asked. 'I hope he's gone now. I don't fancy strangers coming here, not when Mr Morgan's away from home. Who knows what they'd get up to?'

'You'll never guess who's upstairs, Mrs Edwards! It's him, come back from the war. Miss Mariah's husband!'

'Go on with you! We all know them Jerries got him in their nasty old prison camp.'

'It's true! Go and see for yourself if you don't believe me!'

The three women peeped into the drawing-room where Aubrey and Mariah were clasped in each other's arms.

'It certainly looks like him,' Mrs Edwards whispered as they tiptoed away. 'Now I suppose we'll have to wait until somebody sees fit to tell us what's going on!'

'You'll have to possess your soul in patience,' Rosie told her.

'I'll give you patience in a minute, my girl, and that's a promise! Go and put the kettle on. I need a pick-me-up after all this excitement!'

When at last the Mortimers pulled apart, Mariah had a million questions to ask.

'Why did the Germans let you go? How did you get here? And why didn't you let me know you were coming?'

'Whoa! One thing at a time, old girl! I'm afraid that our Teutonic friends don't send their prisoners home on leave! No, I escaped, and made my way back to England. I've been in London these past few days being debriefed. Now I'm here. End of story.'

'Escaped! Aubrey, you might have been shot!'

'Well, I wasn't. Look, it's a long story. I'll

374

fill you in later, but for now I want to hear all about what's been happening here, and then I should go and say hello to Meredith.'

'Meredith isn't here. She's gone to stay with Chad's mother for a bit. The boys are still here, though.'

'The Swansea Six!'

'Yes, they're here too. I meant Chad's sons.'

'Wait a minute. Have I missed something? Sons, plural?'

'Uh huh. I told you all about it in one of my letters.'

'Which obviously didn't reach me.'

'A girl called Dulcie Saunders turned up here a few weeks ago, claiming that her little boy is Chad's son. She produced a birth certificate naming Chad as the father, but of course anyone can give false details when registering a birth so there's really no proof. However, he looks so much like Henry that no one could doubt his paternity. At least, that's what Verona thinks, and she agrees that Chad did know the girl. She wanted money, of course. When she found out that Harry wasn't about to shell out, she disappeared, leaving the child on our hands. Not that I mind,' she added. 'He's a nice little chap, and he doesn't deserve what's happened to him.'

'Poor Meredith.'

'Yes, she's had one blow after another, especially now that Mam and Harry are married. Her nose is thoroughly out of joint.'

'That's another big surprise, those two getting married after living under the same roof all these years. How did she manage to bring him to the point?'

'Unfortunately he had a slight stroke, and he was feeling vulnerable, imagining the grim reaper looking over his shoulder, I suppose. It brought him to his senses, as he explained it to Mam. I'm glad for her, Aubrey. She hasn't had the easiest life, despite living here at Cwmbran House all these years.'

'And it's proof that love will find a way, war or no war,' Aubrey smiled, taking his wife in his arms again.

'Any chance of a bath?' he asked some time later. 'Apart from sitting up all night on the milk train I came part of the way on a farm cart, reeking of manure. I'm stiff as a board and heaven knows what I smell like.'

'I'll see if there's enough hot water. And after that I'll see if Mrs Edwards can produce something extra special for tea. Oh, Aubrey! This is the happiest day of my life!'

'Mine, too,' he said, kissing her on the top

of her head. 'A month ago I wouldn't have believed this possible and now, here I am!'

CHAPTER FORTY-SEVEN

Mariah had a mutiny on her hands. She had planned to send the boys off to bed before settling down with Aubrey for the evening to hear his story, but the Swansea Six had rebelled.

'We want to hear all about it,' Dai Jones insisted, as spokesman for the group. 'Mr Mortimer is a real war hero, escaping from the enemy and all that, while we've been stuck here growing potatoes. You should let him tell us about his adventures.'

'It's not fair!' Ceri Davies piped up.

Aubrey winked at Mariah. 'Well, perhaps a carefully edited version wouldn't do any harm?' He had already made up his mind that some of his experiences were not to be shared with his wife. He wouldn't wish anybody to experience the nightmares he'd been having, let alone the woman he loved. 'I expect you've been told that I was shot down over Dieppe,' he began.

'Bang! Pow!' Ceri cried, eliciting howls of 'Shut up!' from his pals.

'I came down by parachute, of course, and that worried me a bit because I'm not a strong swimmer and I wondered how I'd manage in the sea if I couldn't get out of the harness. As luck would have it I drifted towards the shore, and when I did come down I was waist deep in water and able to wade to land. Unluckily I didn't get very far before I was captured, along with hundreds of other poor wretches.'

'And you ended up in the prison camp,' Mariah interrupted, hoping to forestall any graphic descriptions that Aubrey might reveal without thinking. The boys were too young to hear about bodies lying on the beach in a welter of gore, to quote a rather unpleasant novel she'd recently brought home from the library.

'Was the prison camp horrible, sir?'

'Just boring, actually. Nothing much to do but sit around, waiting for news. We passed the time by forming committees for various activities: sports, entertainment and so on, and one or two people put on classes for anyone who wished to attend. One chap had been a university lecturer before the war and he gave talks on Greek and Roman history, that sort of thing.'

Mariah had to laugh at the horrified expressions on the faces of the Swansea Six. School wasn't high on their list of favourite activities.

'There was also an escape committee, of course,' Aubrey went on, 'although we had to keep that pretty quiet! That was pretty scary, especially since we weren't sure whether there was a mole in the group.'

'What's a mole, sir?'

'Someone planted by the enemy to find out what we were up to and betray us. Some of the men were in favour of tunnelling their way out but I didn't like the idea because of the length of time it would take to do it properly. In the end I teamed up with two other chaps and we managed to get out on a supply truck while the rest of the group created a diversion. Once we reached the outside world we walked for days.'

'I don't see how you could have done that without being caught,' Mariah puzzled. 'People in Britain have to carry their identity cards with them so surely it's the same over there?'

'That's where the escape committee came in. They were quite ingenious at producing all kinds of documents which would see us through at a pinch.'

'But the language difficulty!'

'That was no problem. My German is quite respectable since I studied it at university, and most of the men I was locked up with were French Canadians. Their lingo is a bit different from what they called Parisian French, but it was good enough to fool the Germans any time we were stopped. They got away with it by saying they were from some remote province of France that had its own patois.'

Mariah shivered at the thought of the three men tramping their way through enemy-occupied territory, occasionally being stopped and ordered to show their papers. How they must have trembled as they waited to be waved on, and what it must have cost them in courage to trudge on slowly when every fibre of their nerves was urging them to run!

'Eventually we managed to team up with the French Resistance,' Aubrey went on. 'Those are brave men and women, Ceri, who do what they can in secret to fight the enemy, and to help escaping Allied prisoners such as ourselves.'

'What would have happened if you'd been recaptured, sir?' Dai Jones wondered.

'Just put back in a prison camp, I expect, but if the Resistance people were caught they'd have been shot.' He closed his eyes for a moment, recalling the many stories he'd heard, of reprisals undertaken by the Germans in such cases. Sometimes as many as a hundred men were rounded up from the surrounding countryside and executed, because one or two Germans had been killed during an act of sabotage.

'In the end they got us aboard a fishing boat, and somehow we managed to get back to England in one piece. We were landed not too far from my home, actually, in Kent. That was several days ago.'

'And you didn't choose to telephone me then, Aubrey Mortimer!'

'I couldn't even let Mother know right away, Mariah. We had to report to the proper authorities first. There were questions which had to be answered, and mountains of paperwork to be filled out. After that I was issued with a new uniform, the old one having been left behind, and here we are! Yes, I could have rung up at that point, but I decided to show up in person, as a lovely surprise.'

'Almost giving me a heart attack in the process! Well, boys, off you go to bed. If you have any more questions you can see Mr Mortimer in the morning!'

Off they went, thrilled to the core.

'They'll talk about this for weeks,' Mariah

said. 'Before we settle down for the evening I must call Mam This news is too good to keep!'

'Mariah! What's wrong?' Ellen said at once. She was of the generation that tended to believe that telephones were used only to transmit bad news.

'Nothing's wrong, Mam! In fact, it's very much all right! Aubrey is here. He's come home!' There was a long pause.

'Very funny, Mariah. Now, what did you really call about?'

It was some time before Mariah could convince her mother that she meant what she said. Then Harry had to be brought to the phone so that Mariah could repeat the story once again.

'Here, let me!' Aubrey said, pushing his wife aside so he could come nearer to the mouthpiece. 'Harry! I hear you've been getting married behind my back! Many congratulations, sir!'

Ellen was all for cutting short her honeymoon and rushing back to Cwmbran to share her daughter's joy.

'You'll do nothing of the sort!' her new husband insisted. 'This is our time, and we should make the most of it. And as for Mariah, every moment of Aubrey's leave will be precious to her. The last thing she needs is to have her mother hovering at her elbow!'

'You're right, of course,' Ellen sniffed happily. 'I'm just so glad for them, that's all.'

Mariah awoke very early in the morning. Turning her head she saw that the pillow next to her own was empty. She was overcome with a feeling of such sadness that she could hardly bear it.

'What's the matter with you? You look as if you've lost a shilling and found sixpence!' Aubrey came into the room towelling his hair.

'For a few minutes I really thought I had. I've dreamed about you so many times since you were taken prisoner, only to wake up and find myself alone.'

'Not this time, old girl! I'm all yours for the next few days. Now, what are we going to do with ourselves today?'

Mariah pulled a face. 'I'm so sorry! I have to go to work. The mail still has to be delivered even if my husband has come home from the war.'

'That doesn't present a problem. I'll come along and give you a hand. I shouldn't think anyone will object to that.'

'Just let them try! We've just time for a cuppa and a bite of toast, and then we'll have to get going.'

'Just look at them two!' Mrs Edwards, watching through the window, said to nobody in particular. 'He's riding her bike and she's sitting on the saddle with her legs out to the side. Just like a couple of kids!' She moved aside, wiping away a tear.

Their progress through Cwmbran was slow that morning as the citizens came out into the streets to shake Aubrey by the hand. While he wasn't one of their own, Mariah was popular and they were loud in their praise of her husband.

The greatest welcome came when they reached Megan Jones' house. She could not have been more delighted if Aubrey had been her own son.

'There's lovely to see you, *bach!*' She kissed Mariah and turned to hug Aubrey, 'Does your mam know?'

'We rang up last night. She was all set to come home at once, but Harry managed to calm her down. They may get back before Aubrey has to leave, though.'

'All this in one week,' Megan began, stopping herself in mid-sentence. A true Celt, she was almost afraid to express the happiness she felt, in case the old gods were offended, and struck them down. A fine attitude for a good Christian woman, she chided herself.

'What did you say? I didn't quite hear.'

'Oh, nothing, *bach*. Nothing at all! So when do you go back to work, Aubrey?'

'That's the beauty of it, Mrs Jones. I'm being posted. In their wisdom our masters have decided that I'm not to go back to flying ops. It's my turn to teach the young fry how to pilot a crate!'

'You must be pleased about that, Mariah!' Megan beamed.

'I can't tell you how much.'

That night Aubrey and Mariah went out on the terrace and gazed up at the stars twinkling high above them.

'Just think how many lovers those stars must have looked down on over the centuries,' Mariah murmured. 'How much longer will this war go on for, Aubrey? It's 1943 now. Surely it has to peter out soon?'

From hints he'd been given before leaving for Wales, he suspected that the war was about to heat up, but there was no sense in spoiling the few precious moments left to them. 'Whatever happens, we'll never give up. Of that you may be sure.'

'But people are still worrying about the invasion!'

'We won't let that happen, my love. It's been almost nine hundred years since foreigners took over this soil and it won't happen again.'

'But who's to stop them, Aubrey?'

'Winston Churchill and Aubrey Mortimer,' he said firmly. 'The pair of us are a force to be reckoned with, just you wait and see!'

He put his arm around her shoulders and steered her towards the door.

'Time to go in, my darling. It's getting late, and you have to go to work in the morning.'

We hope you have enjoyed this Large Print book. Other Thorndike, Wheeler, and Chivers Press Large Print books are available at your library or directly from the publishers.

For information about current and upcoming titles, please call or write, without obligation, to:

Publisher
Thorndike Press
295 Kennedy Memorial Drive
Waterville, ME 04901
Tel. (800) 223-1244

or visit our Web site at:

http://gale.cengage.com/thorndike

OR

Chivers Large Print
published by BBC Audiobooks Ltd
St James House, The Square
Lower Bristol Road
Bath BA2 3SB
England
Tel. +44(0) 800 136919
email: bbcaudiobooks@bbc.co.uk
www.bbcaudiobooks.co.uk

All our Large Print titles are designed for easy reading, and all our books are made to last.